the price of everything

also by giles ward

100 ways to improve the world

www.giles-ward.com

the price of everything

giles ward

IMPRESS BOOKS

First published 2008
by Impress Books Ltd
Innovation Centre, Rennes Drive,
University of Exeter Campus, Exeter EX4 4RN

The stories, characters and incidents portrayed in this book are
entirely fictitious. Any similarities to persons or organizations,
actual or not, living or dead, are purely coincidental and unintentional.

Typeset in 10/12 Sabon by Swales and Willis Ltd, Exeter, Devon

Printed and bound in England by imprint-academic.com

British Library Cataloguing in Publication Data
A catalogue record for this book is available from the British Library

For Mum and Dad

*A rich man is nothing but
a poor man with money*

wc fields

1.59 am

Jocelyn Thwaite thrust his hands deep into the pockets of his trench coat and let the numb ends of his fingers root out the comforting warmth of its thick, woollen lining. It was too pathetic. It really was. What was he doing here? Huddled against the wind in this sorry, little train station at such an ungodly hour. He started to hum the opening phrase from Erik Satie's *Gnossiennes No. 1*. It was the piece that he had performed the day he passed his entrance exam to the Royal College and all these years later it still popped into his head at moments like these; the comforting theme tune to his life.

The air about him felt damp and a hard, bitter wind whistled along the platform, searching him out. Jocelyn lifted his collar and lowered his chin into his coat as though in a black and white film. If he had been wearing a fedora he would have pulled it down about his ears. The station was only small, but he had positioned himself as far away from the waiting room as he could – not that anyone had been in it when he had passed earlier. Indeed, he was amazed at how empty and lonely the station felt. But tonight that was fine; he was happy to be inconspicuous.

Jocelyn sidestepped the circle of muted orange light puddling the floor by his feet. Somewhere from the high street came the sound of shattering glass. Moments later the squeal of a siren cut through the darkness. He shivered and trapped his briefcase between his feet. Until now, he had never really given much thought to how intimidating the nocturnal sounds of urban life could be. The cottonwool comfort of his own village life gave him a cosseted sense of the after hours world. On a warm summer's evening he and Elizabeth would leave the bedroom windows ajar to listen to the bats that nested in the redwoods behind their house. But the ambient sounds that filled this man-made habitat were wilder and more fearsome than anything you could find in the country.

A short, two-carriage train pulled up to the platform opposite: a local service, shuffling shift workers and late-night drinkers from town to town. There was something rather quaint about the stub-nosed engine that hissed and screeched its way into the station. It reminded Jocelyn of the Hornby set he had so lovingly assembled and polished as a child. The train paused only briefly to let its few passengers alight. Jocelyn turned his face away and peered far down the track into the darkened void beyond. The 1.54 was late. But that was to be expected in this day and age where nothing seemed to work as it should or fulfil the promises of the adverts. When he turned back there was just a single person left on the platform opposite. The figure shuffled aimlessly from one foot to the other, looking up and down the length of the platform as though expecting someone. He had a careless, stooped gait and even in the station's intermittent half-light Jocelyn could see his hair was disheveled, his chin covered with patches of stubble.

Jocelyn stepped closer to the platform's edge. The dead camera above his head stared vacantly, a single red wire trailing unattached from its belly. There was still no sign of the late-night Plymouth to Paddington service. He snapped the heels of his shoes together and began to hum again. He had tried many times to write a piece the equal of Satie's. Or equal to any of the other great composers he revered. He would sit in awe with the sounds swirling around his head and every bar, every note would remind him of his own frailties as a writer. Forty years and he hadn't even come close. Some of his sycophantic students might beg to differ; yet in his heart of hearts it was his own judgment that counted. He envied his students with their naïve, fledgling minds and boundless, unfettered belief that their lives would lead somewhere and mean something.

The scruffy man wandered back out of the shadows and looked across the tracks. In his hands he clasped a white polystyrene cup. Would Elizabeth be waiting at home for Jocelyn, delicately propped against plumped-up pillows reading one of her saccharine novels? He preferred historical books and biographies: stories of people who had done something with their lives – artists and soldiers, philosophers and politicians; people who had searched their souls and fought to shape the world. The man stepped towards Jocelyn and, instinctively, he tightened his grip on the case. Now he could see him clearly, a photo-fit he could sketch for the police; Caucasian, early thirties, with unkempt shoulder-length mousey hair and small, dark eyes. He was wearing a faded denim jacket and beneath it a T-shirt that Jocelyn was sure carried the logo of some beer brand. Which one, he couldn't confidently say.

It was 1.59am when Jocelyn finally heard the spit and crackle of the metal tracks. He peered down into the gulley at the blackened chippings scattered with discarded fag ends and crisp packets. On the far side, thrust against the wall, was the small twisted body of a decaying pigeon. Jocelyn felt himself gently rock backwards and forwards as he stared at the pigeon's distorted head. One cold, stony eye peered defiantly at him. Didn't birds close their eyes when they died? In his periphery Jocelyn felt the man opposite moving towards the tracks. He thought he heard him shout something, but it was lost in the roar of the approaching train. Jocelyn lifted his head and watched as the train rushed towards the station, its lights casting a sweeping arc across the platform like a spreading fire. The man on the other side of the tracks was waving his arms, but Jocelyn pretended he hadn't noticed, in the same way he might blank someone in Sainsbury's. Briefly, Jocelyn wondered if the crashing noise was the rushing of blood in his ears rather than the train hurtling towards the station. The man opposite crouched at the edge of the platform with his hands on his knees as though he was calling to an errant dog. Jocelyn stepped forward and for a moment his right foot was suspended in space. The train struck his right shoulder first, spinning him one hundred and eighty degrees and propelling him along the track. Stuck like a piece of tissue to the nose of the engine, what was left of Jocelyn's body slowly slid down between the tracks several miles further on. The train didn't stop until it reached its next station, by which time the filmy residue of blood had long been jet-washed clean by the light drizzle that had started to descend just moments earlier.

Double document bullskin briefcase, Asprey London, New Bond Street, £575

112 years before Jocelyn Thwaite's death

Erik Satie gently closed the lid of the piano and leant his forehead against its worn surface. He felt drained of all emotion. This, the first of the pieces he would call Gnossiennes, was his most unrestrained. He had avoided noting the work's 4/4 time signature in the score, or even using bar lines, for just that reason. It was not for him to prescribe how the pianist should interpret the work. Simply he would offer guidance, musical or otherwise. 'Postulez en vous-même,' he wrote in pencil along the margin: – *Wonder about yourself.*

1 minute, 20 seconds after Jocelyn Thwaite's death

At that moment in his life Daniel Lunt felt little sympathy for the dramas of others. But however dark his own world had become, even he had to admit the other guy's had just got a whole lot bleaker. With little thought as to why, and what he might find, Danny jumped onto the tracks. His blood pumped and his temple ached as he stumbled and jerked across the soot-soaked chippings, tripping as he did on the solid immovable sleepers hidden below the grit.

His feet hurt and the swathe of light from the station soon petered out. As his breathing deepened, he became increasingly aware of the cold, dark loneliness smothering him. He half expected others to come screaming from the shadows to help, but there was no one else around. He stopped and let his palms rest on his bony knees. His jeans felt grimy and damp, the sweat of sudden exertion oozing from every pore.

Danny couldn't honestly say what he thought he'd find. It was only now that he paused to consider that a human body hit by the force of eight hundred tons at one hundred miles an hour was never going to look too good. As his pace slowed and he peered into the aching blackness, his mind taunted him with visions of arms and legs scattered along the tracks. The dismembered bodies from Jordan's PlayStation game jumped and danced in front of his eyes. Was that really how a body exploded on impact? He stepped tentatively. A stone rolled beneath his foot and momentarily threatened to send him to the ground. He jerked himself upright and took a deep breath. He must have walked over three hundred yards and still nothing.

In a moment of surreal clarity Danny was left to consider the reality of what might have driven a man to such an extreme act. Was it so irrational to want to instantly and irrevocably draw to close a bad day – a bad life? Danny could sympathise; his had hardly been a resounding success; neither day nor life. An ex-girlfriend who refused to ever speak to him again, a friend who thought so little of him he had kicked him out of his house, no job to speak of and now the lone witness to a scene reminiscent of some late-night Hammer Horror. The cold night air gnawed feverishly at his skin. Maybe he was hallucinating and the stress of the last few hours had finally eaten away at him. Perhaps he would wake up in a stark white room with straps around his wrists and ankles and male nurses on guard by the door. Danny paced the edge of the tracks. There was no sign of anything even slightly untoward; no bloodstains, or fragments of clothing, no personal papers or notes scattered on the breeze.

The possibility that Danny wasn't going to find anything was as disturbing to him as the prospect of what he might find. That a man's life should end so abruptly and, in that moment, take with it even the evidence of his physical existence shocked him. The bottles of Stella and half bottle of whisky he had already downed that evening had the unnerving effect of both blurring everything and clarifying it. He breathed in the smell of burnt diesel and turned to retrace his steps. He felt tired and emotional; inside a voice begged him to scream into the night. To scream at the foolish man who had discarded his life so flip-pantly, but more than that, to scream at himself for being the man that he had become – pitifully alone and homeless. At least the suicidal man's route to self-annihilation had been immediate and not drawn out and protracted like his own.

The station was still empty as he walked towards its orange glow. His eyes, which had sharpened to pierce the dark, now burnt under the lights' glare. Danny felt his way across the platform and let the weight of his body collapse on to one of the wooden benches, as though all strength had been finally sapped from his aching muscles. The damp slats felt cold through his jeans. He tugged his denim jacket about him. He hated himself for letting his temper get the better of him earlier in the evening. He had swung his bag through Steve's window and watched in horror as it bounced off the edge of the frame, shattered the glass and taken Jenny's prized collection of pottery figures with it. Tiny dismem-bered heads littered the flowerbed. Danny had made good his escape like a naughty schoolboy playing ring and run, so that all he had left was the clothes that he stood up in, an empty wallet, driver's licence and a pass-port he'd only ever used twice in his life. He could do with that jumper now. He rested his head back against the advertising hoarding behind him and groaned. Where the hell was he going to sleep? He would freeze here. It was only then, as he raised his head and looked again about him, that he realised he had returned back to the station on the wrong side of the platform. And there, just by the edge was a lone brown leather case.

Had the man left the case? Danny couldn't remember seeing one in his hand. He tried to think back. He was fairly sure that that was the spot the man had been stood fifteen minutes earlier. If nothing else, it proved that Danny hadn't been hallucinating. The responsible thing to do, of course, would be to hand the case in to the police and report the suicide. And that's what he'd do. Wasn't it? Danny looked up and down the platform. He scurried across to where the case stood and picked it up, peering about him like a wild animal about to drag a carcass back to its den. Danny pulled a plastic bag from the metal litter bin beside him. He shook an old crisp wrapper and empty bottle from its bottom and pulled it over the case. He didn't dare examine its contents in the open yawn of the station. With his luck someone was bound to appear the moment he tried to open it. Anyway, he had more pressing concerns on his mind; like finding somewhere to sleep. It was well past two in the morning and the mercilessness of the day had finally brought him to his knees. Let Angie see him now: a shivering, unshaven down-and-out struggling to find a corner of a filthy train station to lay his head. Something in the martyrdom of the situation appealed to him. His only regret was that she wasn't there to see it.

Mortal Kombat Armageddon (PS2), Play.com £11.99 rrp £29.99, you save £18

5 weeks, 3 days before Jocelyn Thwaite's death

Isabella eyed the familiar white calf below the hem of Angie's skirt and made a beeline for it. Threading her tiny fingers in an unbreakable clasp she pressed her face against it with a ferocity that made Angie wince. Worse still, she knew the little girl would be attached to her for the rest of the day. Tanya raised her eyebrows and let a knowing, sympathetic smile pass between them. Having children glued to the leg was nothing more than an occupational hazard. Like falling debris for a roofer or sniper fire for a foreign affairs correspondent. Angie could cope, albeit with strictly limited movement in her right leg.

At twenty-seven, Angela Chase often wondered how she had managed to live at such a pace. It hadn't been deliberate as far as she could recall. It sort of all just happened. One day she had woken up attached to all the same responsibilities her mother had complained about when Angie was a teenager. And she was knackered. She lifted down the plastic sheet and sugar paper from the art shelf and then opened the doors to the paint cupboard. The door was adorned with a collage of brightly splattered daubs of flowers and butterflies – although the casual observer would have difficulty identifying them as such. She pulled the miniature chairs aside and spread the plastic sheet with a great billow over one of the tiny tables. She'd noticed over the past few months how her back had at last started to familiarise itself with the constant bending this job demanded. When she had first started the pain was almost unbearable, the constant stooping to pick up things: crayons, toys, horizontal children.

"Okay, who wants to make their Mums and Dads Easter cards?" she asked, clapping her hands. The room continued to buzz with great indifference. Isabella peered up at her from below her skirt. "Come on, Delilah, Monty … India, don't put the Playdoh in Monty's hair!" Tanya wandered about the room gathering and shepherding children, turning them by the shoulders and gently propelling them in Angie's direction. A small yellowish blur hurtled past her and ran straight into the wall. "Up you get Joshua," she said with a sigh, as Joshua scrambled onto his hands and knees, rearranged his yellow, plastic builder's helmet, wobbled for a moment, then ran full pelt into the wall on the other side of the room.

"Haribo," Angie and Tanya muttered in unison.

"Where's Louise?" Angie asked, standing upright and looking about her. Tanya studied the carpet.

"Um, gone to get Hobnobs," she said.

"Oh, for crying out loud," Angie hissed under her breath.

Tanya and Louise were sweet enough girls, Angie supposed, but my God were they unprepared for the real world. She blamed the boss for employing kids barely older than their charges. She may only have been ten years or so older herself, but at times she felt a gulf of responsibility between them. They barely seemed to have an ounce of common sense between them. And if Angie wasn't corralling the children, she was cajoling her staff. The outside door clicked shut and then the inner playroom door creaked open. Five pudgy fingers curled their way around the edge of the door and eased it open, the familiar moony face finally followed the fingers. Louise clearly hoped Angie wouldn't have missed her. Not easy to do with a fifteen-stone teenager in a short denim skirt, furry moon-boots and a bright pink figure-hugging crop-top that declared her to be a 'Beautilicious Babe'. Angie just rolled her eyes and nodded to the chairs around the table. Louise scuttled into the room.

With ninety per cent attendance at the table, Angie began the painful process of handing out paper and brushes. The skill with any task like this was to keep it simple. Invariably, before they achieved anything even closely resembling Easter cards, there would be two tubs of paint tipped over, a hand-to-hand fight for glitter (probably between two of the girls), a tantrum about missing out on wobbly eyes, a thrown paint brush, a ripped sheet, and enough tears to fill a bucket. The whole process would keep the children entertained for less that ten minutes and result in Angie patching the remnants of what was on the cards into something vaguely passable. It amused her that her handiwork graced the fridge doors of most of the neighbourhood and that glowing parents pointed to her use of texture, space and colour with pride.

With two children of her own to wrestle with the moment she got home, she couldn't argue with her sister's opinion that she was mad taking the job in the first place. But she enjoyed it. She really did. For all her grumbling and moaning, it was the first time in her life that she had been given a purpose. Of course Danny had resented it. She knew he would from the moment she said she wanted to apply for the job. He had feigned indifference, but she knew by the way his shoulders tensed and his eyes narrowed that he hated the thought of her being the main bread-winner. That had always been the problem: he wanted her to stay at home and look after the kids but at the same time didn't actually want to get off his fat backside and get himself a proper job. It made her irritable to think about Danny while at work. And if there was one set of people who didn't deserve the backlash from her annoyance it was these wonderful bumbling, innocent, wide-eyed children that fell over, spilt things, cried, screamed and ran into walls.

Yellow plastic builders helmet, 3–6 years, Woolworths £4.99

4 hours, 48 minutes after Jocelyn Thwaite's death

It doesn't matter where you wake up in the world – Hawaii, Reykjavík, a dirty little train station in middle England – you've still got your own thoughts, your own dreams, paranoias and worries rolling around the inside of your head. For some, the imagination is the only escape they need, for others it is a blank, dark, holding world that suspends them and then unforgivingly spits them back to life time and time again, like some playground bully waiting at the school gate for their lunch money every morning.

Danny lifted his head. The waiting room was barely warmer than outside, but at least it gave shelter from the wind that diligently blew up and down the tunnel of the station. He had fallen asleep hugging the only thing he could find, the plastic-wrapped case. Now as he awoke he realised he wasn't alone. His back was turned to the room and he could hear people shuffling around and the sound of the Tannoy burping instructions outside. He drew the plastic bag closer to him and peered at his watch. It was nearly seven and the station was coming to life. He swung his legs around in front of him and squinted into the light. There were a couple of people in the room with him, but they stayed at the far end trying to avoid catching his eye. So, this is how the tramp in the doorway of Boots felt. Through the smeared glass he could see the shadows of commuters shuffling about with heads down, taking up their regular positions on the platform. Danny could, at least, comfort himself with the thought that he'd never been seduced by that robotic-life trap. To him, work was an irregular necessity, to be avoided where possible and only entered into in extreme circumstances — wherein he demanded maximum reward for minimum effort. Much to Angie's frustration, of course.

A pretty, pale-skinned girl in her late twenties, with auburn-tinted hair and jangling bangles on her right forearm, held out a paper cup of half-drunk coffee for him. Involuntarily, Danny flinched. The look of hurt on the girl's face startled him and he found himself taking the cup from her. The latte may well have been lukewarm and its initial froth already sipped from the top, but to Danny's now achingly empty stomach it was like an elixir. Danny nodded and the girl shuffled away, her altruist deed done for the day. His heart fell; he felt pitiful. Had he become like one of those alcoholics that lose their families and homes and are discovered years later sleeping in a bus shelter on Brighton promenade? No. That wasn't him. That wasn't Daniel Lunt. He was a survivor, a battler. He had been here before, and no doubt he would be here again, but in the meantime he wasn't about to let the world just spit on him because it felt like it. He stood up, wrapped his jacket around him, pulled the case from its plastic coating and marched out onto the platform.

Danny had no idea where the train was going. Nor did he care. He sat down at one of the few available tables and turned to look out of the window. He could feel eyes watching him. The leather briefcase, he was acutely aware, was out of register with his disheveled appearance. Let them stare, he thought: let their imaginations wander, they would never come close to dreaming up the reality. The reflection of his grey, hollow eyes shone back at him from the scratched glass. The station had emptied and the engine jerked itself alive. Danny half expected to see blue uniforms pounding their way down the platform and feel the train screech to a juddering halt. Surely he was playing with fire, holding the dead man's case? He pushed it slightly away from his chest as though attempting to distance himself from the incriminating evidence. It wasn't until the train had drifted past the next station that he let his eyes fall to his hands. They gripped the soft padded handle with such intensity that when he eventually unpeeled his fingers, the imprint of the stitching was embedded in his whitened palms. The girl opposite him placed a paperback book on the table, the distinctive orange trim of a ticket sprouting from its pages. Danny looked about him. It wouldn't be long before the ticket inspector started to make his rounds and, in his stained and crumpled clothes, Danny was unlikely to be able to contrive a convincing alibi. Taking the case with him, he stood up and made his way towards the front of the train. Three carriages of knocking shoulders, and treading on feet later he made it to the buffet car. The sweet smell of burning coffee and stale sugary yeast made his empty stomach ache.

Danny leant against the plastic counter and considered 'borrowing some of the thimble-sized cartons of milk. He could hear two attendants behind the screen loudly discussing a catastrophic shortfall in bread rolls. Without pausing to consider the risk, he lifted the hatchway and slipped in behind the counter. Keeping one eye on the two men moving about in the kitchen he grabbed two muffins and a flapjack and squeezed them into his pocket. He would kick himself later that he hadn't had the presence of mind to choose more carefully. He hated flapjack. He ducked back under the hatch, but as he did so he noticed a discarded Great Western jacket and blue peaked hat. He grabbed them both and made good his escape.

In one of the tiny cramped toilets he slipped out of his denim jacket. He pulled on the dark blue uniform, while taking a healthy chunk from a muffin. He stuffed his old jacket behind the bowl of the toilet and, with the briefcase still in his hand, stepped out of the small compartment. He had just rammed the blue peaked hat on to his head when movement along the corridor caught his eye. The train's ticket inspector peered at him questioningly.

"Alright?" Danny nodded, as dismissively as possible, and edged forward to pass him.

"Do I know you?" the inspector asked with a cock of the head. His thin, black hair looked as though it had been painted on by a small child let loose with a mascara brush. Danny shrugged nonchalantly. "Guy's left this in the loo – better report it," he said, lifting the case as though it was an auction exhibit. "Silly buggers. Anyone could have pinched it." The conductor narrowed his eyes slightly as though weighing up the possibilities that the character in front of him was a phoney. For whatever reason he finally decided it was unlikely.

"You get a fair share of lost on this run – businessmen you see,"

the inspector said. He seemed pleased to have a confidante. "Too preoccu-
pied and stressed to notice … wallets, phones, iPods, even laptops.
Amazing innit? Had the lot on here. Some guy even left his prosthetic leg!
How do you manage that, then?" Danny smiled, shuffling slowly past him.
"I mean he must have walked off here with one leg. You'd notice some-
thing like that, wouldn't you?" Danny nodded. He supposed you would.

"Well, anyway," Danny smiled again, holding the case up in
front of the man's nose, "I'd better …"

"Yes, oh yes, of course." The ticket inspector waved him on. He
was still shaking his head and mumbling "I dunno" to himself by the
time Danny had reached the far end of the carriage.

The rest of Danny's journey was spent bouncing from side to
side outside the toilet compartment between carriages E and F. In his new
disguise he was unable to return to his original seat and he was keen to
avoid meeting his friendly ticket inspector again. Whenever anybody
walked past he busied himself opening and closing the locker doors next
to the toilet, or studiously checking the emergency brake lever. All the
while he made sure the case was carefully secreted by his feet and away
from prying eyes. He still hadn't had the opportunity to open it and its
contents were beginning to become the subject of some fantastical con-
jecture. What if it contained cash, valuable documents or a lottery ticket
worth millions? As unlikely as any of these seemed, it didn't stop
Danny's imagination teasing him. He finally attempted a quick peek, as
the train pulled into what he now saw to be Reading Station. He knelt
down and unclipped the clasp. As he peeled open the lips of the case, he
could see sheets of faded, yellowing paper. At that moment a tall middle-
aged woman bustled past him, a small boy clasping her bony white hand
for all he was worth. She stopped and turned back to look at him. Danny
slammed the case closed a little too abruptly and stood bolt upright. The
speed of his action only made the woman peer down at the case. She
appeared momentarily disorientated.

"Um." She paused. "Coach G, where's coach G?" she
demanded, her voice rattling with accusation. Danny, reeling from a
momentary belief that he'd been rumbled, was unable to speak. He
opened and closed his mouth stupidly, lifted his arm and pointed along
the carriage the way the woman had already been heading. Without
thanking him she tugged at the child's arm.

"Useless," she hissed under her breath and disappeared between
the juddering doors.

It didn't take Danny long to fathom the train's ultimate destination. This was no ordinary train, he realised, carrying its rows of

suit-wearing clones, yawning into their crumpled papers and scratching
their armpits. This was the commuter hell that Danny had spent his life
working – or indeed not working – to avoid. The train hissed and rattled
to an unceremonious stop alongside platform six at Paddington Station.
There were probably worse places for fate to take him: something about
the imposing anonymity of the capital appealed to him right at that
moment. He had no desire to be watched or judged. Rather he was happy
to disappear into the melée and lick his wounds. He would find a hostel
or a bed and breakfast, if he could afford it, and spend a few days trying
to understand what he had just left behind. The thought that he could
just vanish excited him. Let those he'd left behind worry if they wanted,
he didn't care. When he'd needed their trust most they had turned their
backs. Maybe, when he did finally return – if he did – they might listen to
his version of events. Maybe then, just maybe, they could start all over
again.

Clairol Nice 'n Easy Permanent Colour, Dark Auburn £4.79

5 weeks, 1 day before Jocelyn Thwaite's death

It was a week since Angie had calmly stood on the doorstep, her children
holding tightly to her hands, and told Danny to never come back. It had
taken all her resolve and strength to mean the words she spoke. But still,
as her mouth opened and closed, she felt as though she was possessed.
She could feel Jade's shoulders convulse beneath her hand and she knew
her relationship with her daughter was about to change forever.

"He said sorry, Mummy. Don't make him go."

"It's not that simple, love."

"Why not?"

Why not? It was that simple. That was the simple thing to do:
forgive him. Accept him for who he was. After all, she was stupid enough
to fall in love with him in the first place, wasn't she?

"Great, now I've got two ex-Dads," snorted Jordan, breaking
from her clasp and marching back into the house. "You will let us know
when you're moving the next one in, won't you?" he added sarcastically
over his shoulder.

Jade and her mother held hands as they sat together at the
kitchen table. Mel was there with that pitying look she had perfected so

well. The sibling rivalry had never totally faded and at times like this Mel seemed to revel in her big sister's failings. She was becoming more like their mother every day.

"Jade, darling, sometimes grown-ups ..."

"Yeah, yeah," the little girl sang with a roll of her eyes. It frightened Angie when she thought how quickly her children were growing up. One minute they were staring wide-eyed up at you, dependent on you for everything, the next they were shaking their heads with disappointment and answering back. In some ways she was glad they had both been too young to clearly remember their biological father walking out on them. But it didn't stop both of them using this fact as an emotional weight to negotiate whenever the need arose. Mel wrapped her arm around her niece.

"Now, don't go blaming Mummy, it's not her fault."

Did she deliberately leave a little doubt tingeing her voice, Angie wondered?

A week later Angie still didn't feel any more empowered for kicking Danny out of the house. If anything, she actually felt the opposite. The doubts that began as niggles now woke her in cold, drenched sweats at night. Was she denying her children the right to the father they had grown to believe Danny to be? Was she being selfish? Didn't lots of relationships go through this sort of trial and grow to be stronger, better? After all, Danny had confessed his infidelity almost immediately. He could have kept it secret and she would never have been any the wiser. *Chat* magazine was full of exposées of husbands with entire second families tucked away. At least he'd been honest – the one thing she'd always asked him to be.

It was a wet day. And wet days meant sixteen dwarf-height kamikaze sadists in one room for eight solid hours. And people think childcare is the easy option. It didn't help that Louise had called at five to nine with life-threatening influenza – well, a tickly throat – and that they'd had to call in a temp who was more used to creating Excel documents than papier-mâché balloon faces. The small hand was on the five and the large hand slowly approached the six. It had been a long day. Tanya began the protracted, but rewarding, job of realigning children with their possessions in anticipation of the flood of frantic parents who would soon arrive. It was usually at this time of day that Tanya finally became animated: her eyes grew wide and her limbs whirled with newfound energy as she thrust little arms into Puffa jackets and wrapped Barbie scarves tightly around tiny necks. And then through the doors the parents burst. They were mostly mothers, their faces contorted with relief and guilt: relief that their child was still safe after a day with these monstrous strangers and guilt that they could have been so selfish to have left their babies in the first place. After an evening of bath-time tantrums and a night of restless, interrupted sleep, they'd be back tomorrow.

Despite loving the independence the job gave her, deep down Angie felt a stab of resentment that looking after other people's children meant she wasn't there for Jordan and Jade when they walked in from school. Worse still was the fact that since Danny had gone she had had to rely more and more on the favours of friends and family. Not least her sister –"When Danny left, who was there to see you through it all? Me. Me, that's who!" – but Mel hadn't helped see her through it. No one had. Because she wasn't through it!

She started collecting together the Sticklebricks. Somebody had decided it would be very creative to add them to the Plasticene and now the bricks were embedded with mashed brown threads of sticky goo. It wasn't as though the owners couldn't afford a few new story-books and some Plasticene – she knew how much you had to pay for the Tiny Acorns brand of childcare. She also knew how much she and the girls were paid each week. And she could tell you right now the two were a long way from balancing each other out. That, of course, was the rub as far as Danny was concerned. She was looking after 'rich people's kids'.

"Look at the price of houses in that area!" he'd scoff. But it meant nothing to Angie. She didn't care whose children they were. Why should it? Children are children, wherever they're born.

A scream from behind her made her whirl round. It was her worst fear; a sliced finger, a broken foot, a … small boy who couldn't find his yellow workman's helmet. Joshua was distraught – his world had collapsed. How Angie envied the simplicity by which a toddler viewed the world. Lose something, then stand in the middle of a room and scream until someone else sorted it out. Tanya scooped the missing hat from underneath a pile of discarded painting aprons and placed it on his head. Joshua grabbed it with both hands and held it down tight.

The parents started to arrive. Isabella's mum appeared with a Prozac-induced grin at the doorway.

"Baby, where's my baby?" she squealed. Isabella lunged for Angie's leg and hung on for dear life until Angie was able to carefully unpeel each little finger and gently steer the girl back towards her mother. The little girl burst into tears. It was nearly half an hour before the last of the children were successfully escorted from the premises. Only a tiny, thin boy with a little mop of curly blond hair obscuring his furrowed forehead remained in the corner, his face expectantly turned to the door. Max, or Maximillian, as his mother insisted on calling him, was barely evident during the day. He was so disarmingly quite and well behaved that Angie had to remind herself periodically that he was there at all. It was unlike Max's mother to be late.

Angie sat down on one of the miniature chairs beside the boy.

"I'm sure Mum will be here very soon." The boy nodded seriously. "Have you got everything?" Max thought about the question for a minute then held up a little metal car in his hand. "Good," she said giving him a comforting smile. The boy gazed back at her with the eyes of a fifty-year-old. Some children were just born all-knowing.

The temp had left and Tanya was fidgeting by the doorway, her coat already on and her bag clutched to her side. Angie was about to tell her to go, when a banging at the main door followed by a bungle of brown clothes vaguely in human form crashed into the room. Tanya made good her escape, leaving Angie to the man's gasping apology. Max obediently stood up, wandered over to his Dad and clasped his hand.

"Thank you so much for hanging on," the man said, running a hand through his flattened grey hair. He was too tall for the little room and its doll's house furniture. Involuntarily he stooped to make himself appear in proportion to the room. He was also older than most of the parents who arrived to pick up their children.

"It's all been a little bit hectic today, what with one thing and another," he said. Angie stifled a smile, half expecting him to round off his sentence with a 'don't you know' or 'what ho'. Suddenly, he thrust out his hand. "So sorry. Forgetting my manners." Angie tried not to eye it suspiciously but clasped it gently as if to say, 'oh yes, everyone who comes to pick up their child shakes me by the hand'. He held it only briefly but his grip was firm and soft, as though he was wearing well-used leather gloves.

"I'm Maximillian's father," he announced.

"Yes, I gathered," Angie smiled.

"Now then, Max, have you had a good day?" The manner in which he addressed his son was just the same as he might a work colleague. "Let's not take up any more of this good lady's time." Angie couldn't help but smile. The man briefly paused as though to make reference to it, but then decided better of it. Father and son turned to leave, the child a mini facsimile of the adult. Then Max stopped and turned to look at Angie.

"Goodbye Miss Chase," he said very politely.

"Well, goodbye yourself, Mr Maximillian Thwaite," Angie returned with a wave.

Chat magazine, 3 monthly direct debit, £8.75

114 years before Jocelyn Thwaite's death

Nature had once again awoken the colours that flooded Les Tuileries following the dormant winter months. The smell of cherry and apple blossom filled the Parisienne air with a heady scent. Erik Satie carefully folded a single piece of paper from his notebook into the shape of a tiny boat and placed it on the surface of the pond. Suzanne smiled. She stood, hands behind her back, her head tilted upwards, the sleek outline of her neck bared to the sharp early spring chill. Erik moved beside her and pulled her scarf tight. She turned and kissed him lightly on the cheek, the warmth flowing through his skin and down to his fingertips. He felt alive and inspired; as though he could write a thousand pieces the equal of *Gnossiennes*.

7 hours, 12 minutes after Jocelyn Thwaite's death

The gentle spit of warm drizzle welcomed Danny to the capital. He wandered aimlessly through the echoing station, jostled by the purposeful strides of travellers with little trolley bags bouncing skittishly behind them. The noise and smells wafted over him. People veered this way and that, eyes locked ahead with expressions of defiant purpose etched upon their faces. He felt himself being pulled and twisted along by the invisible swell of the crowd – as if continuous movement was necessary to keep the arteries of the city pumping. Move. In any direction, it didn't matter which. Just move.

Danny had only ever been to London a few times in his life: he hadn't really seen the point in visiting the smelly, arrogant place. He would have to find himself somewhere to stay, but for now he was content just to wander the streets. At the end of Praed Street he stood on the corner and stared down Edgeware Road, where the traffic flowed urgently towards Marble Arch. A woman with a wire-framed trolley clipped his heels. The swell of people built behind him in irritation, like he was a rock damming a stream. He needed a coffee.

Danny fingered the stained handle of his mug. Of course he regretted sleeping with that woman. It was stupid. But at the end of the day Angie had to take some of the blame, didn't she? They were her kids, not his. He'd done more that his share hadn't he? He'd certainly been more of a father to the two of them than their so-called father. He slammed his mug down more carelessly than he'd meant and the stocky Asian girl behind the counter shot him a look. He smiled reassuringly and she turned back to buttering thin slices of powdery bread. The rain had developed from a persistent drizzle to an incessant downpour and this had been the first place he had found as sanctuary – a strange Middle-Eastern-Cockney hybrid café, serving both falafel and buttered teacakes.There were only two other people inside and they were preoccupied with their own concerns. Slowly Danny felt the tight muscles across his shoulders begin to relax. He lifted the case from the seat beside him on to his lap and flicked the brass clasp open. It was the old-fashioned, upright kind you could imagine Cary Grant pulling the *Evening Standard* from. But then the man he'd seen step so nonchalantly in front of the Paddington Express had looked like something from a 1950s film. Danny shook the image from his mind and let his fingers search the contents of the case. He pulled out a thick, cardboard folder of loose sheets and starchy papers. They rustled in protest as he pulled them from their protective sheath. He was sure he could smell the musty air of some dark, ancient room. A library, or museum perhaps. The folder was dusty green and splashed with the tell-tale signs of age: bleached blotches of sunlight and shadowy patches of spilled liquid. He pulled it open and shuffled the papers out in front of him as though they were playing cards. It took Danny a moment to recognise the roughly scribbled pencil marks for what they were – musical notations. The pale pre-printed parallel lines that covered the sheets reminded him of the lined exercise books of his schooldays. He might as well have been staring at a bunch of random mathematical symbols for all the sketchy lines and dots meant to him. He sighed. Was this what he'd risked life and limb for? He slapped the folder shut with a shrug of contempt and peered back into the case. There was little else of interest inside: a small plastic Tupperware box containing an empty chocolate bar wrapper and the remnants of an apple core hinted at the previous day's lunch, and a couple of random letters and old bank statements with scribbled phone numbers at the top was all there was to show for the suicidal man's last moments. Pitiful, really, he thought, but still more significant than his own lack of possessions.

The girl at the counter was watching him again. He could feel her beady little eyes probing him. Danny shuffled in his seat and positioned the bag out of view. Maybe he was just being paranoid. After all, it was naïve of him to imagine there was anything more remarkable about him than the dozens of other people who must wander into this faceless little room day in, day out. He was hardly the strange one here. He had just watched a grey-haired old man walk past the window, a plastic parrot sewn on his hat and a filthy blazer covered in metal badges slung over his shoulder. No, the skill would be tracking down the sane person amongst their numbers, not the fidgeting fool in the stained T-shirt, Great Western Railway jacket and leather briefcase. It never failed to amaze him that witnesses on *Crimewatch* remembered the faces of the suspicious, years after an original event: '*Oh, yes, that's her, I remember that face vividly. It was seven o'clock on March the fifth and she was wearing a green blouse ....*' He pushed his hand deep to the bottom of the bag and felt his way along the lining. Apart from a fifty pence piece, which he gratefully pocketed, there was nothing of interest. Danny sighed with disappointment. Just his luck. The girl behind the counter nodded her head gently to the radio and stared vacantly out of the window. A couple of flies buzzed along the sill.

Just as he was considering how or where he might discard the case, his fingers stopped at the unfamiliar coolness of a metal zip. He peered into the case and rubbed his hand up and down its inner lining. He could clearly feel the, albeit shallow, bulge of something just below the surface. Finding the zip's end he slowly pulled it back. Inside he found a slim wallet and a tiny black diary. He laid them carefully on the table and unraveled the little transparent wallet to reveal a selection of colourful plastic cards.

"'Nother cuppa, love?" the girl asked, passing close enough to his shoulder to be able to spy the contents of his hand. He shook his head. The girl lingered close by the next table, pretending to wipe its surface with a grey, greasy cloth. He let her wait – he was in no rush. The café had at last afforded him time to consider his options. He was disappointed to acknowledge they were few and far between. So, what if he found a B&B? What about tomorrow, or the next day? God, he had been rash. Once again he'd let his emotions rule.

The girl tired of her waiting and returned behind her counter where a thin, bespectacled woman was shuffling impatiently for her

Danish pastry. Danny took the opportunity to flick slowly through the wallet of cards. There was a Nectar points card, a library card and a Jaguar service card. He carefully removed them and filed them in his back pocket. He would destroy them later. With what he was about to do, he knew there could be no link back to their original owner. What was he about to do? Steal? Why not? The man who had owned them no longer needed them. No longer wanted them. Clearly the American Express card, the platinum MasterCard and the Barclay card meant nothing to him. Turning one of the shiny slivers of silver plastic over and over in his hand, Danny read the name embossed on the front; Mr J. S. Thwaite. Unusual name, he pondered before picking up the diary and flicking through the gilt-edged pages. He hadn't seen a diary like this since he was a child, with its miniature plastic-topped pencil and thread of ribbon to mark the pages. Danny recognised the scrawl inside to be by the same hand that had written the pages of impenetrable music he had found in the case. Either J. S. Thwaite led a very dull life, or he wasn't very diligent at keeping his notes up to date – most of the pages were blank. Occasionally there was the odd decipherable entry: 10am, dentist; 8pm, drinks Pattersons; 5.30pm, pick up Max. But nothing of earth-shattering note, nor any clues to this elusive character who was apparently so at odds with his own existence that he suddenly decided to end it all. Danny thumbed his way to the back of the diary. As he suspected, what he really wanted to find was scribbled in the inside back cover of the little book. A bit like leaving your front door open and erecting an illuminated sign above it saying 'free valuables this way', Mr Thwaite had scrawled four little numbers in permanent black ink. And then circled them. Twice. Danny shook his head at the foolishness. And then smiled to himself. Two minutes ago he hadn't a clue what he was going to do, but now he had a feeling things were going to get a little bit better for Daniel Lunt. He left the fifty pence piece as a tip for the inquisitive waitress. He wouldn't need that now.

Reading–Paddington, adult standard single, £17.00

4 weeks, 5 days before Jocelyn Thwaite's death

Angie giggled and kicked her legs in the air. Mel smiled with satisfaction. It was the first time she had seen her sister laugh since she had chucked that stupid fool out of the house. And, at the risk of sounding completely selfish, Angie could be a right pain in the proverbial when she was depressed. So Mel instigated the only plan she really knew how to execute effectively – get her sister pissed. Mel poured another glass of sweet German wine. She couldn't stand the stuff herself. She was more of a bottled lager girl.

"Right, are you ready for the show?" Mel squealed, jumping to her feet and clapping her hands.

"Show?" Angie leaned forward on the settee, her legs tucked underneath her. The wine had done its job and for the first time in days she felt her body start to relax. She watched bemused as Mel darted from the room only to return minutes later with a bulging white, plastic Primark bag.

"Mel …," she groaned, "what?"

"Don't worry, about it!" Mel grinned in return, pulling a blue shiny top from the bag and waving it above her head. "Da, daaa!" Angie groaned.

Max's father had collected him again earlier that day. That was the third time in as many days. This time the conversation between them had lasted longer, but had been no less stilted. The man had a strange ability to loiter just behind her shoulder and follow her around the room as she cleared up. Tanya had given her a teasing grin and trotted away giggling. Angie wasn't used to people who said so little. For her, conversational lulls were socially unacceptable.

"Is your wife all right?" she asked, looking up briefly as she wiped the film of little finger marks from one of the stunted plastic tables. Mr Thwaite's reply startled her:

"Oh, no," he said in a low voice, turning so that he was out of Max's earshot, "we're separated." That hadn't been what she meant but she dared not correct him for fear it would send him into a complete panic. Max stopped twisting the cord on his jacket hood and looked up at his Dad with a quizzical frown. "Come on, Champ." Mr Thwaite said, playfully ruffling the boy's blond tuft and leaning to take his hand.

"Tell me you paid for these," Angie groaned while balancing on one foot and pulling a pleated suede skirt up over her tights. Mel didn't answer and Angie threw a ball of packing tissue at her . The skirt barely made its way over her thighs and she twisted to peer at the label. "It's a size eight, Mel!" she exclaimed.

"Beggars can't be wotsits." Mel pulled a thick pink studded belt from the bottom of the bag. "I did pay for this," she smiled. Angie had to admit her sister had quite a talent for petty pilfering. Ever since she had started the job at the Primark store in town, she had perfected the art of removing goods undetected to quite a fine art. Her latest trick was to 'permanently borrow' from the returned garments that people brought back. No security tags see. Only things bought originally by cash, of course, so that once she had slipped the receipt in her pocket, there was no record of the garment's existence.

"Oh, great, and the other five items just fell in to the bag?"

"You like the top, don't you?"

"That's hardly the point." It irritated her, but Angie couldn't help smile at her sister. At times she so envied the naïve simplicity with which she attacked life. She had never taken responsibility for herself. If her mum hadn't been looking after her, Angie had. All she did was move between the two homes, wait until she had outstayed her welcome at one and then return to the other. Heaven knows how she'd ever cope out there in the real world.

"What time is it?" Angie said suddenly, placing her glass down and fumbling between the cushions for her mobile. "Half nine. Jordan should have been back half an hour ago."

"Oh, he'll be fine."

"No Mel, we have rules in this house for a reason – he knows nine's his curfew." Angie pulled the skirt back down and started to fold the clothes up, as if to draw the evening to a close. Mel sighed. It had been good while it lasted. She couldn't help feeling Angie had been a bit tough on the kids for the last week or so and that it was time to cut them a little slack. She refrained from broaching the subject though. That would take a few more glasses.

Jade came bouncing down the stairs.

"Where's Jordie? He should have been home at nine," she said, her voice pinched with injustice.

"Yes, thank you little Miss Perfect," groaned Angie. She swivelled in her seat and pointed upstairs. "You should be asleep."

"Not fair," the girl muttered, and stomped her way back up the stairs. Normally she would stay and fight, but she was wise enough to know that now was not the best time to play her Mum up. There would be other battles. Angie picked up her mobile, punched in the brief message: WHR R U? HM NOW!!!! She threw the phone on to the chair opposite.

"Sod it!" she said with a shrug. "Hand me that belt, let's see if it goes with the skirt." Mel leapt up and handed it to her.

"My name's Jocelyn," the man had said, suddenly turning to face Angie just as his hand reached out for the door handle. Angie, who had already returned to the task in hand, looked up.

"Oh. Right. Yes," she said, standing upright. Then, realising the inference of the gentle nod of his head, continued, "I'm Angie." This revelation seemed to please him and he smiled. A smile that she found herself, infectiously, imitating.

"I'm Tanya," said Tanya. He ignored her and continued to stare at Angie, who blushed self-consciously. *"Well, hello Tanya, how very nice to meet you,"* Tanya mumbled sarcastically under her breath. It was ten minutes to ten when the front door shook with the familiar rattle of loose-fitting glass. The slow shuffle of trainer-softened feet preceded the creak of the living room door. The sisters turned and watched as Jordan sheepishly wandered into the room. His hands were pushed deep into his pockets, his head down and his shoulders rolled up around his ears as though in anticipation of the barrage to come. Since he'd grown his hair into a Green Day fringe, Angie had to squint to see his eyes. She found it frightening, the speed with which he was growing and the daily gulf she felt starting to yawn between them. She merely raised an eyebrow and stared at him. Mel had done a good job of persuading her not to yell at him the moment he walked through the door and to give him the chance to explain. Clearly Jordan hadn't expected this and didn't know how to react. The best he could offer was an inflammatory "Well, get on with it then."

It was like a red rag. Angie jumped from her seat. He took half a step back, feigning indifference.

"Where the hell have you been?" she shouted, aware her authority was slightly compromised by the mixed jumble sale of stolen clothes she was wearing. Jordan let the corner of his lips curl challengingly. Angie stopped short and stared at him quizzically. It took her a moment to place the distinctive, but unfamiliar smell of her son. Then it clicked: mint.

"Have –You – Been – Smoking?" she spat. Jordan lowered his head slightly, a sure sign that her words had struck home. He shrunk back towards the doorway.

"Auntie Mel does," he began in half-hearted protest, but even as he opened and closed his mouth he knew his argument would hold no sway. His mother grabbed him by the arm and propelled him towards the armchair.

"Sit there. Give me your jumper." Jordan wasn't too old to know when he was beaten. Without argument he slipped his arms from his hooded top and handed it to her. The first pocket Angie looked in revealed the half empty packet of Bensons. As she pulled it out she noticed a photograph folded in the palm of her hand. Instinctively, Jordan jumped up from his seat. At first Angie assumed he was making for the cigarettes, but then she realised it was the photo he didn't want her to see. She held it at arms length away from him.

"Hello, hello, what have we got here?" she mocked, assuming she'd unwittingly discovered a new love. But as she unpeeled the image she suddenly realised how wrong she had been. Her face drained of colour, and where once there was a teasing grin, there was now a look of empty shock. Angie stepped forward and took hold of her son. She pulled him close to her. She could feel the softness of his hair against her chin, and suddenly he was a baby in her arms again. It had been a long time since she had hugged him and she felt sickened at how her own self-pitying had swamped her emotions and excluded her own children; the only things left to her in her life that were honest and true. The little boy shrank beneath her arms and she felt his body shake as he gently sobbed.

"I miss him," he said with a simplicity that only a twelve-year-old could communicate. How do you explain to an innocent child the irrational stupidity of the adult? At what point do we lose the ability to see the world in the simple black and white tones of childhood?

"I do too," Angie found herself confessing. She held the crumpled photo in her open palm. She smiled as she looked at the familiar scene; Minorca, six months earlier. Already, it felt like a lifetime ago. And someone else's life at that. She stared at the picture and her heart sank. Jade, brown and smiling, knelt in the foreground, a small yellow and red windmill in her hand; behind her Danny stared defiantly at the camera, his arm proudly wrapped around her son's shoulder. They had been playing football and Jordan's right foot trapped a ball, his arm resting on his hip as though he had just won a trophy. To the casual observer, they looked every part the idyllic family.

"Yes," Angie repeated softly, "I do too."

Nikon Coolpix S210 digital camera, Comet, save £60, £119.99

9 hours, 30 minutes after Jocelyn Thwaite's death

" 'Scuse me mate," Danny said, thrusting his arm out and forcing a tall gangly youth to halt mid-stride. The boy plucked a white cord from his ear and stared at Danny as though he was insane. What had started as a relatively straightforward challenge of asking for directions had suddenly become a test of Danny's nerve and patience. The mass of bodies – tall, short, fat and thin – swept past him with unnerving determination, refusing to look at him or acknowledge his waving arms. This was the famous Oxford Street, Danny thought bemused. The swarming bodies thrust and bounced against each other, nudging the two of them towards the edge of the kerb. The youth flinched at the sudden closeness of the man's body and his foul, stagnant breath. He looked about him for an escape.

"Are there any good hotels near here?" Danny asked. The boy refused to look into Danny's eyes. He fidgeted with the wire of his headphones and stretched to look over Danny's shoulder. The rain had stopped and the clouds had blown apart to reveal a sliver of sunlight reflecting off the shop windows. The youth waved.

"Down there," he said. "Um, near Hyde Park ..." He didn't wait for further interrogation. Instead he stepped off the kerb in front of a screeching taxi and quickly vanished amongst the swelling wave of people. Hyde Park it was then. A blonde girl with huge sunglasses perched on top of her hair caught his eye. Her nose crumpled in disgust and she turned her head away. Danny looked down at his clothes. He removed his jacket, rolled it into a ball and dropped it in to the bin beside him.

Getting the money from the cashpoint had been easy. He had found a machine down a side street behind Selfridges, waited until a couple arguing close by had left, and inserted Mr Thwaite's card. The original daylight robbery. He smiled, as the screen welcomed him like a long-lost friend. His initial worry that the machine might reject the pin number gave way to a renewed confidence and he took the opportunity to study the dead man's finances. He was stunned to find a current account balance in excess of one hundred and thirty thousand pounds. The machine obligingly spat a pile of banknotes into his waiting palm. Mr Thwaite clearly no longer had a need for the money so it was surely better that Danny made use of it. After all, it might sit there unclaimed for years. Was it right that someone should value their money so little that they could kill themselves? At the very least he could have donated it to a charity – homelessness, for example. And what worthier cause than someone who had just been kicked out of his home? Anyway, Danny told himself, it wasn't stealing if the person didn't want it. What was the difference between what he was doing and what hundreds of people did each day when they pulled someone else's old armchair from the skip and sold it at the local car-boot sale? He slipped a handful of notes into his jeans pocket and made his way back towards the bustle of Oxford Street. Someone there would be able to point him towards a hotel for the night. Why settle for a dingy B&B when he had the money to treat himself to something a little bit better?

The Dorchester Hotel, Park Lane: is there a more iconic address? Danny leaned on the wrought iron railings that circumnavigate the open expanse of Hyde Park and viewed his temporary new home. The building itself, however, was something of a disappointment. Strip away the spilling flower boxes, the dancing jets of water and the long line of motor-show display models stretched out in front and to Danny's mind you had little more than a seventies high-rise block of flats. He could never imagine wasting his own money on such a grotesque place. But someone else's? That was a different matter. First things first, however. He wasn't about to book himself a room looking like a homeless tramp. It really didn't matter that he had five hundred pounds of J. S. Thwaite's money rolled up in his pocket. The automated display had been quite insistent that he wasn't entitled to any more than that in a single go. It even threatened to eat his card for good. Still, he couldn't help but think that would be sufficient for the moment. Let the machine revel in its temporary victory. He'd be back tomorrow, and the next day, to win the war.

Danny stepped out between the lanes of traffic that circled the park between Marble Arch and Piccadilly. He wasn't scared of anyone. He was just as good as these people in their Mercs, BMWs and Porsches, squealing their tyres and punching their horns. He grinned at the sound of angry shouts as he calmly stepped onto the pavement in front of the hotel. Danny studied the lie of the land, weighing up his options. A large curved flower display hid him from the view of the two doormen standing guard by the entrance. They wore dark blue jackets and Victorian style top hats. From behind Danny a limousine with tinted windows swept up in front of the hotel's steps. One of the doormen stepped forward and opened the rear door to reveal a tall middle-aged lady. She breezed past him without a glance. Did Danny detect something in the doorman's look as the woman disappeared up the stairs and his colleague pulled the hotel door open? What was it that made these people think they were so special? So much more important than those they had just brushed past? Money. Simply money. Danny's eyes shone. He wanted to feel that power, sense that control.

A black cab pulled up beside him. He leaned through the driver's open window.

"Your back tyre's flat on this side, mate," he said, pointing at the passenger side wheel.

"Bugger," hissed the driver, and the moment he stepped out of the taxi Danny grabbed his jacket and licence badge from the dashboard. Before the driver could look up, Danny had disappeared behind a row of ornamental conifers. The man kicked the wheel's rim.

Danny slipped on the jacket and without breaking his stride, waved the cab driver's badge in front of the doorman.

"Picking up," he said, striding into the foyer. Inside, the urgent groan of the city was instantly silenced by the closing doors behind him. He took a moment to gather his bearings. To his left was the concierge desk, thankfully unmanned, and a row of mirrored lifts; to his right a shallow open seating area scattered with high-backed armchairs, glass tables and tall Art Deco standard lamps. Just beyond was a small illuminated sign directing guests to the spa and pool. Directly in front of him, but obscured by gilt statuettes and palms, was the reception area.

It took him a moment to realise that the pumping sound he could hear filling his ears wasn't the hotel's air conditioning but his own adrenalin. Two men and a woman were waiting at the reception desk. The men wore dark pinstriped suits and thin, brightly coloured silk ties. The woman was tall and slender and the bag over her shoulder looked like it had just been lifted from the shelf of a boutique. She turned her head briefly to look about her, but her eyes refused to settle. Her skin was as pale as milk and, if he pushed her, he was sure she would shatter like china. One of the men moved his hand to her waist protectively and Danny caught the glint of a gold cufflink as his sleeve rode up. Danny slipped his hand in his pocket and felt the roll of notes warm against his palm. It didn't matter how much cash he had, he wasn't going to be able to book a room looking like he did. Turning away from an oncoming porter, Danny sidestepped a china urn and followed the signs to the spa and pool. Ahead of him a pair of glass doors sighed apart to reveal a small, marble-topped desk piled with crisp, fresh towels. The smell of chlorine and coconut oil hit him with an intensity that almost took his breath away. The attendant had his back to the doors and stared aimlessly through the glass that divided him from the pool.

Without letting his eyes leave the attendant, Danny took the three steps needed to reach the male changing room door. Once inside, he made his way along the row of lockers, shaking their handles until he found one that was not only unlocked but was also full of clothes. He didn't linger to consider what might happen if someone entered, instead Danny bundled the contents into his arms and carried them into one of the shower stalls. He undressed, showered, shaved, smoothed his hair down and hurriedly redressed in his new clothes. The tan chinos were uncomfortably tight but not indecently short. He frowned at himself in the mirror: the chequered Van Heusen shirt and pale yellow cashmere jumper made him look like one of those goons on the golf course next to the yard he occasionally worked at. But even he had to admit that, with his hair slicked back and the week's worth of stubble scraped away, he looked more than a little respectable. He tied the laces on his shoes and stood up straight – shoulders back, chest out.

At the main hotel desk the receptionist lifted her head and studied Danny as he approached. She offered a thin condescending smile and nodded lightly to indicate he could speak. Danny feigned indifference and refused to catch her eye. She looked beyond his shoulder and he resisted the urge to turn and look where she was staring. She wore rich red lipstick and her hair was pulled painfully back from her hairline into a tight bun. A coating of fake tan made her skin look as though it had been painted with emulsion. Her badge introduced her as 'Maya'.

"Maya, I'll have one of your finest suites, please." His words belied the juddering of his nerves. She held his gaze, eyebrows arching ever so slightly. Even without the Ballesteros-style get up, his request was unusual.

"Well, sir, we have many fine suites here at the Dorchester." She smiled thinly again. Did she see through him? "We have our Front Suites overlooking Hyde Park Corner, Luxury Suites overlooking Mayfair, our Park Suites with balconies overlooking Hyde Park, or," she smiled challengingly, "we do, of course, have our junior suites." Danny brisled at the inference. Yes, love. I can afford it.

"Hmm," he considered, as if tired by such trifling decisions. "I was hoping for something a little more ..." He let the end of his sentence drift. The girl was taken aback. She was used to smug city types thinking they were something special, that they'd reached the rich league only to discover that, in this tiny microcosm, they were still desperately miles from it. Like the people that request a Park Suite before discovering they can only afford a standard room. Oh, how Maya loved to see their faces crumple under the weight of the reality. It was one of the perks of the job. She would have had the guy in front of her down for one of those any day. Had her fine-tuned instinct deserted her? The man turned his back to the desk. Was he about to leave?

"Well, we do have one of our Signature Suites free at the moment," she countered a little too keenly. This strange man had got her rattled. Danny turned slowly back round. He took a step closer to the desk and leant his arms on it.

"The Harlequin Suite is currently available," Maya continued, clicking buttons on the keyboard in front of her.

"Harlequin Suite?"

"One of our finest. It was Elizabeth Taylor's favourite." Was she blushing? "Dining room, sitting room, terrace …"

"Fine," he replied nonchantly.

"Your name, please sir."

"Thwaite. J. S. Thwaite."

She looked at him again. He didn't look like a J. S. Thwaite. Maya tapped purposefully at her keyboard and then paused to lift her head. "That will be £2,500 a night." She let the challenge hover before going for the kill. "How long will Sir be staying with us?" Danny felt acutely aware of the air constricting around him.

"I'm not sure," he said. "Let's leave it open shall we Maya?" He gently laid the dead man's American Express card on the desk. Maya inserted the card into a hand-held unit and passed it to him. He pressed the tiny rubber buttons. What was the statistic he'd read? Seventy-two per cent of people only have one pin number? Not bad odds. Danny held his breath and ticked the seconds away while the tiny screen flashed defiantly back: processing, processing, processing … A grey-haired man in a pinstriped suit behind him stepped impatiently from one foot to the other. Processing, processing, pin accepted. He let out a sigh that made Maya lift her head. He smiled and she looked back at her monitor screen. Really, there was no telling who had money these days.

Donation to Crisis homeless charity by David Gilmour from sale of his home, £3.6m

6 years, 7 months before Jocelyn Thwaite's death

It was a harsh, biting November evening, the night Angie and Danny met. Does fate bring people together? Luck? Or do you walk past the ones you might fall in love with by the thousand every year? The romantic in Angie would claim the former. She had clicked the Yale behind her as quietly as she could. She had never done this before and she swore to herself over and over as she tugged her coat around her and jogged along the damp pavement that she'd never do it again. One thing you could never accuse Angie of was playing the 'it's not easy being a single mother' card. From the moment her husband had walked out, she had defiantly sworn to protect her children with every last fibre of her strength. Though once, just once tonight, this might need to be her alibi. If Jade woke-up upset she knew Jordan would comfort his little sister. But what Jordan would do then was anybody's guess. Six was a disarmingly unpredictable age. And Jordan, at the best of times, was an unpredictable child. Only two weeks ago Angie had found him chatting happily on the phone to the fire brigade about his Power Ranger doll's missing head. Jordan had taken the split badly, she knew, and she shuddered to think what sort of subconscious rejection her leaving them alone might instil in her son for years to come. She hated and despised her husband for doing this to her, for forcing her to make these choices for her children. She tried to shake the thought from her head and let her sodden feet pound the unrelenting concrete, each pace jolting and jarring her tired legs.

The precinct was nearly a mile from the house, but Angie's adrenalin propelled her all the way without her once stopping for breath. She couldn't remember the last time she had run ten yards, let alone one mile. If the Olympic Federation wanted to know how to break the three and a half minute barrier, all they needed to do was leave the athlete's children alone in a cold house with a fever and see if that didn't make for a new World Record. Outside Halif's Mini Mart Angie involuntarily bent over and clasped her knees, gulping a great lung full of stale autumn air in an attempt to compose herself. She had barely noticed the drizzle that coated everything, her self included, with a varnished sheen. It began to drip from her lank fringe, into her eyes. She blinked the stinging water away. She felt the steam on her cheeks rise and she counted out three more big intakes of air. Now was no time to be self-conscious about her dishevelled state.

A youth leaning by the door studied her with an amused gaze, his eyes travelling up and down her soaked frame. What was he twelve, thirteen at the most? She shivered at the way his stare held hers challengingly. Another youth stepped out from behind his friend and grabbed him playfully around his neck.

"Get us some cans, while you're in there love," he said, waving a crunched up five pound note in his hand. The boys were not much shorter than her, but their spindly, undeveloped frames made their posturing seem childish. Angie was used to the antics of groups of youths gathered near the estate, of course. It was a daily sight, like vandalised phone booths and dog shit. Although something about these two made her feel more uncomfortable than usual. She ignored their request and pushed the shop door open. The familiar clank of the tiny bell above the doorframe heralded her arrival. From his perch behind the counter Mr Halif looked up. Not at the door at first but at the small CCTV screen beside the till. Somehow he preferred the pre-warning that the screen offered. His shoulders slumped with relief when he saw the woman enter on the small flickering black and white screen. Although he did have to double check the live image in front of him to make sure he wasn't imagining the wheezing woman with the wet, plastered hair, cartoon pyjama bottoms and training shoes. Nothing would surprise him anymore. If the Elephant Man strode into his shop wearing a pink tutu, he wouldn't bat an eyelid. Angie placed a bottle of Calpol on the counter, plus a bottle of the Chardonnay that had been on offer just next to it. A shrewd bit of cross-promotion, she noted. Mr Halif eyed her with suspicion. He took the bundle of coins that she held in her shaking palm, but before he could count them, she was gone. All he was left with was the rattle of the bell and the reverb of the door as accompaniment.

The two youths were still waiting by the door and Angie turned away from them. She started to zip her coat up, but it caught and she had to tug at the tiny metal tab. The longer she took trying to pull at the zip, the more unnerved she became. She could feel the stare of the boys' eyes burning into her back. Still pulling at her jacket, she started to walk away from the protection the shop's pool of light gave her. Further along the precinct by the Real Crispy Chicken Hut she heard the tread of shoes from behind and she quickened her pace. She wanted to run, but the combination of her unclasped coat, the bag in her hand and her wobbling legs made her progress stilted.

"Hey, love ..." The shout made her catch her breath. She knew straightaway that it had to be one of the boys who had followed her. His voice was thin and reedy, only just threatening to launch itself head first into puberty. But she was being silly, surely. These were just kids – nothing more. Despite an instinct to the contrary, Angie stopped and slowly turned around. She reasoned that doing so would be enough to make the little upstarts bolt. Angie was surprised to see, however, that a third lad had joined them. No, wait, this third person was a girl. Despite the fact they were all wearing similar jogging trousers and hooded tops, pulled up over their heads, the third face had the familiar, soft roundness of a teenage girl. Her presence gave Angie some comfort.

"Shouldn't you lot be in bed?" she asked with a grin. The taller of the two boys, his eyes now barely visible behind his hood, smirked.

"If you like love," he countered, and his mates giggled. He lowered his head further and peered up at her from below his hood, like a demonic monk from a horror film.

"How old are you?" she demanded, involuntarily stepping

backwards. They didn't answer, but stepped closer until Angie could smell the alcohol on their breaths. The girl was laughing, her smile wide, eyes big and wondering. Shouldn't she be at home mooning over some pop poster on her wall or experimenting with glitter eye-shadow in preparation for her first teen dance?

"We'll look after that," said the tall boy, stretching out his hand towards the bottle in the plastic bag. Instinctively, Angie yelped and pulled the bag away. She didn't care about the wine of course, but she couldn't risk losing Jade's medicine. Foolishly, she might admit in retrospect, she gripped the neck of the bag and swung it in the direction of the boy. He was far more agile than Angie and had seen her intent the moment she raised her arm. In a flash he was out of her reach and then beside her as the bag missed its target and hit down on her own arm. The boy grabbed her and pulled at the bag. All the while the young girl laughed and the second boy stood with his hands in his pockets.

It took Angie a moment to place the sound with the memory. Starsky and Hutch, that was it. The squeal of tyres preceded a flood of light illuminating the scene: a bedraggled woman in pyjamas surrounded by three spindly youths. The effect of the headlights was instantaneous. The three youngsters bolted in all directions, a plan clearly choreographed for just such an occasion. The front of the silver car bounced up onto the verge and displaced chunks of turf, its nose finally resting within inches of a plastic bin. The headlights pointed to the sky and the driver's door swung open. Angie peered through the apocalyptic light at the smudged outline of a figure. The man's voice echoed through the dark.

"If I see you round here again, you're meat," he bellowed after the scampering feet. Even the rain deemed it wise to pause briefly.

Danny turned and looked at the girl, a ripped plastic bag in her hand and a shattered bottle of wine by her feet. Her hair was dark and flattened to the side of her head by a mix of rain and sweat. She was breathing erratically, her shoulders heaving up and down. To her chest she clasped a small pink bottle.

Angie stood rooted to the spot, her jaw open in amazement. So, knights in shining metallic seven series BMWs really did exist.

Danny peered through his windscreen. The girl looked so vulnerable, so helpless, so pretty, even with water dripping from her nose and … was that an Eeyore pyjama top?

Eeyore pyjamas, Bhs, from £12.00

1 day, 8 hours after Jocelyn Thwaite's death

Some people grow to embrace luxury, whilst others wear it like an ill-fitting suit. Danny, for someone who didn't know a Lapsang Souchong from a PG Tips, wore it rather well. Twenty-four hours after spending the night sleeping rough on a piss-stained train station bench, he was sitting slouched in one armchair, his feet propped up on another, in one of the most stately and renowned hotel suites in London. Views had never really been his thing – a trip to Weston-super-Mare was more about the inside of the local bar than the outside of the promenade – but even he had to admit the view from this high up was breathtaking. He pulled his chair up beside the French doors and let them swing open, feeling the cool morning air ruffle his hair. Danny revelled in the fact that since booking the room he had barely moved a muscle. At two and a half grand a night, he saw little point in leaving the room empty. He had spent the first day in a variety of stages of repose: two hours in the bath wallowing chin-deep in a whole bottle of scented bath lotion; four hours on the bed staring agog at the forty-two inch plasma screen – flicking through the channels until the spinning images made him feel nauseous – and three hours on the terrace drinking the contents of the mini bar. Eventually, the sun dipped behind the trees and he fell into a deep, dream-filled sleep. He woke at three in the morning and crawled back into the enveloping folds of the king-sized bed.

By the time he rolled out of the bed, Angie would have been up and about for hours, he mused with satisfaction. If only she could see him now. She would be so jealous … Or would she? She never seemed so seduced by these kinds of trappings in the same way he was. The screen on the wall offered him a menu choice of personally-deliverable delicacies: he'd never tried smoked salmon, let alone lobster. His stomach ached for something solid and comforting. He ignored the menu on the screen and picked up the phone. He could order what the hell he liked. Fifteen minutes later a trolley arrived baring his custom-devised mixed grill of steak, lamb chops, liver, fried egg, sausage, gammon and chips – plus a garnish which he flicked onto the floor – garlic bread, profiteroles and four bottles of chilled German beer. It may have been half ten in the morning, but in the world he had temporarily created, what did that matter?

It was as he was sat at the dining room table balancing on the hind legs of his chair with his hands cradled behind his head that Danny realised he was made for this kind of life. It was how he should always have been. Some are born to it. Others have to fight for it. Or, easier still, steal it. And why, exactly, was that so much worse than those who were given this kind of life on a plate? Nothing more than fate's genetic lottery divided the likes of him with the likes of them: the them that believed nature's hierarchy to be the one true judge. How did those people sleep at night knowing that nothing more than the roll of a die had given them their Gucci shoes, Sunseeker yachts and Tiffany jewels rather than Tesco value beans and Matalan four-quid jeans? Danny dabbed the linen serviette to his lips. He could do posh if need be.

Of course, it wouldn't be long before the management became suspicious of this strange man occupying one of their premium suites: a man who arrived with no luggage and hadn't appeared from his room for twenty-four hours. If he wanted to enjoy his unwitting benefactor's hospitality much longer he was going to have to lay down some ground rules. It was obvious that before long someone was going to miss Mr Thwaite. Was he married? Did he have children who might search him out? And, of course, cashpoints and credit cards made a person instantly traceable. If Danny was going to take this man's life, however temporarily, he was going to have to devise a future for him. No one but Danny had seen the man jump, so no one but Danny knew the man was dead. He may well have been due to appear somewhere the following day – so there was a chance that already Danny had been too slow to react. He pulled the man's case up on to his knees and routed about inside until he found the small black leather diary. To his relief there was no significant entry for that day's date. It didn't mean he was completely out of the woods, of course. To put his plan into place he needed to know where he lived, what he did for a living and who his friends were. Danny was suddenly galvanised with a purpose: he flipped the leather case upside down and let the contents flutter like confetti on to the bed. Cards and papers nestled amongst the mountainous ravines of the bedspread, sheets and notes scattered, some tipping to the floor. He scooped them up and let them fall into an untidy pile. He buzzed room service – he needed a laptop and lots of strong, black coffee. There was work to be done.

Danny slipped his own wallet to the back of one of the desk drawers and held Mr Thwaite's credit card in his hand. He rolled it back and forth between his fingers as he flicked through lists of web pages searching for information about his newly borrowed identity. He was surprised and intrigued to discover that Mr Thwaite was something of a minor celebrity: his searches took him via several impenetrable music sites to references on the Classic FM, EMI and BBC sites before he found a more comprehensive biography on the Royal College of Music website.

Here he learnt all he needed to know about the man whose money was scattered on the bed beside him – his family, his wife's name, his background, even the name of his dog. Danny learnt that as a prodigious young talent the real Mr Thwaite had been trained at the College, before being handed the chance to compose idents and theme tunes for the BBC in the early eighties. These included, amongst others, the irritatingly distinctive sixty-second ticking clock that preceded daytime schools programmes on BBC2 and which afforded their originator a royalty every time they were played. Which was a lot. Demand for film and television scores quickly followed. The royalties from which were still drifting in years later. The 'J. S.', Danny discovered, stood for Jocelyn St John. He stood in front of the mirror and studied his full height. Even with a new wardrobe Danny was going to struggle to make a convincing Jocelyn. He turned to the left, turned to the right, swallowed in his stomach and stuck out his chest. But with a dark suit and his shoulders back, he could make a very passable Joss. Joss Thwaite – he liked that. It was time to go shopping.

Danny straightened his collar in the mirrored glass of the Prada store. Bond Street, he decided, should be Joss's spiritual home. As a wealthy, talented man, envied and admired by people all round the world, this was where he was meant to be. Danny's first task was to ensure the luggage that he promised the Dorchester's receptionist would be delivered, was delivered, and finding the kind of suitcase a man like Joss would own wouldn't be difficult along a road like this. Danny spread his arms wide and breathed in the stinking smell of dirt, fumes and privilege. With a smile he stepped off the pavement, crossed over the road and pushed open the door of the Mulberry shop. Once inside it didn't take him long to select two medium sized leather cases. He had never been much of a browser – much to Angie's regret – and the girl behind the counter was a little taken aback by the speed at which he made his choice and was willing to part with eight hundred pounds. Usually, even the most discerning of clients liked to spend their time selecting and pondering, balancing the bags in one hand, then the other, pulling them backwards and forwards across the squeaky marble floor, opening and closing them. At four hundred pounds each, Danny too might have lingered longer to consider the advantages of triple locking security had it been his money he was spending. But then that was the luxury of using someone else's – not to worry about such trivia.

With his first mission accomplished, Danny went in search of the clothes he needed to fill his new cases. The famous old street offered ample choice: Armani, Ralph Lauren, Louis Vuitton – names he had only ever seen before in Angie's magazines – littered either side of the road. Like a kid dazed by the contents of a sweet shop he stood in the middle of the road and stared about him. Eventually he opted for Gucci. He had always seen himself in Gucci. Much to the bemusement of the magazine-model assistants, he wasted no time in selecting two suits, a casual jacket, a selection of shirts, four ties, socks, shoes, underwear and a set of cuff-links he had no idea how to put on. He opened one of the cases on the floor beside the cash-till and proceeded to fold the clothes up and lay them flat inside. Behind the counter, the assistant store manager didn't let a flicker cross his face. With studied skill he handed the man's card back to him: he might have just spent over three thousand, three hundred pounds, but in a boutique of such repute, discretion was the watchword. He lightly bit his bottom lip. A wealthy individual didn't return to a store that gossiped. And this was clearly one very wealthy individual.

Danny was beginning to enjoy himself. He was certainly enjoying the nervous, envious expressions that followed him. He spent a little longer filling the second case in the Yves Saint Laurent shop, even affording himself the luxury of trying on a couple of the jackets and letting the staff busy themselves around him. And then just as quickly as he had appeared, he was gone. The staff gathered like dummies in the window to watch him disappear across the road and out of site, a suitcase in each hand. At the entrance to the Royal Arcade, Danny flagged down a black cab and instructed the driver to deliver the cases to the hotel.

It was only as he turned back towards Piccadilly and found a small, unassuming wine bar to hide in, that Danny considered what he had actually just done. Not only had he robbed this man of his money, or more accurately his family of their inheritance, but he was slowly robbing him of his identity. Clearly Mr Jocelyn St John Thwaite was someone with a reputation: a reputation Danny was wilfully on course to pull apart. He had read that the real Mr Thwaite had been nominated for a Grammy in 1993 for his film score to *The Water Carrier*, had been honoured with two Ivor Novellos for his TV work and was a Fellow of the Royal College of Music. What would the luminaries make of his little spending spree?

As Danny sipped at his cold, gassy beer he considered how being rich really rather suited him. He'd always known it, of course, it was simply that he'd not been able to do anything about it. Like when he used to deliver those cars for his mate. High-end imported luxury cars, with wound-back clocks and scratched out serial numbers. Behind the wheel of a Range Rover Vogue he was the boss: he was judged by how he appeared, not what he was. The power he felt as he revved the engine and flashed the lights forcing cars to swerve out of the way was addictive then, just as the power of the money in his pocket was now. It had soon become apparent to Angie that Danny didn't own the BMW he had been driving the night they met. Nor the black Mercedes SLK he turned up in the following night, or the Mitsubishi Shogun the next night. When the truth finally revealed itself, more than a week later, the two of them rolled about on Angie's bed in fits of laughter. But although she had never mentioned it since, part of Danny suspected Angie was disappointed he wasn't actually the person she thought he was. Regardless of what she might say, surely even Angie would have preferred him if he had been wealthy and that the cars he drove had really been his?

Danny ordered another beer. A small TV set hung behind the bar babbling inanely to itself. The barman wiped the surface of the bar with the cloth that lay across his shoulder, placed a small disc of paper down and put a fresh beer glass on it. Steve would have laughed at him for spending four quid on a drink that came with a tiny doily stuck to the bottom of it. The bar slowly began to fill – groups of work colleagues jostling for space at the bar with arm-entwined couples. Danny felt conspicuous in his loneliness. He sank the remainder of the beer in one gulp, slid the glass away from him and stood up. In a single svelte move the barman had reclaimed the glass and wiped the surface it had stood on, the memory of Danny's stay removed before he had even walked out the door. Suddenly he had the urge to phone his friend – maybe he could entrust him with his whereabouts. But then his mate's lack of belief in him was still too raw.

Just off Piccadilly, Danny paused to retrieve more cash. As he pressed the sweaty surface of the tiny screen, he half expected the machine to identify his fraud and swallow the card. Instead, it remained obediently silent. At the hotel reception he enquired about his cases, and was informed that they had not only arrived but that the Concierge had had them delivered to his room. He gave Maya a wink. She blushed. He was beginning to enjoy this game. He paused to look at himself in the elevator's mirrored wall. And that's what it was, wasn't it – a game? He brushed the lint from the lapel of his new jacket. His reflection smiled conspiratorially back. At what point did he plan for real life to kick in and drag him back to the mundane? Could he even take himself back there? He had sampled this world now, and more than that, he had discovered it fitted him rather well. He pulled the cuff of his shirt straight under his jacket sleeve and twisted the tiny gold cufflink. The light caught it and it sparkled alive. Why worry? Ignore it, he told himself, stepping from the lift. In his room the cases sat politely at the end of the bed. The curtains had been pulled back and tied, the bed-linen changed and a fresh bowl of fruit placed on the table. He slumped down on the edge of the bed and rubbed the balls of his palms into his eyes. The future would be what he wanted it to be.

Range Rover V8 Supercharged Vogue SE, list price, £63,300 on the road, £74,820

4 weeks, 2 days, fifteen hours before Jocelyn Thwaite's death

Jocelyn Thwaite stared at his reflection in the mirror. He straightened his tie. He liked to wear a tie. Nowadays the fashion seemed to be for untailored jackets and open-necked shirts. Jocelyn didn't want to appear stuffy, but he had to confess that he sometimes struggled with the revelations of the modern world. Was there really a need for things like fashion? A jacket and tie were standard attire for a gentleman. Satie understood; he never left his flat without a starched collar and his grey velvet suit. These days even barristers and doctors wore jeans. Downstairs he could hear Elizabeth bustling about in the kitchen, humming to herself: some tuneless Muzak she had picked up from the radio or TV, no doubt. He had chosen the pale blue striped tie, the one Elizabeth scrunched her nose up at. Maybe the young woman at Max's nursery would appreciate it more.

114 years before Jocelyn Thwaite's death

What little light there was in the room was slowly eaten by the approaching dusk and Suzanne had to narrow her eyes to see. Satie shuffled in his seat and continued writing. Suzanne laid her brush on the edge of the easel and sat back. He made a challenging subject, self-conscious and awkward, his expression sad and distant. Erik always seemed so ill at ease with his work, with people, with life itself. He was unlike the other artists and musicians that gathered around the bars of Montmartre; a part of him constantly removed and shut away from the world as though locked behind an impenetrable door.

4 weeks, 2 days, fourteen hours before
Jocelyn Thwaite's death

Children spilled into the nursery as though flushed through a dam that had burst its banks. Tanya was thrown against the wall as the doors flew open and struggled to regain even a modicum of composure before parents started to ply her with questions. Angie gathered herself and prepared to meet her charges. Monday mornings were always like this – a boiling temper-ridden tussle between wired, coughing kids and tired, stressed parents. It was hard to tell who was the more relieved to escape the intensity of the weekend. There was an unceremonious scramble to relay instructions:

"Isabelle's got a grazed knee. She's got a plaster on it right now, but if you could remove it at lunchtime to let the air at it ..."

"India says she doesn't like the celery sticks ..."

"Theodore is absolutely besotted with his *Wind in the Willows* play set. May be best if the other children don't play with it ..."

Angie nodded with a smile. It seemed enough to satisfy the parents who piled bags, toys and coats into her open arms. It would be a good half an hour before all the children had arrived and, more importantly, all the parents had gone, so that they could shepherd them all to the story area and create some semblance of order out of the chaos. Maximilian appeared at her side and tugged her blouse sleeve. Angie turned and looked down. He was holding up a tiny bunch of twisted bluebells. Some of the bells were missing. He didn't say a word, and appeared a little surprised at her delighted reaction. It's not like it was a new toy or a handful of chocolate. After all, it was his Dad who had instructed him to give them to the woman. Why he wanted to do that, Max really hadn't a clue. Angie stood up and watched the little boy quietly wander into the main room. He ignored the other children running and shrieking about him and found a corner where he could concentrate on his solitary game. Max's father was watching Angie's expression. He nodded at the flowers.

"He insisted," Jocelyn shrugged.

"Oh, how sweet of him," Angie replied. "I must put them in some water ..."

"He's taken quite a shine to you," he continued. There was a pause that Angie felt unsure how to fill. She smiled and waved across the room,

"Well, I must ...," she said.

"Oh, yes, of course," he mumbled apologetically. Someone else might have felt uncomfortable with the way he watched her. But Angie couldn't help but find his bumbling uncertainty endearing. She helped Isabella unwind herself from her scarf, watching Max's Dad kneel down to give his son a kiss as she did. There was something fascinatingly child-like about the way he held his son's face and his awkwardness as he stood back up, as though his long legs and angular arms didn't really belong to him. He wasn't unhandsome, she supposed, in an obvious Hugh-Grant-public-schoolboy kind of way. She found his dusty leather shoes, old-fashioned-cut jacket and pale blue striped tie amusing and, in turn, charming. He wandered back over to where she was straightening books on the shelf. Had he caught her looking at him? He seemed to have a fresh purpose to his stride as though he had resolved an issue in his mind.

Intuition can be a frustrating talent at times. Angie knew, probably long before Jocelyn did, what he was eventually going to ask her. The fact that he didn't get round to it until that evening when he came to pick his son up was no surprise either. After he had left and she could finally shuffle the bolt across on the front door she sat down on one of the miniature plastic chairs and studied the walls around her. The children had drawn pictures of their families. These middle-class offspring had produced fairy tale images of mothers and fathers holding their hands. Maybe there was a kid brother, or the occasional grandparent or a wob-bly-shaped dog. But no ethnic minority or single parent in sight. No wonder so many of them grew up into disillusioned adults. Looking at the pictures made Angie feel sad. Maybe that was the simple reason why she had said 'no' to Maximilian's father. Angie resented the fact that she had had to kick Danny out. And she resented the fact that she felt as though she owed her children a replacement.

Contrary to her better judgment Angie confessed this to her sister the moment she returned home. Mel groaned and playfully knocked her forehead against the fridge door. Little magnetic letters bounced on to the floor. She picked them up and carefully spelt out the word IDIOT.

"But you think he's rich?" she said, waving her arms like her feet might leave the ground. "You know, really rich." Angie turned her back on her and continued to shuffle the children's fish-fingers from baking tray to plate.

"Oh I don't know, I … who cares?"

"He must be. Sending his children there. Does he live near the nursery?"

"I really don't know." Angie was becoming impatient with her sister's nagging. She had been taken aback by the sudden hurt in

Jocelyn's eyes and now it was beginning to play on her conscience. Maybe she should call him and say she'd made a mistake.

"He isn't married is he?" Mel stopped to consider her question, but just as quickly seemed to dismiss the thought. "Whatever, doesn't matter."

"Doesn't matter?" Angie said aghast, shaking her head. "Of course it matters. No, he's separated ... Anyway, it's irrelevant. I've said no."

"Oh," Mel sang triumphantly, "so you know this much about him. Thought you weren't interested." She chuckled to herself as she grabbed
a handful of the children's chips and disappeared into the front room.

Example Child Tax Credit, single parent, two children, earning £10K a year, credit = £6,200.78

3 days, 8 hours after Jocelyn Thwaite's death

Elizabeth Thwaite pushed her thumb under the rim of the envelope's flap and edged it open. She had instantly recognised the scratchy, looped lettering on the front. Momentarily she felt the blood drain from her face only to be replaced by the uncomfortable prickle of sweat on her forehead. She smuggled the letter into her cardigan pocket away from the prying eyes of her housekeeper. Closing the conservatory door behind her she stood beneath the blossoming magnolia and pulled the envelope out of her pocket. Even with the door closed, Elizabeth could make out the rasping sound of the plastic truck's wheels rattling up and down the hallway's polished fifteenth-century floorboards. Maximilian squealed with delight as his truck cornered on two wheels and bounced off the oak skirting. Elizabeth clenched her teeth against the sound. She had told Mrs Jarvis not to let Maximilian ride his truck inside the house a thousand times.

Dear Elizabeth,

Forgive me. You deserve a better explanation of my disappearance than I feel I am able to give right now. You need to know that I am well and have come to no harm. I have not been feeling myself of late and need time to reflect properly. I will write again soon.

All my love,
Jocelyn

Elizabeth felt the heat searing behind her eyes. She wouldn't cry; she refused to. She held the letter down by her side and wobbled briefly on the balls of her feet. She sat down in the high-backed metal garden seat and stared blankly at the paper. There was no doubt the note was from Jocelyn's notebook – a brand of writing paper he stuck to religiously. Much like so many of his habits. Jocelyn was like a tanker in the Channel, impossible to turn without well-scheduled warning. So the spontaneity of his disappearance, if that was what it was, was frightening in itself. There was so much about her husband that she'd failed to understand over the years: his moods and sulks. But they were all part of his creativity, weren't they? Like the women he mooned after; just silly childish crushes really. Nonsense surely? Maybe, as husband and wife, they should have spoken more. But then, did she really want to know what he might tell her? It was true that Jocelyn had been acting strangely for the past few weeks, but that wasn't necessarily anything new. He often had irrational, dark moments. Times when Elizabeth knew to keep her distance and let him evolve from them by himself. He'd even threatened to leave, but that was all part of being married to an artist she supposed. Still, for all her bravado, a keen-eyed observer might spot the creases of worry in the lines on her face. He'd come home. She lifted her Barbour off the hallway peg. The horses wouldn't muck themselves out.

3 days, 8 hours after Jocelyn Thwaite's death

Danny could afford a moment of self-congratulation. Mrs Thwaite would be opening his letter any time now. His career as a master forger was assured. He had carefully studied the contents of Jocelyn Thwaite's case until he was confident that he knew not only how to physically write in the hand of the dead man, but also with his voice. '*You need to know that ....*'. What an inspired phrase that was, and the '*I've not been feeling myself of late*' bit was pure genius. Danny had also made sure the letter was as ambiguous as possible, offering no clues or factual inaccuracies. And although the postmark would reveal he was in London, London, he was happy to report, was a very large place.

4 weeks, 2 days, three hours before
Jocelyn Thwaite's death

It was only as Jocelyn peeled his fingers from the car's steering wheel and stared at his blood-drained fingers that he realised he had been gripping the leather so tightly. He shuffled forward in his seat and peered through the Jag's concave windscreen. Dirt and squashed flies muddied his view and Jocelyn let the washer spit foam to further obscure his view momentarily until the wipers smeared it away. Max rocked back and forth in his seat, levering his body forward in an attempt to reach the plastic dinosaur he had dropped in the foot-well. Usually, he would shout for his Dad's attention, but for some reason his father seemed preoccupied with something beyond the window, and, even at his tender age, he knew instinctively when not to make a fuss. He tugged on his straps and angled his head. From his viewpoint he could just make out the heads of two bigger children bobbing past the window. A boy marched purposefully in front of his sister. He carried a rucksack on his back and wore a football shirt and baggy tracksuit trousers. Neither said a word as they passed the car, crossed the road and disappeared into a small driveway on the other side of the road. Max craned his head to follow them. All the houses seemed so small here, as though someone had dropped a whole handful of them in one tiny place. He wondered how the children would ever find room to race their ride-on toys around. With the children gone, Max returned to the problem of reaching his dinosaur, stretching first his arm and then his leg in its direction.

    It wasn't that Jocelyn had assumed Max's teacher, Miss Chase, would say 'yes' it was just that he hadn't prepared for her to say 'no'. All his planning up until that point had been of what would happen next – as sketchy as that had been. It wasn't as if his confidence was sky-high at the moment as it was. The rejection suddenly plunged him into the kind of introspection that he seemed to spend so much time wallowing in at the moment. At the nursery he had looked down at his son's expectant face and reached out for his hand. Without fear of question or reprisal the little boy had wrapped his fingers around his father's thumb. Had the boy heard him ask his teacher out? If he had, had it meant anything to him? He led Max out of the nursery. So, what if it did? So what, if the boy inadvertently made reference to it at the dinner table? Would Elizabeth really believe a three-year-old? And even if she did, did he care any longer? This was no spontaneous affair. He had considered such an eventuality for years, so it would be difficult to define his actions as irrational or out of character. The fact that he hadn't undertaken an affair before – or indeed, yet – had nothing to do with a lack of premeditation. He had come close, a number of times: the Polish intern student Maria Plaikov with her extravagant fret work, cold blue eyes and long, long alabaster legs; the French au pair, Juliette, who had held his child almost from the moment he was born until the day he could walk, so honest, warm and innocent. Sharing their dinner table one day, gone the next, the victim of Elizabeth's possessive suspicions. Then, last summer he had been minutes away from asking out a girl he didn't even know in the recording studio canteen; a tall auburn haired girl with thin, pensive lips and dark eyebrows. Of course nothing had come of any of these moments. But they were all tell-tale events that lead him to Angela Chase. Angela Chase whose lack of self-awareness and open, happy face snared him the moment he set eyes on her. He turned the key in the ignition and flicked the gear stick into drive. There was nothing to be achieved by sitting outside her house all night. And Max would be getting hungry.

Dino Adventure Set, 3–8 years, www.elc.co.uk, £35.00

4 days, 19 hours after Jocelyn Thwaite's death

Danny had spent three days sampling the best that the Dorchester Hotel could offer. There was certainly no lack of choice with two dedicated bars, three restaurants, a variety of private function rooms, room service at the buzz of a button and a daily restock of the not-so-mini, mini bar. He quickly rejected the imaginatively named Dorchester Bar, with its blue-tinged glass walls and mirror mosaic encrusted grand piano, as he did the restaurants' own cocktail bars with their mandatory dress codes and snooty, unsmiling staff. So, after much research, Danny decided that the Promenade Bar suited Joss, his alter ego, best. He levered himself up onto a stool and leaned across the bar. The bar man placed a crystal glass bowl of anchovy-stuffed Kalamata olives in front of him. Mitchell was the one member of staff who didn't seem to look at Danny as though he was something adhered steadfastly to his heel. It bemused him. In his pocket he had more money than these people probably earned in a year and yet they still looked at him as though he wasn't worthy to breathe the same air. He ordered a vodka Martini. Mitchell grinned at him as he placed a small triangular shaped glass in front of him.

"Mr Thwaite, my man, you planning another night like last night?" His brevity did nothing to disguise the concern in his voice.

"Hell, yeah," Danny grinned back. Mitchell shook his head and turned to serve two women who had just stepped up to the bar. Danny watched carelessly as he served his customers. His hands moved with the patient precision of an artist. He was deceptively unhurried, drawing first from the optics, opening the mixers and then garnishing their glasses with sugar and lime. Danny felt like a school kid spying through the keyhole at an adult world he was yet to understand, but was desperate to join. Moments later the women were joined by their partners. The men's brows were still sweaty with the sheen of exercise. Laughing loudly they waved dismissively at the barman and sent the women to find a table while they leant their elbows on the bar. Danny wondered whether either of the men was the owner of the clothes he had stolen just days before. The one on the right looked the right height. And, actually, now he studied him, he was wearing a very similar blue cashmere jumper. Something about the possibility rather amused Danny.

There was a strange hush to the room, as though everyone was keen to guard their privacy. Heads nodded furtively in corners hidden by high-backed chairs. Thick drapes soaked up any excess sound and squirrelled its secrets into their confidence. Danny watched as a tall, beautiful woman in a simple understated black evening dress and sheer stockings perched herself on one of the stools at the end of the bar. His eye was taken by the small, diamond-encrusted necklace curled in the shape of a leaping dragon around her neck. She ignored both the guests around her and the cocktail list by her arm and lifted her purse to her lap. Without a word passing between them, Mitchell placed a tall glass in front of her and moved away. Before long the bar was completely trimmed by customers and Danny's view of the woman was momentarily blocked. The next time he looked she was gone, her seat filled by an Asian man wearing a white Armani suit.

Danny had already spent £16,832 of Jocelyn Thwaite's money to date – £10,000 on the room alone, over £5,000 on his little shopping spree, several hundred on food and drink over the last few days, and £1,500 on a rather stylish Breitling. Not nearly enough. It was actually proving quite hard to spend the money. If he hadn't still been angry with Angie, he might have rolled up a stack of notes and posted them anonymously to her. But he knew it would be pointless. She was stupid enough to take it straight to the local police station. Angie had never appreciated the value of money like he had. He had always had an astute understanding of what the stuff meant in life, the opportunities and the power it gave. She would grin at him and hum some ridiculously trite little tune like 'Can't buy me love'. He'd scoff, she'd laugh and they'd agree there was a philosophical gulf between them that could never be bridged.

A silver-haired gent with a walking stick and the billowing odour of cigar smoke walked past. He nodded briefly at Mitchell and settled in one of the chairs by the vast plate-glass windows that overlooked the park. Danny raised an eyebrow questioningly.

"Lord Wellborough," Mitchell hissed as he juggled with a forty-seven-year-old bottle of Glengarioch. "Owns most of Norfolk," he explained simply. Danny nodded in an 'ah-yes-of-course-he-does' kind of way and downed the last of his drink. Mitchell delivered Lord Wellborough his whisky.

"You got no other place to go, my friend?" he asked with a smile.

"No, not really," Danny replied. Mitchell nodded noncommittally. Another lonely soul with more money than friends ....

"Well, Mr Thwaite. If you're looking for company ... there are ways and means."

Mitchell saw himself as a healer. Some were leaders or followers. He was a healer: the kind who brought others together, listened to their worries and guided their paths. And that was what made him such a good bar man, not his ability to mix a Bloody Mary although he could do that better than anyone he knew. He had seen it all: from the humble East End boozer to the snooty Maida Vale wine bar. And without doubt the loneliest, unhappiest souls were those he served right here in this bar every night. Mitchell had honed his ability to analyse the characters around him into a fine art. He could tell who they were and how they had made their money by the way they walked, by the way they addressed him, what they drank and where they sat. He had met them all: entrepreneurs, celebrities, old money, new money, drug dealers, gangsters and politicians. But Joss Thwaite had him baffled. His shirt still had those new-from-the-packet creases, his shoes were free from scuff marks and he rattled the watch on his arm like it was the only one in the world. If Mitchell had to take a wild guess, he'd say the man had only very recently come by his wealth: a lottery winner or a gambler, perhaps.

"You see the young lady who was at the end of the bar earlier? Dragon necklace?" Danny nodded and looked over to the seat where the Asian guy sat. "Kira looks after a number of the hotel's most valued guests." It took Danny a moment to grasp the implication. He was still wallowing in the thought of being classified as 'one of the hotel's most valued guests' when the penny finally dropped. Mitchell nodded. So, this was what it really meant to have money: the doors to a totally different world slid open. The realisation – okay, he'd been a little naïve not to spot it earlier – that he could afford to be in the market for such a women left him reeling from the power he had inherited. He waved away Mitchell's offer as nonchalantly as he could.

Mitchell smiled politely and wandered to the end of the bar to collect discarded glasses. The room had begun to empty – the traditional hiatus between aperitifs and liqueurs. It wouldn't start to become busy again until well after ten. Danny rubbed his smooth chin. The face balm he had found in his bathroom hadn't done anything to make his skin feel refreshed and supple as it promised on the label. Instead, it felt raw and itchy. He frowned. Maybe he should get a taxi to the West End. He could sample the trendy wine bars and watch the young foreign girls walk by. He shuffled in his seat. A movement by the doorway caught his attention: Mitchell was greeting a small huddle of people with an exuberant wave of the arm. The group was made up of four people, three men and a girl. Mitchell ushered the group towards the bar. Maya, the receptionist, followed hurriedly behind. Danny lifted his empty glass and peered through its distorted base. The three men leaned against the bar, ignoring the attention they had drawn. The girl wandered further into the room. She leant her head back and looked around her. She was younger than her companions and painfully thin with dark mauve circles around the hollow of her eyes. Limp, twisted threads of hair were loosely held on top of her head by a simple clip. She yawned and stared about her as though she had just discovered herself in some strange wonderland. She stood next to the plate-glass windows and gently spread her fingers against the glass. She appeared fascinated by some tiny detail far away. The shortest of the three men struggled to climb up on to one of the stools, shrugging off an offer of help with an irritated flick of the hand. He bowed his head and hissed from the side of his mouth. His dyed black hair was teased forward in a crew cut that attempted to disguise a receding hairline. The other men, both taller and broader, had to stoop to hear him speak. The one on his right had an earpiece that he conspicuously kept pressing with a fat stubby finger. Every now and then he shot a concerned look about the room. The man on his left continually gasped for air. He had small, dark dots for eyes, flabby pink cheeks and a heavily pockmarked face. The atmosphere in the bar had changed, a whispered hiss played around the room like a Mexican wave. Two women, who had been sat by the window, repositioned themselves on stools by the bar and without the slightest hint of embarrassment, studied the visitors intently. Danny put his glass down and stole another look. The man on the stool raised his head.

"What d'you want to drink Stacey?" he said. The girl pretended not to hear. "Get her an orange juice," he said, swivelling back round in his seat.

"Vodka 'n' Coke," the girl suddenly announced, her hands still glued to the window, her forehead moving slowly back and forth across the glass. The man at the bar rolled his eyes and in that moment Danny recognised exactly who he was; Alex Fry, the Hollywood actor. Alex Fry no more than ten yards from where he sat. He swallowed hard.

"Is that, who I think it is?" he whispered, leaning both elbows on the bar.

"Certainly is Mr Thwaite, sir, the very same," Mitchell said. They both nodded appreciatively.

"Did you see *Brief Liason III*?"

"Mmm, I'm afraid I did." They both shook their heads.

A growing crowd soon gathered. The word had spread quickly amongst both the guests and staff that the famous actor was in the bar. Maya had positioned herself tactfully next to the actor's security guard.

"Just watch them," smiled Mitchell. "Bees 'round a pot." Danny laughed and watched as Maya looped her hair behind her ears and tilted her head. Then, in reply to a question that he couldn't hear, the woman turned and pointed straight at Danny. Alex Fry pushed himself off his stool to see beyond the crowd of people at the bar to where she was pointing. The next thing Danny knew, the actor was in front of him, his hand thrust out. Danny found himself shaking the famous star's surprisingly bony fingers.

"So," Alex Fry coughed, "It's you …" Danny swallowed and looked about him. "It's you that's got my room," he boomed. Danny's mouth moved up and down soundlessly.

"Your room?" he finally managed to ask through gummy lips. Alex broke into a grin and laughed. "The Harlequin Suite. I always stay there when I come to this little town of yours." He slapped Danny on the shoulder. "The look on your face!" He looked about him to make sure his audience was laughing too. They were. "I'm only kidding mate. My fault, only flew in from LA this morning – promo tour." The security guard had sidled round behind Danny and was eyeing him suspiciously. Danny shuffled uncomfortably.

"Alex Fry," the actor announced. "But you knew that, right? Get my friend here a drink," he said pointing at Danny's empty glass.

"Joss Thwaite," Danny replied, taking the drink and gratefully swallowing its contents in a single gulp. "Let me get you one," he added. Alex slapped his hand on the bar.

"A man from my own heart," he laughed. "Line them up barman. My new friend and I are going to get wasted."

He pulled up his chair and grabbed an ashtray from the bar.

"Don't mind do you?" he asked, waving a tiny white stick between his first and second fingers. Danny shook his head.

The two men, fuelled by the constant stream of alcohol, found they had an unlikely camaraderie. Contrary to the boastful, egocentric that he might have expected, Danny found Alex Fry to be self-effacingly insecure, with a nervous habit of continually rubbing the bony nub of his knuckles. The skin, Danny noticed, was almost rubbed raw. Alex introduced him to his companions: his niece Stacey, Larry, his manager, and Dave his security advisor. Stacey, apparently, wanted to be an actor like her uncle and, as a favour to her father, Alex had let her trail along for the experience. He was beginning to regret it. From the moment she had arrived at his house that morning she had been stoned on a cocktail of heaven-knows-what. Even on the flight over she had taken the opportunity to sneak into the toilets. Alex had grabbed her arm and pulled up her sleeve looking for the tell-tale bruising. She had just giggled, lifted her bare foot onto the seat and pointed to the fleshy skin between her toes. Alex hadn't said a word to her since. She hadn't noticed.

The group, now with Danny fully installed as their guest, commandeered a spread of tables by the window. Down on Park Lane the cars kept flowing, the lights painting red and white stripes around the park. Throughout the evening hangers-on came and went, all looking for an excuse to get close to the actor. Some just wanted to shake his hand, others wanted to offer a critique on his latest project. Some out-stayed their welcome and were steered from the table by Security Dave. Alex accepted their banter with a tired resolve. They had just finished their second round of cocktails – all charged to Joss Thwaite's Harlequin Suite – when the film company's PR representative appeared. Belinda spent the best part of an hour running through the actor's heavy promotion schedule for the following day. Alex didn't even pretend to be interested in her minute-by-minute timetable and Larry was left to reassure her.

"It's all cool," Larry smiled. "Alex is really excited about his film, so don't you go fretting your pretty little head." He leaned over and patted Belinda on the knee. "Have a drink." She tugged at her hem, pulling it down as far as it would go. God she hated this job. Just because she was the one in the office that was organised, she ended up with the shitty end of the stick. At dinner parties it all seemed so glamorous, shepherding celebrities around the place. But the reality was nobody else at Grayson Miles PR wanted to do it. She was the one who got it in the neck from the film distributors because some jumped-up little actor suddenly wanted an unscheduled visit to see their own effigy in Madame Tussauds or a surreptitious snort of something illegal in the toilets of the Tate Modern. She sighed loudly. Everyone stopped to look at her. She apologised and flushed pink. The actor and his manager had stopped listening to her altogether. Sod it. She'd have that drink after all.

"Dry white wine," she muttered, resigned. The way Fry and his companions were downing their drinks he'd be in no state for the *GMTV* slot at eight-thirty anyway. She sighed again.

Stacey stood up and wobbled her way to the bar. Her cropped vest hung loosely on her frame, her arms hanging limply by her side as though it was a struggle for her to lift them. This was truly surreal, Danny pondered. Here he was with a guy whose image appeared on billboards, buses, and magazines every single day discussing the merits or otherwise of television interviews.

"That Ross bloke made me look like a dick last time," Alex said, staring pointedly at the PR girl.

"Shit," Belinda hissed under her breath. Terry Miles, her boss, had warned her not to let Fry know who was interviewing him until he was in the green room and it was too late to back out.

"I'm not doing Ross!" he spat challengingly. Larry leaned over and patted his arm. He shot Belinda a withering scowl.

"Al, let's talk about this later, yeah?" he said.

"No, let's talk about this now – who the hell put that idiot on the list?"

"Al, he has regular viewing figures of over six million ..."

"Six mill!" Alex scoffed. "What a tin-pot country. Sorry Joss, " he added turning to Danny. Danny shrugged – yeah, it probably was. "I can get over thirty mill by farting on Jerry Wiseman's show on KBC!" He laughed at his own joke.

"No, seriously," pressed Larry, "you need to do it. If you have to drop something maybe we can dump Emap." Belinda rolled her eyes. Terry Miles would never forgive her if she lost Emap. Tomorrow was going to be the day from hell. Stacey returned with a glowing crimson cocktail in her hand, green leaves sprouting from the top.

"It's a Slippery Nipple," she announced.

"Well, thanks for getting us all a drink," Alex said sarcastically.

"Whatever," the girl replied helpfully.

"I'll get 'em," Danny offered, jumping from his seat.

The remainder of the evening was something of a blur. Eventually, Alex announced he was tired of the bar and wanted to see some nightlife. Belinda had been mid-sentence. Alex's driver was summoned and before Danny knew it he was being bundled into the back door of a private club somewhere just off Great Portland Street. The manager of the club beamed happily and waived the usual annual subscription. Alex leaned his head on the man's shoulder in gratitude, then wiped the residue of spittle he had left on the fabric. With a great fanfare the group spilled into the bar area. Belinda had declined Larry's kind offer of a nightcap at the club and then maybe "back to my suite", in favour of passing on the actor's demands to the Jonathan Ross production team. Larry, sulking from his rebuff, vanished around the corner of the club to make a private call. Moments later he was replaced by a young executive from Warner Bros UK, sent to keep charge of the studios valuable, if erratic, asset. Security Dave lingered by the doorway mumbling up his sleeve.

Sometime before midnight Stacey called a friend who was also over from the States. A giggling, drunken bundle of legs and arms tumbled on to the couch beside them. Behind her a tall, rakish teenaged lad grinned inanely. He pulled his hands from his jacket pocket and pointed at the actor.

"Alex Fry, awesome man," he nodded to himself as though there was a beat in his head. He slid his long legs over the arm of the couch and fell in beside his girlfriend. He propped his feet onto the low wooden coffee table, swung an arm around the girl's shoulder, pulled her to him and thrust his tongue down her throat. Danny stared about him. The plum walls were covered with simple framed black and white photos.

"I'm over there," Alex pointed to a large signed print, sandwiched between Ulrika Johnson and a bald bloke Danny didn't recognise. Alex's niece and her friends sat at the end of the table whispering giddily. The girl had black, short-cropped hair, wild dark eyes and a nose ring. She stared at everyone with disgust, her expression fluctuating from joyous rapture to resigned irritation. Her chest rose and lowered as she laughed. Her boyfriend pulled a small brown square wrapped in cling-film from his leather jacket pocket and placed it on the table in front of them. It looked like a slice of fudge cake. They made for a strange gathering of individuals. As Danny studied the group, he wondered whether they were really much different to the crowd of disparate strangers that gathered back home at the 'Ferret' every Friday night.

"Let's go to the Gaslight!" Alex announced standing up, wobbling on his feet and falling back into his seat. Danny looked at him questioningly. "Girls, girls, girls," the actor giggled.

They never did make it to the lap-dancing club. A call came

through to the bar warning of paparazzi gathering by the front entrance. The young film executive, keen to take his duties seriously, urgently shepherded his charge and friends through the club's fire exit and into the alleyway beyond. The driver was waiting, the engine revving, ready for the quick getaway. A pink neon sign on the other side of the road promised 'exotic dancing' and the actor was momentarily distracted. Security Dave stepped into his path and pointed him in the direction of the car's open door. He collapsed on the back seat and immediately fell into a deep, impenetrable sleep. The car's wheels span. Danny grabbed the passenger door handle and fell in just as the driver released the foot-brake and let the car accelerate away leaving two thick lines of burnt rubber behind on the tarmac. The car was a lot nicer than the Friday night taxis Danny usually ended up in. He closed his eyes tight shut, breathed in the smell of leather and smiled to himself.

Taxi, from the Ferret to home, after 11pm rate, £12.50

3 weeks, 5 days before Jocelyn Thwaite's death

Angie pulled the curtains of the nursery closed and turned to study the spilled contents of the room: only three more children to collect. She smiled down at Max and he nodded knowingly in return. She was exhausted. The day had begun early with an over-eager delivery driver rapping noisily on the front door. Angie had groaned and felt her way downstairs, blinking in the morning sun.

"Somebody's lucky day," a voice said from behind a large bunch of cellophane-wrapped flowers. A spindly youth with a manic grin and plastic framed-glasses appeared from out of the foliage. He puffed azalea leaves from his mouth and huffed. "Biggest bunch of the day, these," he said. The flowers filled the doorway and Angie had to step backwards to let light into the room. The youth unceremoniously thrust a clipboard into Angie's hands and shuffled his feet while she studied the paper. "There," he muttered irritably, pointing to the base of the cover sheet. "Sign there." Angie did what she was told and handed back the clipboard.

The large white flowers sat in a bag of water, tied at the neck with a flourish of brown raffia. Angie placed them on the windowsill and breathed in their sweet scent. It had been nearly three weeks since she kicked Danny out of the house. Since then she hadn't heard a thing from him. Suddenly, out of the blue, he sends flowers - rather nice, expensive flowers. His usual hunting ground was the Esso forecourt. She was, she had to grudgingly admit, impressed. Still, if he thought a bunch of flowers would ... And then she noticed the tiny doll's house sized envelope slid nonchalantly inside the cellophane wrapping. She plucked the card from its sheath and read the inscription:

Sorry if I embarrassed you.
Jocelyn Thwaite (Max's father)

The note made her smile: it was so polite and precise, just like its author. It hadn't occurred to Angie that the flowers could have been from the man at the nursery. She had dismissed his attention as fleeting. She just wasn't the kind of woman that men speared themselves through the heart for. He was persistent, she would say that much for him. Angie sat down on the settee. When was the last time anyone had cared enough to send her flowers? A wave of sadness had swept through her and she fought back the urge to cry.

Angie scooped up an upside-down chair and picked strips of green Playdoh from its seat. She had felt wretched all day. The Thwaite's housekeeper had delivered Max that morning and briefly Angie wondered whether she'd ever see Jocelyn again – she was well aware of how fragile the male ego could be. Max pushed a small metal car up and down the length of the windowsill. He hummed the noise of the car's engine and let the car's wheels spin. It flew off the Lilliput-sized cliff edge and landed in a basket of wooden building bricks. It wasn't the little boy's fault, was it? Angie placed books on the reading shelf. Suddenly Max squealed and clapped his hands. He ran to the door. Angie turned to see Jocelyn leaning against the doorway watching her. Her heart leapt with relief.

"I'm so pleased to see you," she stammered. He dipped his eyes and said something about the traffic.

"Look ..." he began at last.

"No, let me ..." she said. Angie toyed with a lump of Playdoh, rolling it into a twisted ball. Jocelyn looked down at her fingers and she hastily placed it on the table.

"Angie?" He studied the miniature roads and houses on the rug beneath his feet. He paused, scared how she might react. Angie stepped forward. He lifted his eyes and looked straight at her. She knew what he was going to say even before he uttered the words. In that moment he looked so lost and vulnerable, that before she knew it, she found herself nodding and quietly whispering,

"Yes, okay."

114 years before Jocelyn Thwaite's death

'Impossible to stop thinking about your whole being; you are in me complete; everywhere, I see nothing but your exquisite eyes, your gentle hands, and your child's feet.'

3 weeks, 4 days before Jocelyn Thwaite's death

The following evening Jocelyn appeared on Angie's doorstep with yet more flowers in his hand. She laughed; she didn't own one vase, let alone two. She picked Jordan's discarded top from the armchair and went in search of a jug. Jocelyn looked around the tiny front room. Above the gas fire a row of childish scribbles filled the wall: 'Jade, aged 5' 'Mummy on a bisecul, 'Jordan and Danny'.

"They're beautiful, thank you," Angie shouted from the kitchen.

"You're welcome," he replied. "They're delphiniums. The name comes from the Latin delphis, meaning dolphin," Jocelyn continued. Suddenly she felt foolish. What on earth did a man who could recite the Latin names of flowers see in her? She looked at herself in the reflection of the microwave and fussed her hair behind her ear. Maybe she should cut it short. Jocelyn rocked back and forth, his hands behind his back. He fiddled with his tie and readjusted the cuffs of his jacket. One of his cufflinks popped out and he scrambled under the settee to find it. It came out attached to a hair-band and he quickly secreted it behind a stack of DVDs in the corner.

"My sister will be here in a minute," Angie called from the kitchen. She'd forgotten to put the washing machine on and now her hands smelt of stale sweat and dried earth. "She's babysitting," she added, scrubbing her hands beneath the tap. Jocelyn nodded and waited patiently. At the top of the stairs Jordan and Jade hovered, ready to burst downstairs the moment their auntie arrived.

Mel had had her highlights done especially. She bounced in through the front door and before she had even removed her coat, rattled off a list of rehearsed questions. Jocelyn deflected them with aplomb and Angie hissed at her sister. The children sidled into the room and stood and stared at Jocelyn. He made an exaggerated play of shaking their hands. Then Mel and the children stood on the doorstep and watched as

Jocelyn led Angie to his car and held the door open. Angie caught Mel's eye and winked.

"That's a Jaguar XJ," whispered Jordan, jumping from the step and running down the path to peer at the car. He skipped around it, running his hand over the smooth paint. "It's a 4.2 litre V8 Sovereign," he said, running back and grabbing Mel's arm excitedly.

"Is that good?" she asked. Jordan rolled his eyes.

"It's fifty grand's worth of good."

"Oh," Mel replied with an appreciative nod. "Oh." Jade seemed equally impressed. She looked between the car and her auntie.

"Do you think he nicked it?" she asked.

The restaurant was already full when they arrived. A single round table by the window sat empty, shielded from the main door by a tall oak settle. The enterprising owners had converted what from the outside seemed a relatively mundane looking village pub into a restaurant catering for a middle-class clientele who appreciated caper berries, sun-dried tomatoes and celeriac as staple ingredients. A kindly looking waitress directed them to the table. The rest of the room paused to consider their arrival as Jocelyn drew back Angie's chair for her. She picked up the menu and studied it. Then put it down and looked about her at the plates on the other tables.

"They don't usually take bookings in the bar area," Jocelyn said, leaning on his place setting and fiddling with the cutlery.

"Oh," replied Angie, trying to sound impressed.

"The restaurant area's lovely, but a little, oh I don't know – austere." He smiled, judging her expression by her eyes. "I thought you'd find it more comfortable in here."

"It's lovely," she said, thinking how out of place her red dress now seemed. Mel had persuaded her it was perfect, but now she felt cheap. She pulled the hem of the dress to the edge of her knee and trapped it there with her hand. All the other women in the room were wearing muted greys and browns with sensible flat-soled shoes. Red was for the scarlet woman. Wasn't that what she was? Jocelyn pondered the wine list and the waitress hovered beside him as he 'hummed' and 'hahhed', his finger running up and down the list. Was she going to have fish, or pork he asked. She didn't know. Angie shuffled in her seat. Worried that he would laugh at her for not knowing her Sancerre from her Pinot Noir, did he not realise what a disappointment she was going to be? With a great clap of the hands, he announced his choice.

"Oh, yes, ideal," he exclaimed. "Perfect." The girl trotted away satisfied, only to return minutes later with a bottle carefully wrapped in a starched white napkin. "Sorry, I'm an awful bore – but it's something of a hobby of mine." Jocelyn smiled as he savoured the tiny dribble the girl had poured in his glass. He nodded and waved his hand at Angie's glass. As she sipped it he leaned across to study her face for a reaction. She feigned delight as she swallowed what tasted to her like any other white wine she had ever had.

The conversation was relaxed and casual. They talked of nothing and everything. Jocelyn was a generous listener, letting Angie reveal more and more about herself. He rested his chin on his upturned palm and stared at her as though captivated. She couldn't for the life of her understand why, and she wondered, not for the first time that evening, what he saw in her. It was too soon to ask, of course. It was easier to talk of smaller things: their children, education, food, holidays. It wasn't that he didn't talk about himself, it was just that throughout the evening Angie couldn't help feeling he was keeping much of himself hidden from view. He fascinated her. He was charming and kind, awkward and absent-minded. His long, smooth fingers, with tidy, trimmed nails and flawless skin; a walking advertisement for good living. What Angie did learn surprised her. He wasn't arrogant, or obnoxious, but softly-spoken and reticent. Angie was captivated.

"My favourite piece?" Jocelyn let his eyes drift skywards. "Probably the first proper commission I wrote; a piece for a production of Chekhov's *The Memorandum*. Have you seen it? A young friend of mine had written a rather bold adaptation and wanted something ... I was really proud of that. It was a long time ago now of course."

"Wow, you're so clever. You must be so proud."

"Hardly," he scoffed. For a moment Angie wasn't sure whether she had said something stupid; he didn't linger on it. "TV and film seem so glamorous, of course. But it's very compromised. Film work is formulaic, studied and mostly dry." Angie nodded, unsure at what exactly. He was talking to himself as much as to her. "Film executives have their ideas. And directors, don't get me started on directors." He stopped and laughed. "Sorry, I'm going on ..." And from there the conversation wound a very natural path until, before Angie knew it, she was placing her spoon next to the half-eaten apple and raisin strudel and tapping her stomach.

"Oh my goodness, there goes the diet," she exclaimed. They walked side by side to his car, and looked up at the clear night sky.

Jocelyn looked at his watch – force of habit. Time had never been his ally. As a youth he had been desperate to be an adult, and as an adult he had spent all his time wishing he could think like a youth again. He held the car door open for Angie and she smiled that warm smile of hers. He wanted to hug her. He closed her door. It had been as a teenager that he had been at his most creative: at his most unsullied and imaginative. So many emotional and functional barriers had got in the way since then, creating an incurable creative constipation. All that ever dribbled out of his musical rectum these days were the same old familiar bars of trite pap. When he was fifteen he had written his first sonata. It was a very naïve piece, of course, but it was fresh and real. It wasn't tainted with the preconceived expectations of others. It was true to himself. Recently he had found his green college exercise book with its graffiti scrawled cover and childish scribbles inside. He had propped it against the piano's lectern and let his fingers retell his childish musical tale. The notes were as fresh as the previous day's memory and briefly he wondered where the last thirty years had gone. Had he achieved nothing? Had he learnt nothing? To Jocelyn, his music hadn't evolved a single note, it had merely wound itself round and round until it had nowhere left to go. To the uninitiated ear his youthful scribbling may have appeared as nothing remarkable, but to Jocelyn it was magical, even beautiful. In one single piece he had summed up the total of his professional ambition – to describe the emotions swirling inside him through simple notes and chords. But since then he had done nothing but prostitute himself. What else would you call it when he had so easily let himself be seduced by those suits with their perfect white teeth and year-round tans. No, his destiny had always been self-initiated. And now he tutored a new generation of talent. Each and every one of them hungry for the kind of 'success' he had achieved. Awards and adulation. How could he warn them of the hollowness of such things when he hadn't even been able to stop himself?

Jocelyn walked Angie up to her front door and, holding her hand, kissed her lightly on the cheek. He turned to walk down the path. Angie stepped forward.

"Thank you," she said. She meant it. Somehow, without even knowing it, Jocelyn had given her back something she didn't even know she had been missing – her pride. He nodded and said goodnight, promising to call the following day. Angie paused at the door her hand resting on the handle. The evening had seemed so unreal and yet so right. She took a deep breath; there would be a barrage of questions the moment she walked through the front door.

Dressed Dorset crab, with celeriac rémoulade, The Ivy, London, £15.50

5 days, 8 hours after Jocelyn Thwaite's death

The fizzing babble of the unattended TV woke Danny with a start. He found himself spilling from the remnants of a dream in which he had been stood in front of a weather map directing pound signs on the board behind him and forecasting a miserable outlook. He raised his aching head and peered about him. The picture on the screen jumped and span, all the colours of the rainbow flooding the room. It was going to be a cloudy day with intermittent drizzle. Apparently. Danny groaned and reached for his pillow before realising that he was actually balancing precariously on the edge of one of the room's floral armchairs. He struggled to bring to mind the final events of the previous evening. He was relieved to find that he had at least made it back to his own room relatively intact. He put his hand in his pocket and felt the handful of twenty and fifty pound notes spill on to the carpet. How much had he spent last night? Rolling the crumpled notes about in his palm he estimated he had over a thousand pounds left, but that meant he must have spent nearly a thousand during the course of the evening. He had gone out of his way to demonstrate his generosity, he remembered. In fact now he thought about it, he had thrust a wad of notes into the driver's hand at the end of the evening. The mother of all tips for someone who was invariably being paid to do the job anyway. Thank buggery it wasn't his money.

He felt his way to the window and pulled back the curtains. He looked across at the bed, its crisp, white sheets still stretched tight across the giant mattress. It wasn't natural. He threw himself face down on the bed and scrambled the sheets into a heap, pulling the pillows off and dumping them on to the floor. He shouldn't have made that sudden movement. He moaned as his stomach and head rolled in opposing directions. In the bathroom, Danny quickly stripped and plunged himself under the shower. The mirror confirmed his worst suspicions. He phoned down to reception for coffee, then sat down on the end of the bed and idly flicked through the channels. He kicked his clothes across the room and sipped at his freshly filtered finest Colombian. On the screen the female host was bouncing on her hands and gabbling on about the next guest, 'on after the break'. It took a moment for Danny to realise they were talking about Alex Fry. He sat bolt upright and felt for the volume control. He pictured Angie padding round the kitchen in her slippers and her 'boys are smelly' T-shirt. She would be wrestling with protests of missing book-bags and school jumpers, whilst juggling plates full of burnt toast and beakers of milk. In the background this same inane drivel would drone from the tiny portable on the kitchen worktop: the host's incessantly cheerful disposition completely at odds with the fractious atmosphere in their house. Danny always loved the way Angie looked in the mornings – like the gently disturbed surface of a pond. Beautifully ruffled, he called it.

A knock at the door woke him from his malaise. He grunted aloud expecting room service and was startled to see Stacey bounce in through the door waving her arms above her head.

"Dear … God," she announced. "Bonk … Bonk … Bonk." She flung herself into one of the many armchairs dotted around the room. She bounced up and down appreciatively. "Nice …. Room," she purred, looking about her.

"Uh, hello?" he said, cocking his head to look at her. He realised he still only had a towel round his waist.

"Don't mind me," Stacey giggled.

"I won't." He paused, waiting for some explanation.

"Can I stay here a bit – please," she begged, "Those two have been bonking like mad all night. And now they're at it all over again. I can't stand to be in the same room …"

"Those two?"

"My friends from last night. I sneaked them into my room, but they've been going at it like rabbits on speed ever since." She rolled her eyes and thrust two fingers into her open mouth. "So, please, can I stay? Pretty please?" Danny shrugged and nodded at the screen.

"Your uncle's on in a minute …" Stacey appeared wholly unimpressed. "There's coffee over there if you want some," Danny said, disappearing into the bathroom.

Stacey wandered about the room, shuffling the ornaments and opening the drawers. She peered at her reflection in the full-length mirror, tucked her hair behind her ear and grimaced. Turning to study her profile, she breathed in and clenched her buttocks as tightly as she could. She must have put on five pounds just in the last twenty-four hours. Stacey turned to face the mirror full on and pulled her top up to reveal her stomach. The image she studied was the one no-one else saw: rolls of flesh oozing over the waistband of her jogging bottoms. Pushing her hand on her stomach she breathed in as deeply as she could. How did Keira Knightly do it? It wasn't fair, the skinny bitch. Stacey stepped out onto the veranda. She leaned over the edge and stared at the people below scurrying back and forth so purposefully. How wonderful it must be, she thought, to have an aim in life. All those funny little black cabs, like ants, each and every one full of people rushing to be somewhere. Stacey had never rushed to be anywhere in her life. Maybe she should ask her Dad for liposuction. She wouldn't eat another thing all day. Let those lecherous casting agents try saying she was overweight. She could have the figure of a thirteen-year-old if that's what the role demanded. If the worst came to the worst she could have her stomach stapled like her mother. Stacey clenched the rail and squeezed hard. When she was rich she would make sure she would always be the most beautiful woman in the world. She wouldn't let age twist her, like it had her Mum. She would be Audrey Hepburn or Grace Kelly. She would only let herself be photographed in black and white. Stacey pulled a packet of cigarettes from her pocket, pulled one out and threw the packet on to the small wrought-iron table and wandered back into the room. Boy, she needed a fix.

He had half hoped the girl would have got bored and left, but when Danny reappeared from the bathroom Stacey was rolling backwards and forwards on the bed staring at the ceiling.

"Your sheets are all messed up ... bad dreams, or something else?" she teased, rolling on to her stomach and peering at him through her fingers. Danny stared at the pile of papers spread out on the bed beside her. He reached across and grabbed them from her.

"Do you mind?

"Not at all," she grinned.

Danny scooped the papers into his desk drawer and turned the tiny brass key. Stacey sucked on her fingers and stared at him. No doubt this was the method by which she got everything she wanted in life. He stared at her. And despite it all, he was still drawn to her wide, questioning eyes and the hint of naked flesh at the base of her neck, the loop of her loose T-shirt teasing. Not, as he had noted on observation the previous night, that she had much to hide anyway. Was she wearing a bra?

"...Now our guest this morning, Hollywood heart-throb Alex Fry, is apparently caught in traffic but should be with us any moment soon..."

Belinda would be having a fit – behind schedule before the day's even begun. Danny wondered how much his delay was traffic and how much was a hangover. The answer came ten minutes later when the camera panned round to reveal Alex slumped on the bright yellow *GMTV* sofa, a pair of dark Gucci shades balanced on the bridge of his nose. The dusty, bright orange foundation he had been painted with did little to disguise the greying shadow about his eyes and along the line of his jowls.

He grunted monosyllabic answers to the woman's questions. Danny could picture the PR woman off-camera waving her arms and gesticulating wildly.

"... *Alex, your new film* Lethal Exposure, *is already number two at the box office, you must be feeling great?*"

"*Mmm. Prefer to be number one.*"

"*Well, of course... maybe next week. So ...*"

"*Not if people don't stop paying to see that Disney crap ... Minxy the fucking roller-skating hedgehog, I ask you ...*"

"*Oh, um this is live TV, Alex. Apologies to our viewers, especially those with young children ...*"

Danny couldn't bear to watch any more. He picked up the remote and pressed the button.

"Was your uncle really bothered he didn't get this suite?" The thought appealed to him.

"Yeah. Too right." Stacey laughed. "He's a creature of habit is old Uncle Alex. He's got a room at a hotel in Manhatten that he pays for even when he's not there – just so he's sure to get it when he visits. If this new film does well he'll probably do that here. So you'd better enjoy the room while you still can." She paused as though a thought had just popped into her head. "So what do you do exactly, to be so rich?" Stacey lifted herself up and crossed her legs beneath her. They looked like they belonged to a famine victim.

"So rich? What makes you think I'm so rich?"

"Um. Hello!" She answered waving her hands about her. And, as an afterthought added, "You got any gear?" Danny shook his head.

"So?" she pestered. He felt like he was under cross-examination. He wandered over to the window and looked at the scene beyond.

"I'm a musician," he answered.

"Cool," she nodded. "I'm guessing not hip hop, right?"

He smiled. "Right. I write soundtracks to films and stuff."

"Oh yeah, anything I've heard of?" Something in Danny clicked – how far could he push the truth? The silly little girl wanted to be an actor – well, here was her masterclass.

"Have you heard of *The Water Carrier*?"

"Oh, yes Dustin Hoffman ... Wow, you wrote the score for that?" Stacey nodded her appreciation. "Great film, I don't remember the music, of course."

"Of course not. I was nominated for a Crammy for that, I'll have you know."

"Grammy," she corrected, and gave him a funny little frown. She jumped up off the bed and wandered over to where he stood. She deliberately brushed against his arm and stepped out on to the balcony to retrieve her cigarettes. She definitely wasn't wearing a bra. She waved the packet at Danny and he shook his head. Danny hadn't shifted position and she smiled as she squeezed back past him, holding his gaze.

"Joss. Joss. Jossy. Joss." She mumbled half to Danny, half to herself. "I like that. What's it short for? I'm going to call my first child that. I'm going to have, like, twenty kids. But only after I'm famous."

"Jocelyn," he said, but she seemed to have lost interest in her own question. "I'll look out for you at the movies," Danny added. Stacey didn't spot his thick layer of sarcasm.

"Oh yeah, I'm gonna be even more famous than Uncle Alex," she said, without even the slightest hint of doubt. She dragged on her cigarette and blew a great plume of blue smoke up above her head. Stacey was studying him carefully.

"You don't look like a musician," she announced.

"What does a musician look like?" Stacey appeared to consider the question for a moment, but had no obvious answer.

"*The Water Carrier* is years old," she continued. "You must have been very young."

"Yes, I was," he answered simply. "Do you think your friends will have finished their aerobics, by now?"

"Want to get rid of me?"

"You ask too many questions," he replied. Stacey stared at the carpet. Was she annoyed with him? Oh, why the hell should he care? "Want something to eat?" he asked, "I'll call room service."

"Whatever," she sulked, and wandered into the bathroom. "Mind if I take a shower?"

"Go ahead," he answered, but she had already pulled her T-shirt up over her head. She didn't close the door and didn't care that Danny could watch her. Maybe that's what she wanted. He turned away, only to be confronted with her mirror image reflected in the full-length glass. Her shoulders jutted out like splinters of stone, her skin was flawless, but under the harsh white light of the bathroom neon it looked translucent, her vertebrae showing clearly beneath the skin. He watched as she stepped out of her jogging trousers and leant to switch on the shower. He caught sight of the curve of her breast and studied the small, firm shape. It reminded him of Angie's rounded, fuller shape: the shape of a woman, not an emaciated boy. He picked up the phone and rang down to reception.

62

Danny placed the breakfast out on the small table on the veranda, setting two places. The glass door opened and Stacey appeared, wrapped in one of the Dorchester's monograph towelling robes. Her hair was still wet and pulled back off her face. The damp had turned it almost black. She sat down beside him, eyed the contents of the table suspiciously and reached for her cigarettes.

"You should eat something."

"You sound like my Dad," she answered breathing deep lungs full of smoke.

"That's the look for an aspiring actor, is it?" he continued, "a bag of bones?" Stacey looked genuinely shocked.

"Hardly. I'm ten kilos over my ideal weight. My agent said if I didn't lose it in the next few weeks she was going to take me off her books." Danny had obviously resurrected an issue of contention. "Bitch," she added. "She refused to put me forward for a Wendy's commercial 'cause I was the wrong shape. I wouldn't mind, but she looks like John Candy." Danny laughed. "She does," Stacey insisted.

"Well, your weight is just fine," he said. Stacey considered that for a moment.

"Do you want to sleep with me?" she asked.

Twenty pack of Benson & Hedges Gold, special filter, £5.49

6 weeks, 5 days before Jocelyn Thwaite's death

It was snowing the night Danny stumbled from the nightclub, the giggling girl clutching his arm. Her heel caught on the edge of the pavement and she crumpled in a pile beside him, her laughter bringing tears to her eyes. The girl's flat was small and smelled of stale bread and sour milk. Danny fell into the settee, his eyes barely open and his mind barely awake. The girl searched noisily through a pile of CDs on the side. She scattered empty plastic cases about her like confetti and fed a disc into the machine. She danced in front of him, her hands above her head and her eyes closed. Her legs were long and naked and her hips moved from side to side like a swaying tree. The throbbing beat hurt Danny's head and he sunk his face into a cushion. The girl laughed at him and offered him a chipped mug of brandy and then, moments later, her soft, gentle hands.

5 days, 9 hours after Jocelyn Thwaite's death

Danny stared at Stacey. She wasn't joking – she really was asking him if he wanted to sleep with her. Her lips were lightly parted and her robe had slipped from her left shoulder.

"No," he said. "I don't." Stacey pulled her robe back up, hugged it tightly around her and pushed back in her chair. She shrugged and pretended to study something suddenly vitally arresting on the skyline.

6 weeks, 2 days before Jocelyn Thwaite's death

He blamed Angie. Because he loved Angie. He stood in front of her and his shoulders slumped. She could tell something was wrong before he even said a word. He couldn't bring himself to catch her eye. Angie felt a shiver run down the length of her spine. She felt as though someone had plunged their hand into her chest and squeezed the fine tubes that dissected her heart. Danny held out a hand and she pushed it away. She turned away from him and stared out of the window, her world had stopped spinning – everything was still. She closed her eyes but the tears wouldn't come. She refused to turn around and eventually she heard the gentle click of the bedroom door closing.

3 weeks before Jocelyn Thwaite's death

Jocelyn slipped his hand about her waist. He felt the warmth of her skin below the thin fabric of her dress. She looked beautiful tonight. If he was honest he wasn't very keen on the red dress she wore on their first date, but this strapless black one suited her. Around her shoulders she wore a simple chenille scarf. To the casual observer Angie was just another regular follower of Verdi and Puccini. The last time Jocelyn had taken Elizabeth to a concert she had worn a muddy-brown coloured woollen skirt and flats and Jocelyn had felt old beside her. Now, still wearing the same suit, with Angela beside him he felt invigorated. In fact he hadn't enjoyed a concert so much for years. It was a fairly perfunctory rendition of Fauré's *Requiem*. A piece he knew note for note. In fact he often used it to illustrate the mawkish nature of the late nineteenth-century Romantics to his students. But Angela was so wide-eyed. Throughout the performance she sat on the edge of her seat, enthralled. She clapped generously at the interval and turned to hug him. All the way from the hall to the theatre bar she chatted excitedly about what she had seen and heard. Jocelyn envied her innocent appreciation, like a toddler seeing snow for the very first time. "What was that instrument called?" she'd asked. "Why did they have so many different ones?" And "what did the conductor do exactly? Surely if they could all read music why did they need him waving his arms frantically about his head?" Jocelyn laughed, good point, he conceded.

It was as they sipped their interval drinks that Angie managed to pluck up the courage to ask about Jocelyn's wife. How long had they actually been separated, she wanted to know.

"Emotionally, about fifteen years," he replied without a hint of humour. "I'm moving out soon," he added as an afterthought. Angie was taken aback, for some reason she just assumed they no longer lived in the same house. Surely separated meant just that – separated. Jocelyn saw her surprise. He didn't know what to say. He put his arm on Angie's shoulder and steered her away from the crowd huddled beside the small theatre bar.

"Elizabeth and I are, have always been, a marriage of convenience." She studied him. "We live in the same house, for now, but that's about it." Angie twisted her body away from his arm. Was he playing her for a fool? He looked hurt.

"I don't understand," she said. "Does she want you to stay together?"

"Probably," he replied honestly. And probably she did. Because to Elizabeth her social persona was everything. Her village friends, her horsey crowd. You didn't divorce, you just got on with it. All marriages go through … He'd heard it so many times. They were both from an older generation. The difference was, that out of the two of them, he could see how the world had moved on and left them far, far behind. But Max is only three! How long have you …?"

"Max was a mistake." He reconsidered. "Well, as far as my wife was concerned. You see, we'd agreed. No children." He shook his head, it pained him to admit such things about the child he loved. "Max wasn't supposed to be. But Elizabeth is old fashioned, so there was no thought to, you know, to get rid of him.

"But she loves him, right?"

"Loves? Yes, I'm sure. Likes? No, he's nothing more than an inconvenience. She spends more time with her blasted horses." Jocelyn stopped short, as though suddenly aware of how he was exposing himself. "Better finish our drinks, the second half is about to begin."

The wind outside the theatre niggled and teased the audience as they spilled from the entrance. Angie shivered and Jocelyn wrapped his coat round her shoulders. She pulled it closely around her as he disappeared out of sight in search of his car. She pulled the collar to her nose and breathed in his smell. It reminded her of a small box-room in her grandmother's house when she was young.

"I think it's romantic," offered Jade, throwing herself down on the sofa next to her mum the following morning. She flicked through the concert programme that her mum had brought back with her. The women were so beautiful in their large, billowing velvet gowns. The men so smart in shiny black shoes and bow ties. She stared at the glossy pictures and dreamed of being a virtuoso violinist with long flowing strawberry hair, bowing away while all about her fell bouquet after bouquet of beautiful flowers.

"Come on, dreamy head – school." Mum was so boring. Jade huffed and pulled herself out of the settee, her hands still clasping the open programme. Maybe Mum's new boyfriend would take her to the concert next time and she could wear her new silver shoes that Auntie Mel had got her? Angie ruffled her daughter's hair. There was a time when she had daydreamed like Jade: a time when the world seemed so full of romantic possibilities. When did she stop dreaming that some day her hero would arrive unannounced to whisk her away from it all? Life had got so complicated. Even if he did arrive, she would have to organise after-school care, a home for the hamster, clean washing for the next day's school ... Life somehow had got in the way. She sighed and handed Jordan his PE bag.

"Are you seeing Prince Charles again tonight?" he asked, snatching the bag from her hand.

"Jordan!" Angie remonstrated.

"Thanks," he mumbled. Mel was probably right. Every man has his flaw, so why not take what you can and move on. But somehow that just didn't seem to be any kind of answer in life. Yes, Danny was thoughtless, over-bearing, obnoxious, pig-headed. And no, he had no job. But they had been good together, hadn't they? And the children loved him – and, then, the stupid idiot had ruined it.

"Do you think he'll take us on holiday?" Jordan teased, as he hoisted his bag on to his shoulder.

"No. Now off to school – wait for your sister." Jordan grumbled something under his breath and flicked the hood of his top over his head. She could hardly blame her children for thinking such things. If Jocelyn offered to take them away, would she refuse? Didn't they deserve to be spoiled? Just once?

Jocelyn turned the key to the back door and silently let himself in. He had spent the night asleep in the front seat of his car in the garage. The night had been too perfect to be ruined by lying next to his wife. Elizabeth represented the ordinary; last night had been extraordinary. The room hummed with the familiar buzz of the oil-fired Aga. Jasper their thirteen-year-old English Setter nuzzled Jocelyn's hand as he pulled out a chair and sat down. The dog, satisfied that his master was home, lolloped back to his basket and curled into a ball. Something to be said for being a dog, Jocelyn mused. He would take a dog's life over a spineless musician's any day. The sound of creaking boards above his head heralded the start of another day in the Thwaite household. Had Elizabeth even noticed he hadn't been there?

Elizabeth pulled the bone-handled brush through her hair. Every day two or three more grey strands appeared trapped in the bristles. She would never have described herself as a pretty woman: handsome, maybe, in a sophisticated, well-bred way, but her body was altogether too unwieldy, her hands too large, to be called attractive. She was realistic. Men looked at other women, they all did, she knew that. But Jocelyn – he hadn't a clue how to woo a woman. So, why should she be worried? The sound of the kitchen door catch was enough to tell her he was home. She would make a cassoulet for supper; it was his favourite.

Pedigree English Setter bitch, Staffordshire, £650

114 years before Jocelyn Thwaite's death

Satie studied the manuscript in front of him. It was a piece he was struggling to complete and he chewed on the end of his pencil in frustration. He let his mind wander, staring at the Parisian skyline beyond his room.

A dove settled on the sill and peered in at him. "She is perfection," he wrote along the edge of the paper, "her whole being, lovely eyes, gentle hands, and tiny feet." He let his index finger run across the bars of music and wished the tune into his head. The room was dark and cold but the warmth he felt inside stirred him. She hadn't accepted his proposal on that first day together, as he thought she might. It saddened him, but he knew not to rush her. He would ask her again, soon.

12 months, 3 weeks before Jocelyn Thwaite's death

The inside of the old Georgian building off Wardour Street no longer matched the grandeur of the outside. It had long been raped of its original ornate fixings and was now nothing more than an empty, soulless, shell filled with glass, metal and plastic. When Jocelyn arrived at the dubbing suite, the director and editor were busy huddled over a huge, sprawling mixing desk. It looked like something from the bridge of the SS Enterprise. The pair stared at the wiggly sound shapes on one of the many computer monitors, the sound editor squinting in an attempt to find the breath between two notes where he could make a cut. Had he even the slightest inkling of musical timing? Jocelyn groaned as he placed his leather case on the large velour couch in the corner and stepped forward to see what butchery they were undertaking. Some films were merely bad. This latest one was a travesty. The director leant back in his chair, cupped his hands behind his head and swivelled around to greet him.

"Joss mate, great to see you."

"I prefer Jocelyn, if you don't mind …"

"Yeah, whatever, mate. Running through the heist scene … love the tempo."

"Great"

"Yeah. We just need to shorten it – so Guy here's brought up the violins a tad sooner and overlaid the oboe –"

"Clarinet."

"Yeah, right, and looped that lovely little tinkling theme you've got going from the love scene." Jocelyn was incredulous, was the idiot serious?

"The love theme?" He did a poor job of disguising his disgust. "Does that fit there?" The director was unperturbed. He swung his chair back round to face the vast projection screen against the far wall of the suite.

"Listen," the director instructed. It was an abomination. A splice and cut slaughter of his hard work.

"I'll be in the canteen," Jocelyn said, resigned. Why should he care? With any luck no one would ever linger in their cinema seat long enough to spy his name scrolling at the end. Invariably the soundtrack would become a best-seller in some remote country like Azerbaijan and Elizabeth could buy herself another horse.

In the canteen – actually a dozen plastic chairs and four cube-shaped tables – the rushes from the dubbing suite were flickering on a small monitor in the corner. There was little else to look at and Jocelyn's eye kept being drawn to the psychotic movement and bright colour. No wonder the kids of today had the attention spans of goldfish, everything they saw moved so quickly. Directors didn't want a sweeping twenty-minute piece of music that dipped and swelled, involved the viewer and created an ambience. Instead, all they wanted were short sharp phrases that covered every gamut of emotion in two minutes flat and included a hummable chorus. 'Something like the Star Wars tune would be good'. Bloody John Williams, he had a lot to answer for. Jocelyn helped himself to a cappuccino from the machine and settled down to read the *Broadcast* magazine that had been discarded on the table. They could call him if they needed his opinion. They wouldn't.

For a moment he thought he recognised one of the two women who walked into the room. She reminded him of one of his students. Both were in their late twenties, Jocelyn guessed, one tall with curled, red hair, the other shorter with straight, blonde hair. They sat down together, the blonde woman leaning forward and handing her friend a booklet. Jocelyn stared at them. The tall woman looked up and met his gaze – and he looked away a bit too sharply. He had been pleased with the score originally. Now, he couldn't care less what happened to it. The original love theme had been a simple phrase he had developed on the piano in the drawing room at home. He remembered it clearly because it had been late at night and the windows had rattled with the rain outside. The day had been a write-off: piles of scrawled notations had been left stacked on top of the piano. Then suddenly, almost as he had given up hope, he had hit upon a simple, cyclical rhythm of five descending notes. At first the tune appeared so obvious he was convinced he must have borrowed it from somewhere. The notes were so melancholy, simple, yet shocking in their resonance together. At the time he had stopped and gripped the edge of the keyboard, aware that he had discovered something special. There had been a time when he had contemplated saving this piece for himself, but then the film had sounded so promising with its celebrity cast. How he regretted that decision now. The blonde woman had left. Her friend was staring at the booklet in her hand and chewing the underside of her lip as if concentrating intently. A sound on the screen diverted his attention. The lead actor was stood on the edge of a cliff as a bright red Ferrari plunged off the edge. Jocelyn shook his head. What crap.

"Not a fan?" The red-head had been watching him.

"Somebody must like it."

"Ah," she said, picking up her coffee and coming over to sit where he was. "But do they. Or do they just think they should?" Jocelyn was impressed. He studied her angular face and dark, unplucked eyebrows.

"Are you an actress?" he said. She laughed. He hadn't meant it as a chat-up line but to his horror he realised that that was exactly what it sounded like.

"I work for one of the investors, checking how the editing's going." She paused and rifled in her bag for chewing gum. "It's a little behind schedule, apparently." Jocelyn nodded.

"Yes, they're busy rearranging a sixty piece orchestra. That's always going to take time."

She laughed.

He could fall in love with this woman, he thought. With her fair skin and slim, delicate wrists. If he closed his eyes he could imprint the memory of her on the inside of his eyelids. Was she the muse that he had dreamed of when he wrote the film's love theme? Had fate drawn them together? He remembered recording the demo in his small studio and scribbling the title of the piece on the sleeve of the DAT tape: *The Moment of Love*. The producers, of course, had insisted that the piece share the name of the film: *Extreme Passion*. Trite. He could hardly refuse, but what did the music have to do with the wooden caricatures on the screen? Jocelyn wiped his palms on his trousers and shifted forward in his seat. He glanced at the woman. He would ask her out.

Her friend reappeared beside them. She turned her back on Jocelyn and held out a pile of colourful brochures.

The red-head took them from her and stood up.

"Nice meeting you," she said, turning to Jocelyn with a smile. Before he could stand and tell her about their future together, she had gone.

George Lucas's revenue from Star Wars licensing rights $20 billion

2 weeks, 4 days, 17 hours before Jocelyn Thwaite's death

Angie leant against the kitchen work surface and looked around. If this had been a cartoon there would have been a gentle fluttering of paper settling to the ground as the front door rattled in its frame. The change was instant the moment the children left the house, like a button on the soul of the place being switched off. And every time she was left alone, Angie felt a shallow ache deep inside, as though a part of her was missing. She sighed, flicked the switch on the kettle and lifted down a mug from the cupboard. Wednesday was her day off from work, her day off from life. First, she would make herself a cup of tea and have five minutes in the company of *Trisha*, before she battled with the tornado-battered remnants of the house. The phone startled her, but she didn't make a move to answer it. She let it rattle in its cradle until the answer phone eventually clicked in. Jocelyn's familiar clipped accent cut in and she sat and listened to his message. His voice was hushed as though he was speaking behind the bowled cup of his hand. Angie could picture him huddled behind a door somewhere out of earshot of his wife whispering his urgent declarations. She considered reaching over, picking up the phone and putting him out of his agony, but didn't. All at once his hissing, urgent pleading annoyed her. She stood up, walked out of the kitchen and closed the door.

Jocelyn tried Angela's home number three times and her mobile twice. He left messages on both. He flicked his phone closed and looked up at the nursery's door. Max held onto his fingers as though he was scared to let go. The short fat girl in the tight denim skirt – whose name Jocelyn could never remember – grunted a greeting and prised Max from his father's hand. The place was a shambles on Wednesdays without Angela. Was there a chance she was ignoring his calls on purpose? She had enjoyed the concert, hadn't she? The girl was looking pointedly at the tiny plastic Thunderbirds lunchbox in Jocelyn's hand.

"Oh," he said, and handed it to her. No, he was being paranoid, she could just have easily left the house without her phone. He considered ordering her flowers but then remembered his previous gifts still sat on the windowsill stealing the light from the tiny room. Was it right to appear so keen? Why not? There is no time frame for love. It didn't just appear after six months of courting. It could be instant. It could also never appear. Jocelyn watched the chubby girl disappear inside with his son reluctantly hanging from her hand. Yes, of course, love could be instant. If music had shown him one thing through all these years it was that very fact. It was romantics, just as he, still believing in such things that kept them alive. The world was too cynical and unbelieving. He saw it in Angela's eyes – at the restaurant, during the concert – skittish fear of everything around her. It was as though she expected things to go wrong. As though she didn't think she deserved to be happy, or to have someone like him take her out. It made him smile at how little she thought of herself and how unaware she was of her own consuming beauty. He would show her, he resolved. He would make it his aim to bring her to the mirror and show her the person she could be. And then she would thank him, love him and forever be indebted to him. Max was waving at him from the nursery window. He didn't notice. He thrust his hands deep in his pockets and marched purposefully back to his car. He would keep calling. She was just shy, nervous of how their relationship was unfolding. He could understand that. If that meant he had to work a bit harder, so be it. She deserved it. Angela would be grateful in the end.

MotoRazr V3 mobile phone, pay as you go, Carphone Warehouse, from £29.95

5 days, 16 hours after Jocelyn Thwaite's death

"Joss, my man. Am I relieved to see a friendly face." Alex jumped out of his chair and pulled the tiny button mic from his shirt. "Get me a drink." The interviewer, a teenage girl in a corduroy skirt and thick black tights squealed in horror. Her producer whirled round and tried to reach out for the actor's arm. This was to be the finale of Sunday morning's show. The biggee! And, as it was the last interview of the day, they had even been honoured with an interview in the star's luxury hotel. But from the moment the star had slumped down in front of them, he had done nothing to disguise his disinterest. The girl had struggled to engage him, although the questions hadn't helped her cause: How big was his on-set trailer? Did he have any pets? And what was on his Ipod? Alex had had enough. He ignored the protestations behind him and leant on the bar beside Danny and his niece.

"No. Thank you. Go away." He said raising his hand and preempting Belinda's arrival at his shoulder. Without saying a word she spun on her heels and returned to placate the film crew. Danny watched as the young presenter burst into tears, her producer and cameraman shuffling equipment into bags and skulking from the room.

They'd have to run with the Abi Titmuss piece after all. Mitchell lined up the glasses.

It hadn't taken Stacey long to get over Danny's rebuff. She had swung her legs up on to the chair beside her and flicked the ash from the end of her cigarette.

"Well, if you're not going to shag me, take me shopping instead," she had said. Danny stared at her incredulously. "Take me to Harrods. I want to go to Harrods. Order a taxi. I'm going back to my room to get changed. I'll see you in reception in five." Before Danny could wonder how the hell this spoilt little bitch had managed to manipulate him so easily, she was gone, leaving a pile of fag ends and huge wet footprints across his carpet. Of course, he should probably tell her to get lost. But the thought of spending the day with the girl intrigued him. Anyway he didn't have much else to do, did he?

In Selfridges Stacey skipped from department to department like a puppy chasing a tennis ball. She swept up armfuls of neatly folded blouses and tops and dumped them back down in crumpled piles. Danny followed behind her making an ineffectual attempt to reorder them. Stacey didn't notice, she had already moved on to the next display of silk jackets. A tall, slim sales assistant in black observed the strange couple with a studious eye. Her hooked, crow-like nose followed the pair as the young girl scooped up the items, gave them little more than a cursory glance and put them back down. "Ooh, what about this ... it's gorgeous!" she squealed, waving a pink top in Danny's face. "What do you think?" Danny didn't have a clue what he thought. Was it nice? Not really.

"Gorgeous," he confirmed. Stacey screwed her face up.

"Nah, too, you know," she said and placed it in his hand. He stared at the label – £289. Angie had a top very similar didn't she? How much had that been? £15? Twenty at the most? And what was the difference? Danny twirled the fabric in his hands, he could see the outline of his fingers beneath the material. What was so special about this top? It was very ordinary. Very pink. It helpfully came with two arms and a hole to put your neck through. So why the extra £269? He did his best to refold it. Stacey had disappeared. He wandered up and down until he heard her familiar high-pitched squeal by the changing rooms. The curtain to one of the cubicles was pulled right back to reveal her skeletal frame in front of the mirror. She was turning this way and that seemingly unable to get a satisfactory view of her flat, shapeless body. She grimaced at the assistant next to her.

"That's far too small – it makes me look like I'm pregnant," she spat. "Get me a bigger size." Stacey spotted Danny approaching and rolled her eyes.

"I'm so impossibly fat. Look at this mirror." Danny peered in the mirror. If anything he would swear the reflection was a slimmed version of the reality. The assistant returned, appearing not in the least sympathetic to Stacey's trauma, with a variety of sizes draped over her arm.

"You taking the piss?" Stacey scowled and grabbed the dresses from the girl. The shop assistant shot Danny a resigned look as she pushed back past him.

By the time the couple had made it to Harrods Danny thought his feet were going to bleed. His fingers burnt from the weight of her bags, the thin string handles eating into his skin. Somehow, despite the privileges his newfound money had earned him, this girl had relegated him to nothing better than a bag carrier. He sulked by the sunglasses whilst she proceeded to try on every conceivable style before discarding them all with a derisory wave. They strode between the perfume and make-up counters as though they were racing a ticking clock. At the underwear counter, Stacey stopped to pick up a tiny piece of lacy fabric. She held the thong to her crotch enjoying Danny's obvious discomfort.

"What do you think?" she giggled, gyrating her hips. He tried to maintain his composure.

"Not very warm in winter."

Stacey laughed and skipped away. He followed at a distance, studying the bizarre mix of customers that had congregated around the underwear. Which customer was he: the sophisticate with his wealthy girlfriend, the attentive uncle with his young niece, or the manipulative pervert grooming a child? Danny leant next to a full sized cardboard cutout of an attractive model in a red basque and French knickers.

"So what's the deal with you?" Stacey reappeared at his side still holding the skimpy thong. She was fiddling with the diamante attachment on its side.

"Deal?" Danny said, pushing himself upright and bending to pick up the ever-gathering collection of bags that had started to appear like bin liners around a gatepost.

"Gay or girlfriend?"

"Pardon?"

"Pardon?" Stacey mimicked in a contrived English accent. "Well, you've either got a girlfriend that you're pining after, or you're gay."

"Why? Because I didn't immediately jump into bed with you?" Danny laughed and continued to pick up the bags. Stacey placed the underwear on the cash-desk. She ignored the assistant and continued teasing Danny.

"Well?" She insisted. Danny shook his head.

"If you must know, I'm engaged." Stacey nodded her head knowingly.

"Guessed as much." He hated the smug way she looked at him. "What's her name?"

"Angela," Danny answered carelessly. Stacey was like a terrier with a rag, nagging him with questions about his fictitious fiancé. Regardless of what she asked, however, she had a talent for appearing disinterested in the actual answer. The more she asked, the more Danny found himself elaborating, enjoying this extra layer of pretence, as though, somehow, this new fabrication rounded his growing character. So Joss Thwaite was now not only a successful, talented and wealthy musician, he was also incredibly popular with a beautiful, model fiancé. Model? He couldn't resist.

"Really?" Stacey exclaimed with excitement. "Which labels has she done?"

"She's in Milan at the moment, that's why she's not on this trip with me." He couldn't stop himself. It was too easy. The girl lapped it up. "She's just finished a show with, uh, McCartney's girl …"

"Stella …"

"It is, isn't it?" Danny replied. Stacey looked momentarily confused. He patted her on the arm. "I should buy her a gift really. What do you suggest?"

"Wow," Stacey nodded. "Well, let's see. Diamonds. You can't beat diamonds."

"Diamonds it is then." The doorman held open the doors to the front of the store. Danny turned to him – a red-faced buffoon in green topper and overcoat. "I say, my good man, where can I buy diamonds?" The man looked not the slightest bit perturbed by the ludicrous question. He faced Danny with a blank expression and steely eyes. "You might try Hatton Garden, sir."

"So, you two spent the day together, huh?" Alex smirked at Danny then across at his niece. Stacey grabbed Danny's arm and hugged him close.

"He's lovely," she cooed. Danny shook her off his arm and she laughed. Mitchell poured a slushy, pre-mixed green concoction into the three glasses on the bar.

"My own recipe – I think you'll like it, my friends."

Unbeknown to Danny, Hatton Garden has long held the reputation as London's jewellery quarter. Since feudal times, a community of market traders and gem dealers have grown up side by side in an area stretching from Holborn Circus to Clerkenwell Road. Danny stepped out of the black cab and spun around on himself. Both sides of the street were edged by rows of shops with austere black fascias and gold copperplate lettering. Subtle mesh grills covered the windows. Stacey appeared more taken with the taxi she had just ridden in. She had spent the whole journey jumping between seats.

"These flippy seats are so cute." Danny paid the twelve pound fare with a twenty pound note and waved away the change. The driver threw him a hearty 'Cheers guv'.

Ruben Sachs stared out between the tiny leaded-glass panels at the world moving by. A mismatched couple laden with shopping bags burst from a hackney cab on the far side of the road. Let fate blow them this way, he silently prayed. It was a cutthroat business the jewellery trade. There was a time when stones and gems were the ultimate investment. That was before bonds and shares and bricks and mortar became the pensions of choice. He cursed his great-grandfather every day for this inheritance. And he in turn might well be spinning in his grave at how his business had shrivelled. The Sachs family business had hardly changed in over a hundred years, whilst all around trendy, modern jewellers with smoked-glass windows and inferior low-grade gold had sprung up to seduce the tourist trade. He turned and wandered back behind the counter. There was a one in fifty chance the couple might enter his shop. Better odds than the lottery. What else might he have been in life? An actor? A musician? No, his worldly path had been preordained long before he was even born.

The bell above the door was the antique kind on a large metal spring. It rattled rather than rang as the couple bundled in through the door. Ruben bit his lip and silently thanked the powers above. His mother had always believed in prayer. Maybe, he now realised somewhat belatedly in life, she might have been right all along. The man piled his bags by the front window, stood up straight and grinned at Ruben. The girl behind him seemed preoccupied with something caught in the lank strands of her hair.

"You got a loo?" she hissed, crossing her legs and bouncing on tip toe. Ruben directed her along the small corridor behind the counter to the 'Customer's powder-room.' Were they time-wasters? Ruben shook his head; he couldn't bear the thought. Two solid days without a customer and the first ones to arrive just wanted to use his toilet. It would sum up the spiralling decline of the business. He should have sold five years ago when his father died and Sharps Pixley had offered to buy him out. He spied the collection of bags by the door. Still, they had money, the names on the bags told him that much: Carvella, Versace, Jimmy Choo.

The girl returned. She stared about her as though she was walking amongst one of the Seven Wonders of the World. If she had spent six days a week in this dark, claustrophobic little room for the last forty years she wouldn't find it quite so intriguing. Everything she saw in the room demanded a 'wow' or a 'gee'. Rich and American and stupid. Could there be a better sales opportunity? Ruben was unsure whether he still had the fight in him.

"Sir? Madam?" Stacey leant against one of the small glass cabinets and stared at the tiny twinkling lights below. She tapped the top of the case with childish excitement.

"Let me see that one!" she said. Ruben revealed a small key hung from a chain attached to the button hole of his waistcoat. With a flick of his wrist he unlocked the case and plucked the tiny antique ring from a blue velvet pad. It was no more than a couple of millimeters thick and on top sat a single glowing sapphire nestled among a ring of tiny diamonds. Stacey rolled it around and around in her fingers watching what little light there was in the room, dance on its smooth surface. Danny paced the room looking at the mini, hand-written labels attached to each of the items. Most of the labels were bigger than the pieces they were tied to and not a single one below nine hundred pounds. Danny studied a display of silver pocket watches while Stacey continued to ask the assistant to take out items that she then draped about herself. She studied her face in the small round antique mirror on the counter.

The sales assistant shuffled from foot to foot irritably. Ruben had long given up on complimenting 'madam' on her latest choice, she had chosen so many. There was barely an item in the shop that she hadn't tried on. And, if he was truthful, which with a customer he rarely was, she looked awful in every single one. Her scrawny, pale neck couldn't hold a necklace and her bony wrists made every bracelet dangle grossly. It didn't help that she was clearly either drunk or stoned. Stacey wobbled and nearly dropped a £150,000 ring that the sales assistant, against his better judgment, had let her try on.

"It belonged to Queen Victoria's daughter-in-law, Princess Alexandra of Denmark. Her engagement ring."

"Did you take something back there?" Danny hissed in her ear.

"Just a little pick-me-up," she mumbled and pulled a bracelet off her wrist. Danny shook his head.

"Come on, let's get out of here," he said. The manager looked crestfallen, but by the time he had come round to the other side of the counter to plead with them they had already started to gather their bags.

"If there's anything in particular you're looking for," he continued, holding out his hands. He was aware that he was perhaps coming over a little desperate – but, what the hell, these were desperate times. "We do customised pieces as well, so if …" The door was open and the couple were already out in the street, they didn't even notice him. Something about the girl didn't seem right. Apart from the fact she was giggling uncontrollably and appeared to be struggling to stay vertical. And then it clicked – she was still wearing Princess Alexandra's ring. He raised his arm, but in a synchronised moment the girl clasped her hand in realisation.

"Run!" she screamed and suddenly shot off down the pavement. Danny, torn between explaining or running as an accomplice, turned and did the latter. It would be hard enough explaining the stoned girl's actions, let alone who he was and how he happened to be there. Still with the bags in his hand he struggled to keep up with Stacey as, at full pelt, she disappeared down an alleyway between a bookshop and an old-fashioned pawnbrokers.

"You did what?" gasped Alex, moving his head between the two of them, waiting for one of them to give up and confess the joke. "You stole a one hundred and fifty grand ring? Oh shit." He rolled back on his hands. "Right, well you're taking that right back in the morning Stacey." Stacey laughed and pulled her bag on to her knee.

"But unc, it's so lovely," she said, pulling the ring from her bag and placing it on her finger.

"Put it away, you idiot," he hissed, looking to see if anyone had noticed. Mitchell had tactfully repositioned himself at the end of the bar.

They had run the full length of Grenville Street before taking a short cut that joined with Farringdon Road. A red double-decker had blocked their path, waiting to pull into the bus stop just beyond. Stacey finally bent double to catch her breath. Danny had to admit he was impressed with the girl's stamina – probably the performance-enhancing drugs swirling around in her blood stream, he decided.

"Come on," Danny had urged, slapping her on the back and jogging to the end of the waiting queue. There was no sign of the jewellery store manager behind them. They didn't even know whether he had bothered to follow. He hadn't looked the fittest of people. Anyway he would probably just rely on the police, the extensive selection of CCTV cameras Danny had noticed in and outside the shop and his insurance company. With such armaments, why bother giving himself a coronary? He'd probably exaggerate the value of the thing anyway and screw the insurance. They'd probably done him a favour. Still gasping for air, they climbed onto the bus. Stacey ignored the driver and looked about her as though there was a bad smell. As it happened there was – an old woman with a pigeon in a hold-all sat at the back – but everyone on the bus, apart from Stacey, pretended not to notice. Danny paid the driver with a ten-pound note and pulled at Stacey's arm.

"Stop staring," he said. Stacey, resting her hand on one of the seat rests, found it to have some strange greasy residue on it and wiped it on her leg. She shuddered.

"Couldn't we have got a taxi?" she snorted.

"Just sit down," Danny said under his breath. They were starting to become something of a sideshow. A black lady and her two tiny children watched them with blank expressions as they jammed their expensive-looking shopping in between their legs. Along the way he had lost a couple of the bags and Stacey threw him a punch.

"My Dior glasses," she moaned.

Ruben Sachs made himself a fresh pot of strong tea. He wouldn't drink it, of course. It was merely a comforting action, like pulling on a familiar coat. He stared at the oil portrait of his great-grandfather in his carved ebony frame. If he sold the painting it might have bought him premiums for a month or so. But which two months? Insurance was an expensive luxury in this day and age. Ruben scratched his chin. Well that didn't matter now. He pulled one of his father's carver chairs from beside the dining room table and placed it near the window. Drawing the heavy woollen curtains, he unravelled the length of rope he had found secreted beneath the stairs. The overwhelming sense of relief he felt was like a drug and he smiled to himself – if only that strange couple knew what a favour they had just done him. He should have done this years ago.

"Where the hell did you end up?" Alex continued, shaking his head.

"Islington," Danny replied. It meant nothing to Alex but he rolled his eyes all the same. Stacey stood up, looked about her as though she had forgotten something and said:

"It was crap. Vile place." She wiped her nose on her sleeve and wandered off to see if her friends were still entertaining themselves in her room.

Winona Ryder, bail whilst charged with shoplifting, $20,000

2 weeks, 4 days, 9 hours before Jocelyn Thwaite's death

Angie's mobile buzzed for the fourth time in as many minutes. She pulled it from her coat pocket, looked at its illuminated face and pressed the red button. The 'My Humps' ringtone that Jordan had put on it was starting to really annoy her. An elderly couple by the cold meats counter gave her a withering look. She probably should have paid more attention when her son was showing her how to modify the ring. What was it? Profiles, select, tone, no … She didn't even know how to silence it. Angie pushed the phone to the bottom of her bag and let the contents smother it. Better than a mute button. Sometimes she felt as though the modern world threatened to run away from her. Was that what happened? Life suddenly drifting away from you? Maybe she would wake up one day and her children would be spoon-feeding her reconstituted puréed mush. That reminded her, they were out of fish-fingers.

Jocelyn placed the phone's handset back down and tapped it with his forefinger. He hummed a passage from Satie's *Gnossiennes*. This certainly qualified as a moment of stress. The student in the chair opposite watched him expectantly. He'd forgotten she was there. Michelle was a first-year student on a scholarship, with poor parents and a barely average talent. As far as he was concerned, she was nothing more than an exercise in how to waste valuable college funds. Too many students were thrust in and out of university these days. There was no grounding for real ability and talent to shine. It was quickly smothered by mediocracy. All they really wanted was to get on to god-awful pop reality shows, anyway. What did they understand of the passion of Wagner or the wit of Satie? Jocelyn closed the folder in front of him and handed it back to Michelle.

"Be clear about Berlioz's motivations. He wasn't just a Romantic, he *was* romantic …" Michelle nodded enthusiastically. Jocelyn doubted she understood the subtlety of the inference. She took the folder from him and flicked to see what scribbling notes he had etched at the bottom of her essay. Actually he had written very little: a couple of reference notes and a simple 'good' in green pen. He hadn't even read the thing properly – no need, he already knew what trite juvenile nonsense it contained.

"Thank you, sir," she said, crossing her legs. Was she flirting with him? He had been setting course notes on Louis-Hector Berlioz for years. There was only so many ways you could sum up his genius. And in all that time he hadn't come across a single student who had really understood the strange, warped passion of the man. Critics quickly dismissed him as an obsessive, even a stalker, but there was more to him than that, he was bewitched, seduced by the object of his desire, the Irish actress Harriet Smithson. He had watched her performance of Ophelia in *Hamlet* and becoming instantly entranced. He followed her day and night like a love-struck puppy. But she rebuffed him. Did any of these barely pubescent kids understand what it was to be so deeply under someone's spell that they could not eat, could not sleep at night? Of course they didn't. They described his actions as, at best 'passionate', at worst, 'freaky'. But Berlioz was none of these things – he was the embodiment of both the darkest and lightest parts of human desire all at once.

Michelle hugged her folder to her chest and Jocelyn peered at her. She was a plain-looking thing. Her clothes were drab and her face drained of colour. Funny how those girls who should wear make-up, don't, and those that shouldn't do. Berlioz wouldn't have wrenched his soul over a creature like her. She scooped the lank strands of her mousey hair behind her ear and shuffled her glasses up her nose. Was that an attempt at a pout?

"Sir," she began, and then paused as though questioning herself.

"Yes," he said a little too abruptly. She looked momentarily unnerved.

"Oh, nothing," she replied, getting out of her seat. She hesitated by the door as though searching for some reason to stay.

"Try Poulenc's *Les Biches*," he said.

"Oh yes, I will," she gushed, her cheeks finally submitting to a little colour. "Thank you. Poulenc? Yes." She pulled the door closed behind her. Jocelyn leant on his desk and rubbed his eyes. He smiled at the thought of this timid shrew attempting to unravel the sordid erotica of Poulenc's surrealist orgy of horny youths and lesbians. He picked the phone back up and tapped out Angela's mobile number.

How two half-sized human beings could consume so much food, Angie would never know. By aisle ten – sauces and pickles – she had enlisted a second trolley to help take the load. Her bag started to vibrate wildly. Angie fumbled to pull her phone free. Jocelyn. Again. This time she pressed green.

"Hi," she said, trying to balance the tone of her voice some-where on the edge just between aloof and friendly. There was a pause while Jocelyn attempted to gather his breath. He hadn't, in all honesty, expected her to answer.

"Where have you been?" he asked abruptly. He sat upright in his chair and pulled the phone as close to his ear as he could. "I thought you might have been in an accident, or something." Angie felt bad. It hadn't occurred to her that Jocelyn might have been worrying about her. It had been a long time since she had been used to such a feeling.

"Sorry, I ..." She didn't know what to say. She could hardly admit to deliberately ignoring his calls. It wasn't as though Jocelyn had done anything wrong. "My mobile's not been ringing. Jordan must have been playing with the ring-tone."

"But, I phoned your home as well."

"Sorry," Angie said again. Jocelyn had an acute way of making her feel guilty. Was she wrong? Danny had the same ability to make her doubt herself whenever they had an argument. Suddenly he would turn logic on its head and Angie was left wondering whether she was the one being unfair. Men could sense doubt and they knew when to leap for the jugular.

"Well, as long as you're okay," he said suddenly, in a softer voice.

"Of course I am," she laughed trying to lighten the mood. "Just stocking up on enough food to feed the five thousand – or two hungry children." Jocelyn smiled. Now, that was why he liked her. Such simple cares. He picked up the old picture-frame on his desk and looked at the faded portrait of his wife. He barely recognised the smiling young woman with the dishevelled hair. He sighed, pulled the drawer of his desk open and slipped it among a pile of student notebooks. He should really have a picture of Angela on his desk.

"Look, Angela," he began. Angela? She wished he would stop calling her that. That was what her mother called her as a child when she was naughty. Her name was Angie. "Look, I wondered if you were free on Friday?" Angie hesitated and Jocelyn sensed it in her voice. "I understand if you're busy." There was that hurt little boy's voice again.

"No, no, that would be great," she said. She looked at her nails. The colour was chipped. What did this man see in her? There were so many women out there who would be better suited to him: women who knew about violin concertos and Cubism, interest rates and SIPs and which knife and fork to use with the entrées. "But nothing fancy. What about just a drink?"

"Okay," Jocelyn said with uncertainty.

"I mean it – no fancy meals or concerts. Let's just go somewhere quiet and talk. Okay?"

Jocelyn paused.

"Okay," he agreed. "Nothing *fancy*."

Angie laughed at the way he said fancy as though it was a filthy word. "I'll pick you up. Seven?" he added. Angie flipped the cover of her phone closed and stared at it. How had that happened?

Jocelyn smiled to himself. Maybe he should tell Elizabeth about the affair now. That's what it was, wasn't it, an affair? Then he could move out of the house. Maybe the Dean would let him stay in one of the tutor's flats on the campus. He would book a table at 'Le Jardin'. He knew a friend of the head chef; he would be able to get them a table at such short notice. Jocelyn looked about him at the tiny room. To the untutored eye it was a quite beautiful place. It had wonderful deep-ledged mullion windows and thick velvety wallpaper that was barely visible beyond the shelves and shelves of books, CDs and manuscripts. In one corner Jocelyn even still kept an old Grundig record player and an unarranged stack of vinyl recordings of Mahler and Bach, Sondheim and Bacharach. A film crew searching for the archetypal music professor's study would never need to invest in props again. There was a knock at the door. Jocelyn was tugged from his thoughts.

"Yes," he barked in irritation. A lanky, ill-proportioned youth with large, veined hands and spindly legs edged into the room. Ralph was probably the most talented of what was a singly average year group, a quiet audacious oboist. But unfortunately, with his awkward gait and annoying habit of being unable to utter more than two words together at one time, he had no chance of surviving the cut-throat world of wood-wind. Jocelyn flung his A grade dissertation at him.

"Try listening to Poulenc's *Les Biches*," he grinned.

The teenage supermarket assistant smirked as Angie mentally tallied the total on the small screen with her monthly budget. How could a simple food shop for three cost £165.32p?

"Sorry, can I leave these," she apologised, handing the checkout girl two boxes of cereal, a bag of pears the children would never eat anyway, a frozen lasagne and a bottle of wine. The old man behind her shuffled irritably from foot to foot. "Sorry," she said again. The man refused to catch her eye. How many times a day did she find herself apologising? She put the bottle of wine back on the conveyor belt. Sod the money. Maybe she should just string Jocelyn along and enjoy his cash.

She doubted whether Mrs Thwaite ever had to 'just-do' with the super-market's own value-range cornflakes.

My Humps polyphonic ringtone, calls cost £1.50/min

2 weeks, 1 day before Jocelyn Thwaite's death

"I said nowhere fancy!" Angie exclaimed.

"It's only a *little* fancy," Jocelyn teased. "Anyway, Angela, you deserve the best." Angie smiled. She had to admit the place was stunning. Waiters busied themselves, swarming from table to table with proficient urgency. The brightly coloured walls were covered in beautifully chalked script, offering the day's freshest catches. At the back of the main dining area, the open-plan kitchen bristled with starched white chef hats. Occasionally the hiss of steam broke the hushed chatter as some fresh delicacy was tossed into a frying pan. Every now and then Angie caught sight of a flame leaping into the air. It was certainly a step up from Pizza Hut.

"You look wonderful tonight," Jocelyn said, leaning across the table.

"Thank you kind sir," she smiled back. Jocelyn certainly knew how to make her feel special. She felt herself blush and chided herself. She was probably just the next in a long line of women he had expertly smooth-talked. But, no, Angie didn't really believe that – however hard she tried she couldn't marry that possibility with the slightly bumbling, softly spoken man that sat in front of her. As clichéd as the phrase was, when Jocelyn said 'you look wonderful tonight', she felt he really meant it.

"Look, Jocelyn." Angie took a moment to find the words. "I really appreciate all this. But ..."

"But?"

"But, it's not really me." Angie picked the napkin off her knee and wrung it around her fingers. How did they get them so clean? One wash of Jordan's T-shirt and it was tinged a shade of old-pants grey. Jocelyn laughed. A big bellowing laugh that turned heads. What had she said that was so funny?

"Well, it's not," she said irritably. "Sorry." Must stop apologis-ing. Jocelyn shook his head and made a great play of wiping invisible tears from his eyes. With nothing to see, the surrounding diners returned to their scallops.

"How can a little luxury not *be* someone? That's ridiculous. Just because you haven't had the chance to enjoy food like this before doesn't mean you can't appreciate it." Angie resented the implication. Maybe she hadn't had rocket and blue cheese salad with walnut oil before, but that wasn't the point. "It's hardly your fault," he continued, "that you live where you do."

She stared at him aghast.

"There's nothing wrong with where I live," she hissed. Jocelyn realised his mistake at once and raised his palms.

"You know what I mean," he said. She really did look wonderful tonight. He much preferred her hair down than pulled up into a ponytail as it was at work. She looked too stern like that and it revealed worry lines. A girl like her shouldn't have worry lines. "I think everyone deserves the chance to experience the best in life," he continued. "People are so quick to dismiss what they don't know. Do you like oysters?" Angie twisted her face in revulsion. "See. How do you know? Have you tried them?" She felt like one of her own children, confronted with a plate of green vegetables. "Anyway," Jocelyn said, aware that he was perhaps being unfair. He waved his hand dismissively, "I'm glad you're here now."

And she was, wasn't she? She wanted the best in life, didn't she? Surely the reality was that, had she been born into his kind of privilege, she wouldn't have refused it. It is easy to belittle the value of money when you haven't got any. Wasn't that what Danny used to tell her all the time: 'Ang, we're as good as anyone else. Don't let people walk all over you.' She'd never believed it of course. Angie looked around the room. Nobody looked particularly happy. Well, apart from the fat, red-faced guy in the window with the blonde girl a fraction of his age. If he made it past the raspberry pavlova without needing a defibrillator it would be a miracle. Jocelyn took his time pondering the possible choice of liqueurs, persuading Angie to try some sweet orange drink. After his jibe about the oysters she felt compelled to try whatever he suggested. It tasted like cough mixture and stuck to the top of her mouth.

"This is for you," Jocelyn said, pulling a long, thin box from the inside pocket of his jacket. He slid it across the table. Angie stared at the box then back at Jocelyn. She picked it up and slowly opened it as though something might jump out and grab her by the throat at any moment.

"Jocelyn," she exclaimed, "it's beautiful."

From the box she pulled a silver necklace encrusted with two fine lines of tiny diamonds. She rolled it between her fingers, letting the light play along its length. She had never seen anything so perfect in her life. "I can't accept this," she said. She wanted to return the necklace to the box and give it back, but her hands refused to let it go.

"Try it on."

"I'm not keeping it," she said laying it across her throat. Jocelyn stood up and lifted her hair off the nape of her neck. He gently secured the clasp. Angie stared at her image in the bowl of a dessertspoon.

"It really suits you," Jocelyn said, sitting back down. "Do you like it?"

"Yes. No ... I," Angie didn't know what to say. It must have cost a fortune. If she accepted it did that mean she was acknowledging that the two of them had a future together? If she handed it back would he stand up and walk out?

"It's absolutely gorgeous Jocelyn." She felt hot under his gaze. "But I can't have you spending your money on me like this."

"Why not?" he asked. "It's my money. What's the point of having money if you can't enjoy it."

"If I accept it..."

"If?"

"If. That doesn't mean you've bought me." Jocelyn laughed again.

"What a bizarre thing to say." He smiled. "Whatever do you mean?"

"That's what rich people think, isn't it? That they can buy everything – everyone?" Jocelyn shook his head.

"Look Angela, I really, really care for you. You've opened my eyes. Don't you see that? You mean the world to me."

Angie unclasped the necklace and laid it out carefully on the place setting in front of her.

"And I care for you," she said. "You've been so generous, but it's all going a little fast for me."

She studied his expression looking for some sign of what he was thinking. Was he being genuine? Or was this just some elaborate ruse to get her into bed? She doubted it. From the start he had been nothing but the perfect gentleman. Jocelyn pushed his chair back from the table and laid his hands in his lap.

"It's a gift, nothing more," he said. "I'm sorry, if I've upset you."

"No, no, of course, not."

Once again Angie felt as though she was the one being unfair. She gently laid the necklace in its case and put it beside her cutlery.

"Thank you," she said, and Jocelyn smiled.

Of course, he hadn't wanted to 'buy' her. What a suggestion. It had never even occurred to him. However, if pressed, Jocelyn would have to admit to deliberately choosing 'Le Jardin' for its hotel next door. And a small bribe had secured him a beautiful double room over-looking the town square at very short notice. It was a shame the bottle of 1999 Laurent-Perrier Cuvée waiting in the room would be wasted, but he had no doubt the spotty maid that came to clean the room in the morning would make the most of it. Jocelyn ordered a taxi instead. As they stepped out onto the pavement, he sighed with resignation. Another night lying awake beside his wife. No, enough was enough. He would tell Elizabeth all about the affair. He would tell her how he had fallen so totally and completely in love and finally he would be able to draw that tired chapter of his life to a close. Elizabeth, he had no doubt, would struggle to understand his passion. She would be shocked, bemused, upset, but even then she would keep her emotions hidden from him and, for all he could guess, from herself as well. It was too bad. He felt sorry for his wife, of course, but he had to release himself from the cold, lifeless shell he had become cocooned in. Sometimes sacrifices had to be made. Satie would have understood.

Pizza Hut weekday lunchtime buffet, pizza only, £4.49

114 years before Jocelyn Thwaite's death

After they made love on the single thin blanket, the warmth of their bodies heating the tiny room, Satie lifted himself from the bed and sat at his desk. He studied his face in the scratched looking-glass on the wall. "My expression is very serious. When I laugh, it is unintentional and I always apologise, very politely." He turned the notepaper over and continued to write on the reverse. He paused the flow of his pen. Absent-mindedly he had scribbled the outline of Suzanne's slight, genteel features. He lifted the paper to his lips and kissed it lightly. He wanted to hide her away from the world and keep her safe.

6 days, 12 hours after Jocelyn Thwaite's death

It was nearly a week since Danny had witnessed the real Jocelyn Thwaite throw himself in front of the Paddington Express in the early hours of the morning. What would he make of the man who had assumed his identity and was enjoying the very finest hospitality British Airway's Business Class could offer on a Boeing 747 bound for LAX? Quite an achievement for a previously unemployable, homeless, cheat. If this had been an initiative test in which you are dropped off in the middle of a Scottish moor to find your way home with nothing but the clothes on your back, Danny would surely have passed with honours. The skittish, stewardesses didn't even attempt to hide their enthusiasm for the famous Hollywood actor and his party. By association, Danny himself was a celebrity amongst these brazen *Hello*-magazine-worshipping sycophants. And he loved it. They beamed at him through shimmering pink lipstick, their white teeth gleaming. They chuckled when he asked for a drink, winked when they handed him his magazine. Danny's chest heaved with pride under the scrutiny of their complete attention: if he coughed they were beside his seat with a glass of chilled water. Ironically, on page fifty-four of the in-flight magazine Danny read with interest an article on Irina Abramovic's extensive Fabergé collection. Not bad for an ex-Aeroflot air stewardess. The plane lunged momentarily before righting itself and the ice in Danny's whisky swirled about the glass. His stomach heaved and he peered out of the tiny window at the feathered clouds below. The second drink finally helped soothe the tension biting between his shoulder blades. There was a time at the check-in desk when he was convinced his new life was about to come to a juddering halt. Alex had been stood close beside him as he handed the girl his passport – Mr Daniel James Lunt's passport. He mentally counted backwards from ten, waiting for the girl behind the desk to bid him 'a pleasant journey, Mr Lunt'. Instead she merely offered him a thin well-practised smile and handed him his passport. He took it with grateful, sticky, fingers. Danny sighed and tilted his seat back. He flicked aimlessly through the pages of the magazine. He was both horrified and amused by the article about the man who had sold his house and given everything to charity. Fine if you could afford to do that. The man, Peter Staines, looked out of the page with a disarmingly contented shrug. He was happy now. Yeah, right.

Across the aisle Alex and Stacey were bickering in hushed voices and beside him Larry snored loudly. A stewardess appeared by Danny's side. He could see the dark roots beneath her bleached blonde hair scraped back from her forehead. She had plucked her eyebrows until there was nothing more than the faintest line left. She looked permanently startled. She smiled and handed him a small white canvas bag.

"Compliments of British Airways," she smiled like a mannequin Danny peered suspiciously in to the bag. He pulled out a bottle of Hugo Boss aftershave, sniffed the contents and slid it into his jacket pocket.

Alex's invitation had come totally out of the blue. One minute they were in a lap dancing club chatting meaningfully about the correlation between beautiful women and true happiness, the next, Alex was inviting Danny to stay at his home. Danny struggled to disguise his surprise. Surely this famous actor had friends falling over themselves to party at his Beverly Hills mansion? They had slammed their tequilas together and watched the smooth golden thighs of the dancer gyrate. The girl's body twisted and rippled like the flow of water, every muscle alive and moving. But her eyes maintained a cool, reflective distance. The body might well have been there for the voyeur's enjoyment, but the mind was still free and running wild somewhere far, far away.

"Come and join me," Alex said, leaning across and shouting in Danny's ear. "I'm spending the next couple of weeks there before I start pre-production talks on my next project." The incessant thump of music was beginning to give Danny a headache. "You'll love it, it's not far from Long Beach. Do you know it?" Danny did his best impersonation of someone who didn't but might well have. The actor seemed convinced. The girl thrust her arse close to Danny's face. He felt obliged to thread a twenty-pound note under the thin thread of her G-string.

On the plane, Stacey clambered over her uncle's legs. He pretended to be asleep and she kicked him with the pointed toe of her stiletto and threw him a filthy look. Danny watched her disappear up the aisle towards the toilet. She pushed her way past one of the attendants who turned and peered at her with cold, steely eyes. At one of the airport stalls Danny had picked up a postcard. He pulled it from its small plastic sheath and studied the image on the front. What kind of picture did a husband having a breakdown send his wife? Danny shrugged. It would have to do. Mrs Thwaite would start to come suspicious of her husband's disappearance without further communication. Maybe if he pretended to have taken an overseas break it would not only buy Danny more time, but also explain his gradually shrinking bank balance. Goodness knows what Jocelyn's wife would make of her husband's credit card trail: binge drinking and lap-dancing were unlikely to be the real Mr Thwaite's pastimes of choice. A postcard should be enough to prevent her from searching for him for now and while Jocelyn's credit card was willing to oblige his demands, Danny was free from suspicion. He leant his head back and tapped the postcard with his fingers. Stacey reappeared at his side and balanced on his armrest.

"Hmm, very nice, baby elephants," she smirked sarcastically, pulling the card from Danny's hand. Danny grabbed it back in irritation. "Is that for your fiancé? Not very romantic." Stacey let the word fiancé roll off her tongue as though she was spitting out a ball of old gum. He turned the postcard face down. "Ooh, sorry," Stacey said, taking the hint and standing back up. She grabbed a drink off the passing stewardess's tray and squeezed past Alex into her seat. Danny unclipped the pen from inside his jacket pocket and bit its end. Dear Elizabeth, he wrote.

There was something that didn't make sense about Joss Thwaite. But then, even by his own admission, Alex Fry had never been a very good judge of character. For every genuine, honest dealmaker out there, there was a charlatan trying to rip him off. For every friend, there was a kiss-and-tell merchant. He'd long given up pretending to know people. But this guy? Well, he wasn't after his money – he clearly had enough of his own. And he wasn't a fawning fan. He'd made it quite clear that first drunken evening, exactly what he thought of his *Brief Laisons* films. Joss had leant over, jabbed a forefinger in his face and with beer-soaked breath said, 'Terrible story, dreadful acting, rubbish effects'. Alex had difficulty contradicting his review: harsh but fair. His honesty was at least refreshing if not completely welcome. Joss didn't act like a millionaire. And Alex had met a few – sportsmen, businessmen, spoiled brats – all looking for some of his celebrity to rub off on them: a photo in the society pages of *Vanity Fair* or a ticket invite to front seats at the Niks. Very rarely was it because they actually wanted to get to know Alex Fry. A tall, Titian-haired stewardess appeared at his arm. She knelt down beside him. Alex sighed inwardly.

"Do you mind Mr Fry?" She held out one of the BA branded cotton serviettes and a pen. "My friend's daughter is such a big fan. She thinks you're gorgeous."

"And what about you?" Alex couldn't help it. It was obvious, really. She giggled and looked deep into his eyes. Of course, she did.

The landing was bumpy; pockets of turbulence rattling cups and dislodging papers. Danny gripped his armrest and briefly closed his eyes. If he died here would anyone ever know? Or if he was eventually identified, his cold, blue face revealed from beneath a plastic zip, would anyone be able to understand how he got there? The wheels bounced half a dozen times before squealing in a ball of blue smoke. Stacey just laughed. Alex looked ashen and Larry mumbled a prayer. The plane unloaded its cargo of wobbling legs. Danny paused at the top of the steps and the wall of heat that met him made him gasp. If Angie had been here she would have already begun to rifle in her bag for the factor 65.

The drive from the airport was slow and torturous and Danny found himself thrust between Stacey and Larry in the back seat. Stacey insisted on opening her window and leaning her forehead against the frame, opening and closing her mouth against what little breeze the movement of the car generated. The warm air from outside the car won the duel with the air conditioning inside and left the occupants in puddles of their own sweat. As they skirted the edge of the city, Alex made it his duty to relay the key sights and Danny stared out of the window at the scene beyond. The grey concrete strip of highway eventually gave way to smaller roads and the lush green of carefully trimmed lawns. Either side of the road sprinklers maintained the steady drizzle of rain that nature had neglected to provide. The homes were set back from the road and each one rose up impressively against the rich blue sky, a mix of large white three storey colonial buildings and mock-Georgian mansions. Just as it seemed as though they were about to run out of road, the driver cranked the wheel to the right and pulled up in front of tall, black iron gates. Opening his window he mumbled something into the tiny grilled box on the gatepost and the gates slowly swept apart to reveal the drive-way beyond. The drive cut through grass trimmed like a golf course green. It was dotted with ocean palms and eventually opened onto a large circular drive in front of the house. The central 'roundabout' sprouted exotic large leaved flowers. The building itself was a squat two storey brick affair, designed without a single curve or soft line to break it's symmetrical form, and sprawling as far as the eye could see to the left and right of the Doric pillars framing the front door. It reminded Danny of a much taller building that had been sat on.

Danny removed his Versace baseball cap and wiped his forehead. He had only been in California thirty minutes and already the heat was starting to drain him. His trousers stuck to his calves and sweat puddled under his arms. Dalton, the driver, opened the car's door and let the contents of the rear seat spill out. Danny was relieved to untangle himself from between Stacey's bony legs and Larry's sweaty thighs. A small Hispanic lady in a black smock and white starched apron curtsied and held the door open as Alex led his entourage up the steps and into the house. He led them through the echoing marble-floored hallway and into the vast open-plan sitting room with its massive glass windows that stared out over the sea beyond. The walls were pure white and what little furniture there was, was covered in muted shades of brown and cream. Every now and then the yawning walls were broken up by huge canvases splashed with bold, rich colours.

"I need a lie down," Alex groaned, waving his hand. "Paulita will show you to your room." The maid looked up at Danny expectantly.

"Vees wai señor," she gestured with a flick of the wrist.

Danny threw himself down onto the low-slung double bed. The doors were open on to the balcony and he could feel the breeze from the Pacific ripple across his face like someone pulling a muslin sheet over him. He closed his eyes and let the distant sound of the sea rise and all with his own breathing. He woke with a start and peered at his watch.

British Airways cabin crew starting salary, £10,815 p.a., plus flying allowances

1 week, 1 day after Jocelyn Thwaite's death

He had been asleep for over fourteen hours, jet lag and emotion conspiring to pull him down into a deep untroubled sleep. He rolled from the bed and rubbed at his dry eyes. The sound of hushed, urgent voices wafted from the open windows and he felt his way out onto the balcony. Danny leant over the rail and peered down at the pool below. Its surface rippled gently as though someone had recently thrown a blue silk sheet across its full length. Stacey dangled her feet at the edge, her back to the house. Danny watched her thin, tanned shoulders rise and fall with the kick of her legs. Behind her a youth in oversized khaki shorts, hung low at the crotch, paced up and down. He occasionally lifted his head to look at her between scratching his long greasy hair and peering at his scuffed baseball boots. Unlike Stacey, the boy had yet to outgrow the awkward gait of the pubescent. He crouched down on his haunches beside Stacey and said something Danny couldn't hear. Stacey shrugged in return. He stood up and shuffled away, his head bowed and his feet scraping the pool's smooth tiled edge.

"Good morning," Danny called down over the rail and Stacey looked up over her shoulder.

"Oh, you've not died then?" she scoffed. Paulita appeared at the sound of voices and held a large crystal jug aloft.

"Orinj, Senor?" Danny nodded and reached for one of the new shirts waiting for him in the wardrobe.

By mid-morning the sun already glowed white in the azure sky. The tiles beneath Danny's bare feet were blistering hot and he was forced to tiptoe to the pool's edge. He thrust his grateful feet into the water beside Stacey.

"Who was that?" he asked.

"My boyfriend."

"I didn't know you had a boyfriend."

"I haven't."

Danny stared at her blankly. Stacey grinned mischievously. "Well Taylor thinks he's my boyfriend. And his Dad does own nearly half of Santa Monica, so I'm just keeping my options open." He shook his head ruefully – she wasn't joking.

"Well, he seems like a nice lad," he said. Stacey laughed.

"What are you, my Dad? *A nice lad?*"

She kicked the surface of the water and it spat droplets onto her bare knees. She rubbed them with her palms, moisturising her dry skin. Stacey looked at Danny with something almost resembling sincerity.

"He's a dork. But I'll probably marry him," she said, with more than a passing note of resignation.

"Well, surely you don't have to if you don't want to." A single small dark cloud appeared in the sky, toyed with the idea of blocking the sun, thought better of it and floated westwards. Stacey smiled again – that insincere, plastic smile was back.

"I need to be kept in the style I've become used to, you know." Danny nodded. He supposed so.

"So, how come you're here – I thought you lived with your parents?"

"I do," she replied, leaning back on her hands and exposing her middriff. Danny let his eyes fall to the smooth skin ratcheted taut across the bone of her ribcage. From her navel sprouted a tiny sparkling stud.

"It's a two carat asscher diamond," she said, following his gaze. Danny pretended to study it rather than the loop of her shorts where the bone of her hips created an echoing space that revealed the white lace below.

"Uncle Alex lets me stay here whenever I like. So I live between the two places."

She peered into his eyes as though gauging his thoughts. Did he think her just a stupid little girl? She'd hate that.

"If I lived with my parents twenty-four-seven I'd end up doing a Manson."

Taylor watched from the living room window. Stacey was flirting with the man beside her on the edge of the pool. He knew the signs. Thrusting out her chest, pulling her hair behind her ear, rubbing the smooth skin of her legs. He was old enough to be her father. Taylor twisted his fingers through the chain around his neck. She was impossible, she really was. There were girls at school who would fall over themselves to go out with him. The skinny, childish groupies that squealed and jumped up and down at his band's college gigs. They giggled and flirted and talked of making-out and prom night. That wasn't Stacey. She was so much wiser, shrewder. Taylor let the blind drop and turned from the window.

Alex stepped out beside the pool. Behind him Paulita shuffled attentively, ushering a tall thin man in a black suit, white polo neck and dark wraparound sunglasses out into the sunlight. A leather-bound folder clasped shut by an ornate gold binding was trapped under his arm.

"Joss, my man, you're with us," Alex said, stepping forward and shaking Danny's hand excitedly. "Sorry I left you to it last night – I was beat." He grinned and slapped him on the back.

"Marcelo, I want you to meet a good friend of mine." Alex turned and waved the man in the suit over. Marcelo pulled his shades half way down his nose and peered at Danny. "This is Joss Thwaite. He's a film composer. A potential new client for you." The man didn't say a word but took a moment to weigh him up. He nodded as if to suggest he might tolerate an audience. "Joss, this is my art agent Marcelo Le Trouche. A quite formidable buyer. In fact," Alex added, wrapping his arm about Marcelo's shoulder, "this man here has made me a small fortune." Danny shook the man's hand. It was bony and cold. Danny resisted the compulsion to shudder. "You *have* seen my collection?" Alex continued waving his hand back towards the living area's glass plate windows. He spotted Danny's hesitation. "Oh, come on, you must see these." Danny wasn't exactly sure what it was he was supposed to have seen, but suddenly he felt an apprehensive knot in his stomach. The man in the suit was studying him attentively. He still hadn't said a word and even more disarmingly his pale skin refused to sweat even in the intensity of the sun's direct glare. Stacey unfolded herself and climbed to her feet. "Boring, boring," she sung and kicked her way across the grass and out of sight.

The reflection from the pool bounced off the vast windows, creating a stunning liquid wheel projection across the room's stark white walls. Danny stepped towards them and stared out at the ocean beyond. As though hurriedly described by a brush, the sea and sky merged into a watery blur. Alex and Marcelo were busy discussing one of the large canvasses on the far wall.

"... don't you think?" Alex said looking over his shoulder. Danny turned. "Sorry. Oh, yes. Very colourful." Marcelo had removed his glasses and his eyes were like little pinpricks of black. He sneered at Danny.

"Warhol," Marcelo slowly explained. Philistine. Marcelo was skilled at judging his clientele: excitable amateurs, investors and ignoramuses. This 'composer' clearly fell into the latter category. Honestly, imagine being confronted with one of Warhol's original 'Dollar Bills' and calling it 'very colourful'. It was like Neil Armstrong stepping on to the moon and claiming it to be 'fairly pleasant'.

"Marcelo found me this in New York. It was in a private collection." Marcelo nodded solemnly. "It's from his early sixties period – before he started creating so many replica versions." The agent stepped back away from the painting, wrapped his hands behind his back and frowned.

"His genius, of course, comes from his almost clairvoyant understanding of iconic imagery." Alex leapt to his side and looked at the painting. Marcelo leaned slightly to his right and Alex followed suit. "He had a wonderfully iconoclastic notion of what colours could do to a naked black and white image and how repeated patterns could defamiliarise received truths." Danny looked again at the painting. Was he missing something? The canvas was undoubtedly well, big – reaching over seven foot in height. The replicated black and white image of a single US dollar bill was repeated in rows to create an almost hypnotic pattern with blocks of muted green and gold silk-screened randomly across the texture. Danny resisted the temptation to point out that actually it looked like the artist had been in too much of a rush to print the image in register.

"Of course, I met Warhol." Marcelo paused for Danny to gasp. He didn't. "Amazing man. I visited his 'Factory', a debauched place – a throbbing heart of creativity, scandal, money and sex." Alex hung attentively to his every word. "He understood the relationship between art and money. He used to wake up on a Sunday morning and say, 'let's go shopping for masterpieces'."

"Worth nearly two mill, this little baby," Alex grinned, nudging Danny with his elbow. At last Danny let out an involuntary gasp. Two million? For that?

"Look, over here. You'll love this – a Jasper Johns." A what? "I've also got two Frank Stellas, a Cy Twombly, a, er…"

"Rauchenberg." Marcelo prompted.

"Oh, yes a Rauchenberg and two other smaller Warhols." He studied Danny's expression expectantly. Did nothing impress him? Marcelo shook his head and turned to a smaller image on the far wall.

"This has got to be one of my personal favourites. The De Kooning. Ah, the father of abstract expressionism." Danny looked at the small piece of dusty paper clenched between two pieces of glass. A bunch of random pencil scribbles, over-coloured with pastels.

2 weeks, 2 days before Jocelyn Thwaite's death

The little boy put down his crayons and looked at the portrait in front of him with satisfaction. It wasn't exactly a realistic image of his mother, but for a three-year-old he liked to think it was a pretty good attempt. He handed the sheet of blue sugar-paper to Miss Louise, the plump lady in the tight denim skirt. Surely she would add this one to the gallery of original illustrations that adorned the hallway wall? Louise took the paper from Joshua's hand and without looking at it placed it by the sink where a gust of wind immediately picked it up and deposited it in the bowl of soapy water. Louise retrieved it by the corner and dangled the wet dripping mess over the waste paper bin before letting it drop. Joshua watched, crestfallen. That might have been worth millions when he became a famous artist. He shook his tiny shock of curly hair and shrugged. Maybe he'd become a racing driver instead.

1 week, 1 day after Jocelyn Thwaite's death

Who was the real thief in the room? At least Danny waited until his victim was dead. This De Kooning chap was eating off the hand of the gullible in broad daylight. Marcelo smiled and tapped the leather-bound folder in his hand.

"Now, I've got a few other little prospects you may be interested in." Alex jumped up and down like an excitable schoolboy at a toyshop counter. "There's another Warhol coming up at the Sotherby's New York sale in a couple of weeks." Marcelo sat down in one of the curved leather couches and spread the folder out on the table in front of him. He drew a single sheet of thick matt card from it, took a moment to look at it himself, purred, then twisted it round and handed it carefully to Alex as though it was the actual painting. Alex lifted it up and studied it. "It's a self-portrait, signed and dated," Marcelo continued, "acrylic and silkscreen ink on linen. Twenty two inch square." Danny peered over his shoulder at the offset red and pink print. "Estimate of six hundred and fifty to seven hundred and fifty. Although to be honest with you, it could touch the right side of a mill." Alex fidgeted excitably on the edge of the couch.

"What do you think Joss, pretty impressive, huh?"

Marcelo continued to pick out a selection of images from his magic folder. Not a single one valued at below a quarter of a million.

"So, what about you Joss?" Alex smiled, handing him a sheet of paper that contained nothing more than a blue square. Danny turned it over to see if he was missing something.

"Yves Klein," added Marcelo patiently.

"Well, I'm not really a collector, myself," he answered while considering how he might escape from the conversation.

"I can assure you it's a shrewd investment," Marcelo beamed with a patronising grin; challenging Danny to disagree. "A lot more reliable than bonds and shares, that's for sure." Alex joined in with the agent's dry-throated cackle. "I think you'll find all the truly clever investors place their trust in works of art," Marcelo continued, "I could open a small portfolio for you if you liked." The hairs on the back of Danny's hands started to itch. Was Marcelo challenging him?

"I'm not sure these are really to my taste," he found himself saying. "I prefer something, a little, more classical myself." Marcelo's eyebrow arched. Ah ha, the fool had picked up the gauntlet. He nodded slowly.

"I see. Impressionist? Pre-Raphaelite? No, let me guess." He paused, toying with Danny. "Post-impressionist," Marcelo announced. Danny didn't say a word and the art dealer took his silence as confirmation. He grinned to himself. He hadn't lost his touch. "Cezanne, Gaugain. Mmm, expensive taste." Marcelo stood up and wandered around the room, pausing occasionally to peer at the vista beyond the window. "Well. I doubt you'd be able to afford either of those guys. But of course there was a whole school of followers working in their style. Sisley, for example, or Courbet – a very disciplined painter ..."

"Cezanne," Danny announced, sitting back in his seat and cupping his hands behind his head. "I like Cezanne." Marcelo swallowed a mouthful of dry air.

"Cezanne?" he repeated, his voice inflected just the wrong side of incredulous. Danny warmed to the man's discomfort.

"Certainly. I've often thought about starting a collection ... But, you know, time and everything." Marcelo felt the tips of his fingers moisten. He looked over to Alex for confirmation that his friend was serious. Alex shrugged. Was Fry's English buddy for real? Cezanne? This was a painter who's *Still Life With Curtain, Pitcher and Bowl* was sold by the estate of Betsey Whitney for nearly $61 million just a few years back.

"Of course you do realise, erm ..." Marcelo ventured cautiously, as though feeding his fingers between the bars of a gorilla cage, "just how in demand Cezanne can be? Over $60 million for a recent piece?" Danny said nothing. But inside he felt his stomach revolve one hundred and eighty degrees. Even Jocelyn Thwaite's bank account might struggle with that. He stared blankly at the dealer. Marcelo's red face looked like it might pop like an overripe pimple.

"And he's very much in demand," Marcelo continued. "Very few of his works come on the open market. You're rather dependent on a private collector realising his assets – for death duties and the like." He rubbed his palms together and studied the dry, red skin.

"Well, if it's difficult for you," Danny continued slowly, "I could get my own people on to it ..."

"No, no," Marcelo blurted desperately, "absolutely not. No not at all." The air felt hot and stagnant, his head spun with the wonder of possibilities. This was the big league. With the commission he could make on a Cezanne, he could retire for life and treat his boyfriend to that around the world cruise they had talked about. Marcelo leant forward to place a hand on Danny's knee, saw the look in the Englishman's eye and thought better of it.

"I'll get my contacts on to it right away."

"You do that."

"You want to avoid the auction houses – go straight to source ..."

"Whatever," Danny replied curtly. The conversation was dead; Danny had won. Alex breathed in sharply between his teeth. He never realised there was so much money in film scores.

Winton Oil Paint Starter Set, 10 × 37ml tubes, £19.88 (including VAT at 17.5%)

1 week, 5 days before Jocelyn Thwaite's death

Angie opened the phone book for the third time in as many minutes. Did you call 999 or your local police station at times like these? Times like what? It was only just past six o'clock – it wasn't even dark yet. And the children often took a diversion on their way home from school – a friend's house, the precinct, the playing fields. She closed the book and sat back down. She was being ridiculous. Angie wrapped her hands around her cold mug of tea. She chipped the glaze from the mug with her fingernail and studied the swirl of oily brown liquid.

Logic came as little comfort. Ever since Danny had left, Angie had felt a desperate, cloying need to keep her children close. If she could have bolted the doors, pulled down the blinds and never let her family from her sight again she would have. But they needed to breathe, to be the children they were, she knew that.

And then the front door was flying back on its hinges, the glass threatening to leap from its frame. Screams and shouts filled the house like a black and white film suddenly turning technicolour. Angie felt her heart jump with relief and frustration.

"Where the hell have you been?" she shouted, jumping from her chair. The tea spilled from the mug and soaked her hand. "Jordan?" she hissed, more curtly than she'd meant.

"Sorry, sorry, my fault."

Angie looked up. To her surprise Jocelyn filled the frame of the door. "I met them on the High Street," he said, casually slipping his jacket off his shoulder. Angie found herself taking it from him and wrapping it over the post of the banister. "So we went for a coke, and before we knew it …" He looked at her concerned frown. "Really, I'm sorry if we worried you. We had a great time, didn't we kids?" Jade was pulling at Angie's arm, jumping up and down excitedly.

"Look, look, Jocelyn bought me a Sportz Yasmin!" Jade proudly held aloft the tiny doll, her hair already hanging in sweaty clumps.

"I'm going to play my new game," Jordan announced, bounding up the stairs and out of view before Angie had time to take it from him.

"You bought them toys?" Angie exclaimed, "Jocelyn, really …"

"What? What?" he laughed, edging past her into the living room. Angie followed. "I know," he said. "I knew you'd be annoyed, but they're such great children."

Angie suddenly felt acutely aware of the weight of her arms and legs. She slumped into the sofa and put her face in her hands. What could she say? How could she be angry with him for wanting to spend time with her children? After all, they'd had so precious little attention recently. They missed having a man around the house. Jocelyn stood over her and gazed at the top of her head. He could see where the roots of her hair sprouted from the crown.

"They're a credit to you," he said, reaching out a hand to touch her shoulder. Her body flinched under his touch and he pulled his hand away. Jade stood by his leg looking up at him expectantly. He looked down at her small round face, like a puppy dog desperate for approval.

"Leave your mother and I alone," he breathed quietly. Jade wandered slowly from the room. Jocelyn stepped over to the window and looked out at the view beyond. It was desperate, sad and grey. A burning red sunset threatened to bathe the streets in fire. No bad thing, he thought. It reminded him of some unforgiving apocalyptic world beyond civilisation. How could Angela possibly be annoyed that he should want to help drag her and her needy children away from such a soulless place? He turned to her tear-streaked face.

"I'm sorry," she said, "I was being silly." Jocelyn nodded gently. He was sure the room was getting smaller every time he visited. The flowers he had sent nearly two weeks earlier were wilting in their vase. He looked at the TV screen, its picture jumping aimlessly, the sound barely audible. Well, there was no turning back now. He sat down beside Angie and picked up her hand. He clasped it between his own and shuffled his knees together so he could turn to face her. "Anyway," he began, "I've got something to tell you." Angie looked up. His expression had turned serious. He reminded her of Max, concentrating on some tiny detail of a picture he was drawing. He paused for a moment just as someone with great news might do in a cheap Australian soap. Angie felt the gallows-humour urge to burst out laughing.

"I've done it," he said, his voice defiant, as though challenging a denial. Angie stared at him blankly. What had she missed? "I've finally done it. I've left Elizabeth," he announced.

1 week, 6 days before Jocelyn Thwaite's death

How to tell your wife you want to bring to a close years of shared decisions? Years of two people sharing everything – toothpaste, cornflakes, a new human life. The kitchen was warm and airless. A row of tea towels warmed on the Aga. Jasper circled twice before settling on the old woven rug beside it. Jocelyn lifted the lid on the hot plate and placed the full kettle on it. He could hear Max splashing about in the bath above his head, his joyous squeals at odds with the stale quiet of the rest of the house. In the hallway, the long-case clock moved its hands slowly in time with the earth's predetermined roll through space. The kettle began its gentle whisper and Jocelyn leant back on the cooker's rail and looked out at the garden beyond. The lawn had been cut that afternoon and he marvelled at the straightness of line that wound its way from the back of the house down towards the stretch of water beyond. With a slightly embarrassed shrug Jocelyn referred to it as a pond; Elizabeth called it a lake. He poured two coffees, sipped at one and left the other to sit on the edge of the Aga for Elizabeth's return. Would she scream and shout at him or cry with relief? Would she take Max away somewhere he would never see him again or dump him in his arms? Jocelyn had to admit, rather tellingly, that he didn't know.

Elizabeth appeared at the kitchen door holding Max in her arms. Still damp from the bath his blond hair was matted brown. He thrust his face into his mother's chest. Elizabeth handed him to Jocelyn and brushed her top where the damp of his hair had left a darkening stain. The boy refused to look at his father and bent his head to stare at the small plastic car in his hand.

"I think we need to speak," Jocelyn said. Elizabeth maintained a blank, distant expression.

"Okay," she replied. Together they put Max into his bed and tucked him in. It was the first time the couple had done such a simple task together for months, like two warring parties momentarily suspending their hostilities to kick a football around in the mud of no-man's land. Jocelyn smoothed the hair from his son's forehead and kissed it. They returned downstairs and sat opposite each other in the drawing room.

So many of Jocelyn's memories were fractured, incomplete or missing, but he could instantly bring to mind the memory of the moment he first saw his wife. She was the most beautiful woman in the auditorium. The most beautiful woman in the world. All at once everything else in his life seemed irrelevant. The music in the hall was relegated to a toneless background hum. He knew he would marry her. The ache he felt swamped him and bred an awful realisation that his life, his passion, his music was about to change forever. There she was – his future. An old friend had begged moral support for what was the opening night of a four-date tour. Whilst Jocelyn had carved himself a highly respected and lucrative path, his friend had struggled from one unsatisfactory touring party to the next. If forced, Jocelyn would confess a smug satisfaction at the course their two lives had taken: not least because, out of the two of them, it was his friend who harboured the most natural ability. As composers, both students had demonstrated their audacious flair. But one had the confidence in his ability and the other didn't. So Jocelyn had spent years watching his friend's talent slowly seep away on laboured renditions of popularistic pap like Elgar and Vivaldi, every night playing to audiences that didn't know an andante from an allegro. Jocelyn watched his friend's nimble fingers work across the fret board and realised he hadn't heard a single note for the last ten minutes. The tune was so familiar, so embedded in his psyche, it meant nothing – like an Arctic explorer with snow blindness. Instead, he had found himself staring at the nape of the girl's neck in front of him. It worried him that his overriding concern was not the phrasing of the pizzicato in the forty-fourth bar but whether the woman was as pretty from the front as from the back. Jocelyn edged his way along the line of seats and contrived to return from the gents at an angle that revealed the girl's full profile.

Jocelyn stared at Elizabeth again just as he had that night. She was a different person now. Or was she? Was it just that he saw her differently. Was she still pretty? Had she ever actually been? She looked so plain, so randomly asexual. She was certainly no Angela. Or Maria Plaikov. Or Juliette, the au pair. Or the red-haired woman at the studio. Was it so wrong of him to be honest?

"Why?" was all Elizabeth could say. And that summed it up. Where was the passion? The regret? Jocelyn would have had more sympathy for his wife, if for once, just once, she screamed at him, threw things at him. Showed that their marriage was more than just the process of living day to day. Wagner didn't just live day to day. Bach didn't just live day to day. Satie didn't just live day to day. They had drive, ambition, passion. Jocelyn stood up and walked over to the walnut-topped drinks cabinet and unplugged the port decanter. He waved a glass at his wife and she shook her head. Of course she did. She would never let her guard down not for a minute. Not even when her husband said he was leaving for good.

Inside, Elizabeth Thwaite felt a little bit of her die. She didn't understand what it was that her husband wanted from her. She had tried hard to be a strong wife for him; to accept his moods and whims. Surely this was nothing more than another of his silly little rebellions? He needed them every once in a while, didn't he? She would let him have his tantrum. If necessary, she would let him go. He'd be back, she knew he would. Jocelyn would never really leave her, she had to believe that. It wasn't her he was angry with, it was himself, his music, his life.

On the stairs, Maximilian Thwaite cried gently to himself. He'd be strong. That's what Mummy and Daddy would want. He wouldn't cry out loud or shout. He would sneak back up stairs and crawl under his bed. It was warm and safe there, where he had stuffed all his cuddly animals. They would look after him.

Harry Danks, viola player, BBC Symphony Orchestra, first factory job, 10s 8d a week

1 week, 3 days after Jocelyn Thwaite's death

The youth scratched his chin, admiring the thin growth of hair in the reflection of his computer screen. Maybe he'd look tougher if he grew a goatee. As he idly punched the keys on his MacBook, Taylor studied the view beyond his room. On the beach, a group of youths were playing volleyball. Every now and then a shout pierced the air followed by cheering and the clapping of hands. Ignorant jocks and airhead cheerleaders. He looked down at the small flat screen. He had to tilt it towards him to alleviate the glare of the sun that slowly rose directly above his head. He had lived in Los Angeles all his life but still his skin remained resolutely pale save for the occasional blotch of unsightly red. Taylor contemplated surfing for porn, thought better of it and logged on to his band's MySpace site. There was only one new comment. RaveChick32 had left some indecent suggestions for the band's lead singer. Really, these girls were so shallow. Didn't they realise it was always the guitarist in the band who was the one with the talent? Maybe if he called Stacey, she'd come on over. Although, the way she was taken with the new English guy staying at her uncle's, he doubted it. What did she say the man's name was? Joss Thwaite? Taylor clicked on his google bookmark and typed in the musician's name. Joss Thwaite looked more like a drug dealer than a classical composer and the uncultured English accent didn't help – making him sound like every Hollywood casting agent's idea of the perfect villain. In response to his request, the search engine spat out an eclectic mix of family trees, book titles, random news articles and online stores, but nothing that linked the names Thwaite and Joss together. Taylor leaned forward in his seat, his interest piqued. Perhaps this guy was a fraud after all. It wasn't beyond the realms of possibility that Stacey was funding her own personal drug dealer. Many celebs had their own personal amphetimine suppliers in the same way that they had trainers, spiritual gurus and agents. He scrolled down a second and then a third page of suggested sites until near the bottom of the third page, he spotted the name Jocelyn Thwaite. The meta-tags beside it listed the words con-certos, film scores and Royal College. It was surely too much of a coinci-dence that both a Joss and Jocelyn Thwaite were composers. He clicked on the link and studied the musician's biography. There was no photo and only a brief outline of Joss's career highlights including a number of television credits that Taylor had never heard of. Although he was impressed to learn he had written the score to *The Water Carrier*. He clicked through a selection of sites until he found a copy of the sound-track and downloaded it to iTunes. The opening overture built slowly from a winsome, almost tuneless, flute solo into a watery crescendo of layered percussion and simple, under-stated strings. It was actually rather good. The main theme carried a tune that Taylor could even imag-ine his band sampling. None of what he saw or heard, however, seemed particularly consistent with the man's extravagant lifestyle or his ability to afford the friendship of someone like Alex Fry.

MacBook Pro 15 inch, 2.4Ghz, £1,299

1 week, 4 days after Jocelyn Thwaite's death

The salt-scented coastal breeze had begun to build lightly. It gently ruffled the flaps of the great white awning that had been erected at the back of the actor's mansion. Beneath the canvas three chefs in beautifully crisp, starched white uniforms and tall white hats toyed with succulent cuts of meat. At one end a large platter of glistening chunks of ice held aloft a bed of raw fish, shellfish and boneless tentacles. At the other, huge glass domes covered beautiful desserts. A tall Jamaican woman in a sharp-collared black suit and white silk cravat directed proceedings with a wave of her arm.

It was well past dusk by the time the majority of guests had arrived, offered kisses and edged their way through the house to the gar-den beyond. In that passing window of time the pool had turned from shimmering translucent blue to a glowing reservoir of orange, illumi-nated by the lights sunken into the tiled floor. A slender bikini-clad girl cut back and forth through the water, stopping occasionally at one end to flirt with a group of three guys. She scooped her long black hair off her forehead and leant her forearms on the edge of the pool as her admirers in three-quarter length trousers and floral short-sleeve shirts drank in the free entertainment.

Danny leant against a misshapen lump of polished anodised aluminium that jutted from one of the garden beds and studied the guests about him. He sipped at his vodka Martini and placed it on the sculpture's wooden plinth. It didn't taste as good as Mitchell's. A woman in a wrap-around skirt, bikini top and bare middriff kept looking across at him from beside the fruit platter. The slightest glance was enough to draw her next to him. From a distance she may have been thirty-five, on closer inspection she was nearer fifty-five. Her skin was tanned and smooth. It shone with an unnatural sheen, as though coated with varnish.

"Don't let Al spot you doing that," she said, and Danny followed her gaze to where he'd placed his glass.

"It's an Isamu Noguchi …"

"Of course it is," Danny said, quickly picking his glass back up. It had left the soft outline of a circle.

"I'm Christie," Christie announced thrusting out her arm. The collection of gold bangles on her wrist jangled noisily as she pumped his hand up and down. Her teeth sparkled like a row of brand new Lego pieces on one of Jordan's models. "It's a piece of crap, isn't it?!" she cackled, nodding at the twisted shape beside them. The dryness caught in her throat and she spluttered for a moment unable to get her breath. A waiter handed her a glass of pink champagne and she swallowed it with a single gulp. Danny turned to look at the sculpture. He wasn't sure. Was it? Was that a professional critique or a personal opinion?

"So you're the famous English composer I've heard so much about. How wonderful." Her skin was the colour of badly mixed orange paint. It was smooth like the seat of a worn leather chair, but pulled so tight that its original texture had been allowed to completely vanish.

"I've heard so much about you."

"Really? All good I hope," he replied ineffectually.

"But, of course," she said, trying to affect a coquettish tilt of the head. For a fleeting moment her expression seemed strangely familiar.

"Oh I love England. It's such a sweet place," she continued, almost oblivious to Danny. "Tell me, tell me, I must know …" She leant in close to him as though about to indulge in a great conspiracy. "Have you ever met the Royal Family? Oh, you must have done." Danny felt unable to disappoint her. He raised his eye and rolled his head in an 'I can neither confirm nor deny' kind of way. "You have? You have?" She squealed with delight. "Ooh, ooh, tell me, tell me. Did you ever meet …" She leant even closer to him until Danny could smell the faint tang of old smoke and alcohol on her breath. " … Princess Diana?"

"Well ..." he began. An ear-piercing screech cut through the gentle Californian breeze. The party stopped and turned as one. Danny instinctively placed his hand over the top of his glass to stop it shattering. Christie clasped her hands together.

"Oh. My. God. Did you? *Did* you?"

The overwhelming urge to be the person Christie wanted him to be flooded over him. In that moment, he was actually 'somebody'. The drink was the fuel, but his imagination was the engine. Yes, he had met the princess many times. Would he call himself a friend? Yes, certainly. At first he was merely her advisor on music for state functions and banquets held at Kensington Palace. But over time, yes, she came to confide in him more and more. That was all. Nothing more ...

Christie looked like she might weep. Or kiss him. Or, worryingly, both. The hypnotic spell he held her under was intoxicating. And like a jumper near the precipice, he was unable to hold himself back. It was careless, reckless, stupid even. But in that single slice of time he was the man he always knew he was meant to be. He held Christie by the shoulder and spun her around, leaning in and whispering conspiratorially. She, in turn, played her part hanging on to his every word, her eyes wide and her mouth open.

"Oh mother, leave Joss alone," said Stacey, stepping from the shadow of a nearby huddle. She looped her arm through Danny's and pulled him possessively towards her. Her mother stared at her as though she might at any moment leap at her and claw her eyes out. Stacey smiled. "I see you've met my wonderful mother," she said, making no attempt to disguise her sarcasm.

"Do you mind darling?" her mother replied bitterly, "Joss and I were having a private conversation ..." She couldn't stop herself, she leant forward and hissed, "... about his friendship with Princess Diana. Prin-cess Di-ana," she repeated as though by saying it twice it made the revelation even more incredible.

"Really?" Stacey said, her surprise momentarily stealing away her composure. She hastily contrived a frown. "Mother's impressed by things like that." Christie ignored her and turned her shoulder to block her daughter.

"Are the affairs true?" she hissed. Stacey shook her head. Her mother was so pathetic. She turned and studied the guests laughing around her. She would never understand why her uncle surrounded himself with these people. Did he really consider them friends, or just playful competition? Either way they hardly seemed to make him happy. Alex was stood on the far side of the pool staring aimlessly at the sea beyond.

By his side a blonde-haired girl in a sheer black dress was clapping her hands like a baby sea lion waiting to be thrown half a mackerel. Alex caught Stacey watching him and raised his champagne flute.

Alex drained his glass and sighed. This was no substitute for life. Throwing money away on parties like these was hardly the answer, but the house was so quiet without people in it. There was only so much one person could do with twelve bedrooms, six reception rooms, two kitchens, ten bathrooms, a games room, cellar, servants quarters and boat house. Even with Paulita permanently in residence he could go hours without seeing her. Admittedly there were plenty of visitors: the gardeners twice a week, the pool man, the laundry truck, his manager and entourage, his mother, his brother and wife and daughter, not to mention a long line of aspiring models, actresses and potential partners to be vetted. But the house still rattled like a dry pea in a tin can. Sometimes Alex pondered whether, in reality, his home wasn't much more than a glorified cell. A very nice cell, but a cell all the same. He would sit and stare at the large Frank Stella canvas above the fire mantel, twisting the bourbon glass in his palm and wonder whether the one point two million dollars Marcelo had convinced him to spend really related to one point two million dollars worth of visual enjoyment. Still, parties were good. They acted to remind him that he wasn't lonely and that he was actually, contrary to his own suspicions, very popular. And, of course, it was a good opportunity to get Larry to negotiate with Mena Suvari's management. There had been a number of muted suggestions that the PR generated by a relationship – real or otherwise – would be mutually beneficial. He peered at his watch. She was late. Alex peeled back a crab claw and sucked the meat from inside. He studied the guests about him. Over by the Noguchi, Joss, Stacey and her mum were deep in animated conversation.

A waiter with a silver salver balanced high on his upturned palm passed by the group. With a well-practised move, Christie swapped her empty champagne flute for a full one. The waiter didn't break a stride. Stacey sniffed and rubbed at the end of her nose with the back of her hand and her mother rolled her eyes skywards.

"What? What?' Stacey threw her arms in the air.

"Oh, nothing," Christie scoffed staring beyond her. She paused briefly as though contemplating whether to continue. She couldn't resist. "Got a cold darling?" She looked to Joss for confirmation. Danny raised his hands in surrender as if to say 'don't look at me'.

"You're a fine one to have a go," Stacey spat. Her mother smiled thinly. "Where do you think I get it from?" she continued, nodding at the already empty glass in her mother's hand. Danny could sense the electricity charging the air.

"Stacey," he hissed, aware of the amused eyes watching them.

"Oh, that's right, blame everyone else but yourself. Little-Miss-Always-Hard-Done-by," her mother retorted.

"Well, I've had a great teacher, haven't I?" Stacey laughed humourlessly, turning her head away as though appealing to the gathering audience. Conversations around the pool died to a respectful hush. Stacey slowly shook her head in mock disappointment.

"You stupid little girl. What do you know about anything?" Christie shouted. Stacey put her hands on her hips and stared her mother full in the face.

"Well I know Dad's bored of you." It was like a knife through her mother's heart. Christie squealed and in one svelte move threw herself at her daughter. She dug her nails deep into the mass of hair and pulled for all she was worth. Stacey stumbled away from her, tearing her mother's hands from her body and throwing her backwards. Christie yelled and bolted forward a second time, this time with her head down and her arms flailing about her. Stacey, with the natural agility of youth on her side, easily sidestepped her and Christie's arm connected with the twisted limb of Alex's precious sculpture. The hollow aluminum rang out and Christie grabbed at her aching wrist. Danny stepped forward and clasped her about the waist, her arms still whirling madly. He turned to put out an arm, anticipating a counter-attack, but Stacey just stood watching her mother. At first he thought she was crying but then he realised that she was in fact laughing. Tears streamed down her face as her mother cursed and swore at her. Stacey stopped laughing, took one step towards her mother and, with a sneer, spat in her face.

"Pathetic bitch," she said, before twisting on her heels and walking away.

From a distance Taylor watched Stacey disappear from view and smiled to himself as her mother slumped against the sculpture. Christie threw her arm dramatically to her forehead, her shoulders heaving up and down in wretched sobs. Joss stepped forward and wrapped his arm around her and she let the tortured moment last as long as she could, eking out the sympathy of the gathered crowd. Taylor smirked. He had been witness to enough of these ridiculous mother and daughter battles. It didn't take a psychologist to work out that theirs was a pathetic attempt to win the approval of an increasingly absent father and husband. And the man responsible for their slowly imploding selves was probably at home consoling himself with the undemanding warmth of someone else. Taylor sipped at a Coke. He didn't touch alcohol, thanks to people like them. And people like his parents. He watched amused as the party guests slowly stripped themselves of their inhibitions, willingly revealing the fragile layers beneath. He fiddled with the knotted leather wristband looped around his arm, twisting its soft entrails between his second and third fingers. He had picked it off Stacey's dressing table and asked if he could keep it. He took her absent-minded nod as confirmation. Stacey didn't like Taylor very much. He knew that. But that was okay. People, he assumed, could grow to like each other and, if he held back in her shadow long enough, maybe the occasion would come when she would need him. It would probably take an overdose, or an unwanted pregnancy. But in that dark moment when she needed a friend, he would be there. Taylor crossed his arms, felt the awkwardness of his body against the doorframe and unfolded them again. He tried to make himself as invisible as possible; he'd always preferred to be an observer rather than a participator

The party began to fracture into groups. Some remained by the pool, dipping their feet into the warm mirrored water, others, new to Alex Fry's infamous gatherings, had taken up the option of a guided tour of the estate. And the hardcore, mainly men who had gathered about the actor and stuck to him like Velcro, watched with delight as he flicked a switch that illuminated a pathway leading from the house to a large slated building a hundred yards from where they all stood. With the flick of a second switch, the grass in front of the building was bathed with a bright white light. Like children, the men giddily pushed each other out of the way and bounded down the path to the golf-driving range below. Taylor shook his head in derision at the sound of the testosterone-fuelled jeers that floated up on the otherwise silent sea air. Joss Thwaite, Taylor noted, hung back a moment, unsure whether to follow or not. Larry, his uncle's agent, slapped the composer on the back and with no option of escape, he followed the group down the pathway.

Stacey sat on the edge of the lawn where it dipped away, rolling down towards the ocean. If you desensitised to the sound of the party, you could just make out the soft rhythmic pulse of the surf stroking the shoreline. Taylor appeared by her side. He sat down beside her and took hold of her hand. She didn't turn to look at him. The coastline was trimmed with millions of tiny lights like the strings of white bulbs that edged their Christmas tree each year. As a child she would spend hours staring at them. Slowly she would close the lids of her eyes so that the small lights jumped about, sending sharp white shards in front of her. Sometimes she'd even rub her eyes to make them water and then watch as the lights swam and spun in the watery blur. Then, just for a moment, she would believe she was no longer in her parents' house, but in some magical land thousands of miles away. Stacey tried squinting her eyes, but the lights refused to dance. She hated this place with its plastic, shiny trees, finely trimmed lawns and litter-free beaches.

"Got any gear?" she asked and Taylor pulled out a small round tobacco tin from his back pocket. His fingers chased a tiny white pill around its base. He picked it out and handed it to her. She would make those lights twinkle again.

Charles and Diana wedding mug 1981, slight wear, car boot sale, £2

1 week before Jocelyn Thwaite's death

Established in 1882, by the then Prince of Wales, the Royal College of Music sits in the heart of South Kensington's cultural and scientific quarter. It was opened to the sound of rapturous applause and a sixty-piece orchestra. Jocelyn's arrival at the main entrance on this occasion, like every other, was met with resounding silence. He stared up at the pillars towering above and contemplated the trajectory that a free-fall attempt from its highest point might describe. A large banner draped across the right-hand wing of the building announced a forthcoming Mozart festival. Opposite, Jocelyn could admire the imposing shape of the Royal Albert Hall. He still vividly remembered the first time he had stood there and the enormity of the sensations it provoked. He had rocked on his feet, closed his eyes briefly and attempted to gather his feelings. On those very steps, the likes of Holst, Britten and Vaughan Williams had passed, their shadows cast long across the imposing entrance way. From there on, theirs would be a shared history: passing through the building's vast arched doorway together, across its ornate mosaic floor, between its towering marble pillars and up its sweeping stone stairways. Maybe he too would be immortalised in oil and hung high on the wall for generations of mesmerised students to stare at in wonder. Then again …. He pulled a freshly ironed handkerchief from his jacket pocket and blew his nose. He would have to learn to iron them himself – he couldn't be seen with a crumpled handkerchief in his top pocket, the College would know at once that he'd left his wife. Or worse, think she had left him. Either way, such personal 'problems' were heavily frowned upon. Academia was not so liberal-minded as some walks of life – at least not on the exterior. One of Jocelyn's fellow lecturers nodded a welcome as he pushed open the heavy doors. Elizabeth's reaction hadn't surprised him. She hadn't argued or shouted. She had even helped him find his small leather overnight bag, the one he used when he was away from home recording or when he was staying near the College. She placed fresh socks and underwear and two clean, ironed shirts in the bag while he gathered his toiletries from the bathroom. Max was still asleep as he quietly closed the door behind him. Since then he had stayed at a small hotel on the Gloucester Road. Of course, he knew she was merely indulging him, just like she did with Max when he had a screaming fit about wearing his wellingtons. She assumed he would soon return, a sheepish expression on his face and a bunch of flowers in his hand. But not this time. Not this time.

"Mr Thwaite, sir, just the fellow …" Jocelyn turned and stared at his assailant. "Need your help. Got a bunch of strings grads on a composition assignment, plucking away like billy-o." The man patted Jocelyn on the shoulder. "Honestly you've never heard anything like it." Jocelyn continued to stare at him blankly. "Let the composers compose and the musicians play, I say. This course swap nonsense is quite the most dreadful idea." The man studied Jocelyn for a moment and cocked his head to one side. "You okay, old chap?"

Laurence Bailey (DMus, FRCM) led the way. The jaunty bounce of his step ensuring that Jocelyn had to quicken his pace to keep up. The warren of tunnels and pathways wound their way through the intestines of the mighty building, until together they popped out into the belly of the Recital Hall. There they discovered a huddle of students centre-stage, madly scribbling on sheets of music paper, their instruments balanced on their knees. Laurence pushed the doors open with a great flourish and clapped his hands.

"Now then ladies and jelly-spoons, you are greatly honoured …" He ushered Jocelyn out of the shadows and into the glare of the hall's spotlight. "Mr Jocelyn Thwaite, Research Fellow in Composition, has kindly agreed to lend you his highly experienced and highly regarded ear. So let's not waste his time people." Before he had left the house, Jocelyn had briefly sat at his Steinway in the drawing room. It was a wedding present from Elizabeth – a 1927 Grand in Louis XV Walnut. At the time he had considered it a lucky charm. But, if truth be told, he hadn't written a single decent piece on it.

"Right, who would like to be the first to unveil the results of their great musical deliberations? Miss Wallington-Jones?" He would send for the piano. The moment his Steinway had left the house, Elizabeth would know for sure that their relationship was over. Then he would sell it and sever his ties with the constrictive past, once and for all.

The house he had found to move into was a tiresomely predictable new-build within walking distance of Max's nursery. He knew the moment he saw it that Elizabeth would hate it, with its mock Tudor leaded-windows, plastic front door and brass carriage lamps. Without a doubt, the thought of her face crumpled in disgust was a significant part of the house's charm. Jocelyn hadn't wanted to look inside, but the estate agent insisted. So he followed patiently as Colin, Call-Me-Colin, Peterson waved excitedly and pointed at every single plug socket, turning what should have been a five-minute perusal into a forty-minute tour. Staring from the front bedroom window at the house's mirror image across the road, Jocelyn wondered if had finally given up on life. Would Erik Satie have been seduced by the comfortable inertia of such a soulless place? The Barley, a four-bedroom detached house with integrated double garage and south facing aspect. Did Satie dream of a home like this as he sat alone in his one room hovel in Arcueil, a single damp mattress and his upright piano for company? Would he have succumbed to the 'charms' of laminated flooring and dimmer-switch lighting had his Gymnopedie No.1 reaped him the money when he was alive that it had for others since his death? Colin, Call-Me-Colin, took Jocelyn's ironic smirk as one of enthusiasm and guided him to the main bedroom. He was at pains to point out the surprising 'roominess' of the upstairs. In the undercover back porch – laughingly described as a luxury executive conservatory – Jocelyn stood and studied the garden. Recently laid to lawn, it jutted out from the back of the house and was edged on all sides by six-foot high timber panels – a view that differed little from that of a B&Q car park. Jocelyn was hoping for something a little, well, larger. Colin Peterson waved his arms excitedly, enthusing the dream – a *Ground Force* vision of Japanese pebble beds, cascading barrel water features and rustic decking.

Beatrice Wallington-Jones bowed her way effortlessly through her composition. With legs unceremoniously apart she bent and twisted her body to flow with the sound of her violin. Her long hair, bunched in a pony-tail, flicked this way and that in time to the rhythm. Beatrice had been playing violin since the age of six and, much to her mother's delight, had earned a scholarship to the College that her parents could have afforded a dozen times over. Still, their annual ski holiday was safe. With a grand flourish that brought a spontaneous, albeit reserved round of applause from her fellow students, Beatrice beamed with her trademark *aren't-I-clever* grin.

"Hmm," frowned Jocelyn. "Not totally dissimilar to Sibelius' *Finlandia*. Or am I mistaken, Miss Wallington-Jones?" Laurence was a little taken back by the directness of his colleague's critique. Admittedly there were similarities to the forementioned piece, but it surely had a quite mature structure and … "Trite and predictable. Next." Tears filled the young girl's eyes. The student next to her looked terrified. Jocelyn stared at him. The lad, prematurely balding and wearing small round spectacles, looked at the instrument in his hands as though he had no idea how it got there. He lifted it under his chin, misread the first three notes, coughed, mumbled an apology under his breath and began again. Jocelyn paced back and forth in front of the stage, his eyes cast down as though studying the tips of his shoes. Laurence Bailey leant forward in his seat, his elbows propped on his knees, and silently willed on the young student's performance. Thwaite had a reputation, it was true, for being at times –how to put it delicately – robust with his views, but even he would have to admit he was being a touch hard on what were, after all, a relatively fresh intake of young performers. Jocelyn abruptly stopped pacing, turned to face the stage and with a dramatic movement let his chin drop to his chest and his head shake from side to side. The boy's playing came to a juddering, uncertain stop.

"Pleasant enough, I suppose, if you were scoring a film about a coma victim," he scoffed.

"Um. I really liked the deceptive cadence …," Laurence offered, lifting himself from his seat. But Jocelyn gave him no chance to expand, having already pointed to the next student in line. She, in turn, launched into a screeching rendition of her composition. Jocelyn raised his hand.

"Are you all so empty? Where's the inspiration? The originality? Stop copying what everyone's done a hundred times before …" He paused, looking for at least some spark of understanding. "… only better. You're young. Your minds are supposed to be fresh and open – inventive. Instead you're recycling the same old crap." Jocelyn rolled his eyes and marched along the edge of the stage, turning to look at the bemused, blank expressions. He was a commander, a general rousing his troops – the mighty battle of inspiration versus the guerrilla tactic of mediocrity. People so easily accept the bland sounds they are spoon-fed. And it was their job, as musicians, to jolt them alive. "Where's the passion? The heart?" he continued. No one braved a reply. The heat in the room felt like a crushing weight, the air thick and clogged. "Start listening with your hearts, not just your ears." He stopped and looked around him. Laurence had a baffled expression on his face. Jocelyn was aware of a thin trickle of sweat running along the ridge of his eyebrow, threatening to sting his eyes. He could feel his heart thumping beneath his ribcage, much, he thought, as it might if he was having a heart attack.

"Are you alright, old chap?" Laurence asked, standing and putting an arm on his shoulder. The students moved their heads expectantly, relieved at no longer being centre-stage. Jocelyn looked down at the varnished hall floor.

"Oh, what's the point," he hissed under his breath. He turned, and without looking back, walked straight from the room.

The car's front tyre dragged along the edge of the kerb and juddered to a halt. Jocelyn jumped from the front seat and held the door open for his passengers. Angie threw him a baffled look, her sister and children obediently climbing out behind her.

"Come on, come on," Jocelyn urged. Angie had never seen him so animated. One minute she had been in the kitchen wrestling with a pile of filthy clothes, the sound of children squabbling over the remote control in the front room in one ear, her sister's inane rambling in the other, the next Jocelyn was at the door excitedly ushering them all outside. Angie wrapped an arm protectively around the children and stared about her. This was not a part of town she knew well; it wasn't far from the nursery and many of her children came from tidy, beautifully manicured streets like these. The gravel driveway led up to a double garage, a strip of immaculately laid lush green lawn to either side. She had forgotten that grass could be this green: the park near their house was not much more than a patchwork of dried earth, yellowing weeds and crusty white dog turds. The gentle hush of the street enveloped her, as though someone had muffled all sound by laying a giant silk sheet over the top of the whole place – like a model railway lying unused in the attic. Instead of police sirens and the thud of boom boxes, the quiet was only broken by the hoot of a woodpigeon. Beside the antique Victorian lamp at the end of the driveway a 'For Sale' sign had recently had added to it a large red 'Sold' sticker. A young man with tall, spiky waxed hair in a cheap dark suit and purple tie slammed shut the door of his silver Vauxhall Astra, its front wheels balanced along the edge of the pavement. He thrust out his hand.

"Mrs Thwaite, nice to meet you," he grinned. The loose gold strap of his watch rattled as he moved his hand up and down. "I'm Colin, please call me Colin, Peterson, Right Moves. I think you'll just love the house…" He didn't give Angie opportunity to doubt anything he said, stepping purposefully towards the door and swinging it wide open.

"Please. After you." The family trailed in. Mel, Jordan and Jade following behind like a row of ducklings.

"Wow," Mel offered thoughtfully as the estate agent pushed open the living room door.

"This is the main family room, with a north aspect from the conservatory to the garden beyond." Jordan yelped with joy and ran to the window.

"Can I go outside, Mum?" he asked, without waiting for an answer. Jade ran around and around the room, running her fingers across the smooth, freshly painted plaster.

"All the rooms have been finished to a very high spec. Dado rails throughout. Plus intricately carved classic egg and dart cornicing in the two reception rooms," Colin, Call-Me-Colin, announced. Mel and Angie hung on his every word.

"Cornicing? Wow!" Mel teased. In the kitchen she opened and closed every single cupboard and drawer. The dishwasher, hidden behind a fake chipboard door, eased open. "Nice movement," she nodded appreciatively. The group gathered in the conservatory. The sun had chosen just the right moment to reveal itself, sending golden rays across the red tiled floor. The doors to the back garden swung on their hinges where Jordan had burst through them. A single shiny-leaved rubber plant sat on the window ledge.

"Mum, it's a lot bigger than our house," hissed Jade, gripping her mother's hand. Angie had to concede she had a point. She couldn't help wondering what on earth Jocelyn was going to do with so much space. Usually men who separated couldn't wait to relive their bachelor lifestyle in some trendy little penthouse flat – one of those new developments by the canal basin with its personalised parking spaces, intercoms and nodding doormen.

Jocelyn studied Angela's face carefully. Did she genuinely like it? Or was she being polite? It had been the very first place he had circled in the property pages and the only one he had actually visited. But had he gauged her right? Possibly he should have asked her to help choose – but that of course would have spoiled the surprise. The surprise, after all, was the grand gesture. She'd understand that, wouldn't she? The odious estate agent was grinning inanely and going on and on about neighbourhood watch and school catchments and how house values were constantly on the rise in such a 'sought-after' area. Angela appeared convinced. That reminded him, he must transfer the deposit into his current account. Not that he liked it sitting there too long, he didn't trust those cashpoint machines; You never quite knew who could gain access to that little box on the wall and enjoy the profits of your hard work. Jocelyn leaned against the conservatory's door frame and watched Angela and her family in the garden.

"Well, they seem to like it," Colin, Call-Me-Colin, grinned, his hands thrust into his suit trousers. His mobile phone juddered awake to the tune of the French assault on the Russian troops from Tchaikovsky's *1812 Overture* and he plucked it from his pocket. Jocelyn winced at the sound and stepped onto the thin strip of decking that edged the garden. Jordan had found a football and was kicking it between two fence posts. Jade and Mel were rolling around on the grass giggling with joy as the little girl tried to tickle her aunt.

"I love to see them laugh like that," said Angie. Jocelyn didn't reply. He held out his hand to take hers. Mel struggled to get the better of her niece and pinned her to the ground. Jade shrieked and Mel pulled up her top to blow a raspberry on her stomach. Jordan, hearing his sister's plight, threw himself on Mel's back and looped his arms around her neck.

"It's a lovely house," Angie said.

"You're sure you like it?" Jocelyn said with a delighted smile, turning to face her.

"Yes, of course," she replied, adding with a shrug, "but it doesn't matter what I think, does it?" Jocelyn looked genuinely taken aback.

"Well, of course it matters," he said. "It matters so much." He put his hands on her shoulders. "It's for you. It's for the children. It's for us." Angie felt her head spin. The sun was right in her eyes and she had to squint to see him properly. Jocelyn's dark shape rose above her, a strand of hair stuck out from the side of his head rendering his silhouette misshapen. Was he seriously suggesting they move into this house? Together? A church bell somewhere patiently punctuated the moment. The tumble of figures on the grass mutually agreed an unconditional surrender and lay back on their elbows gasping for breath. This was the home that Angie had always dreamed of: a swing in the far corner, a paddling pool and slide by the fence, barbecues and parties in the summer. It was all she ever wanted for the children. Jordan could play football without having to dribble around broken glass and used needles. Jade could invite her friends for dressing-up parties and sleep-overs. Here it all was, suddenly, laid out in front of her. All she had to do was reach out and grasp it. Wasn't it what she deserved? What her children deserved? All she had to say was 'yes'.

"No," she said – quietly at first, as though to herself. "No Jocelyn. It's not right." Mel and the children looked up at her and she pulled away from Jocelyn's grasp and turned to go back inside the house. "What do you think you're playing at?" she hissed. She was aware that her question was more abrupt than she meant, but Jocelyn hadn't appeared to notice; he leant against the windowsill, spread his arms out wide and smiled.

She was overreacting, of course. Jocelyn knew she would at first. Well, it was a shock, wasn't it? Angela didn't like charity. But this wasn't charity, this was their future and she'd understand that. It wasn't as though he couldn't afford it. Elizabeth and Max could keep the big house and they'd have this. Surely Angela would see how perfect it was for everyone?

"We can't move in here," she continued, turning her back on him and peering out of the window at her children in the garden. Her cardigan had slipped from her left shoulder. He loved it when she got angry – so passionate – he couldn't help but laugh.

"Of course you can," he said, pushing away from the window and offering her his hand. She slapped it away. "I'll sort everything out. The move. Furniture. Everything ..."

He really didn't get it did he? How could he force her into making such a decision? They had barely known each other a couple of weeks and now he was blackmailing her into making a choice between her children's future and her own happiness. Where did men get off trying to control your life? It had been the same with Danny: male pride dominating so many of their decisions together. Well, not this time. So what if her house didn't have en-suite bathrooms, hand-painted splash-back tiles and sensor reactive outdoor lighting? It was hers. She had bought it, and made it into a home for her family. There were some things you couldn't just walk into a shop and buy – like self-respect for example. Angie was not about to live off someone else's goodwill. Jordan's face appeared in the doorway.

"Are we moving in here?" he cried, "Are we? Yeeeess! Jade, Jade," he shouted, and before Angie could stem the flow, her children were at her side jumping up and down. Mel stood in the doorway, her hand on her hip, an eyebrow raised.

"Look. No. Kids, it's not as simple as that." Jordan slapped his arms by his side and dipped his head. Jade, taking a little longer to grasp the meaning of her mother's comment, continued to stare up at her expectantly. She looked from her Mum to Jocelyn to Auntie Mel and then back along the row of adult faces.

"Come on Angela," laughed Jocelyn, stepping forward and reaching out his arms. She shook her shoulders and wriggled free from him.

"Jocelyn, you don't understand. You can't just expect us to move in here like that."

"Why on earth not?" he said irritably. But then what did she expect? He had gone to all this trouble for her. For them.

"Yes Mum, why not?" mimicked her daughter, her eyes wide and accusing. Even at her age she could tell a good thing when it appeared in front of her. She'd never forgive her mum if she let this go. It had been just the same with Danny, hadn't it? Her Mum being unreasonable and not letting him back in the house. Although she still suspected she was partly to blame for Danny leaving in the first place, what with her spilling Ribena on the carpet and everything. Jade didn't like to think about it – she might cry. And now was not a time to cry. If she did, Jocelyn might walk out. And then there'd just be the three of them again. And there'd be no treats, no new toys and no new house.

"No. That's my final word. Come on, let's go," her mother said, and Jade felt the tears start to burn behind her eyes. She bit her bottom lip and squeezed her eyes shut. Why exactly did grown-ups insist on making everything so complicated?

Tickets to see Irina Kolesnikova in The Nutcracker at The Royal Albert Hall, rear circle, £22.50

114 years before Jocelyn Thwaite's death

Suzanne span round and round like a wooden top, her body light and careless as though untroubled by nature's laws of movement. She was a sprite, a gypsy, unstoppable, like a newly emerged butterfly. Satie understood that about her, had fallen in love with her because of it, yet he still couldn't temper his hatred for the baying men and clapping hands that greeted her. His jealousy roared away inside him like the cheap liquor that burnt his throat.

1 week, 5 days after Jocelyn Thwaite's death

The following morning Danny woke with a start. The echo of a memory edged away from him. He could still feel the warmth of Angie's bare arm wrapped around his chest, pulling him close, as real as though she was there with him. He stretched out his hand, only to feel the cold empty hollow of the space beside him. The pure white bleach of the West Coast sun splintered the room and he guarded his eyes with his forearm, groaned and rolled over onto his front.

Outside the evidence of the previous night's party had been cleared away. Even the ring stain from Danny's glass had been carefully erased from the sculpture's plinth. Paulita appeared at his side, a glass of chilled orange juice in her hand. Breakfast, she announced, would be served in the summer room. Danny studied the plate of eggs she placed in front him. His stomach rolled in protest as he prodded tentatively at them. Alex, Paulita explained, had left early for an urgent campaign meeting with Larry and his studio's press officer. Apparently Miss Suvari's failure to appear at the party has caused something of a stir – being seen as a deliberate snub that could potentially have far-reaching consequences. If the gossip columns picked up on the story, Alex Fry's celebrity-stock could fall heavily. Who you were seen with was every bit as important as who you were. Danny smiled absent-mindedly as Paulita chatted merrily in her disjointed English – a strange stilted mix of Hispanic and Californian. She slid more eggs onto his plate. Alex, she said, had made it clear that Danny was to make use of his driver to explore the city if he so wished. Danny gazed at the empty house. For all its expensive designer furniture and hi-tech time-efficient gadgets, the building echoed with the sterile chill of a hospital. The gentle, insistent hum of electricity plagued his ears like tinnitus. What this house needed was real noise, he concluded. What it needed was a family. Jordan and Jade screaming and shouting, sliding across the varnished wooden floor on their knees, throwing cushions and toys at each other and leaving puddles of pens, crayons and Ribena all over the floor. What this house needed ... what he needed ... He shook the thought from his head and went in search of Dalton.

Danny's dream had left him with a strange, unresolved feeling. It was not unlike the sensation you get when you think you've forgotten to do something but just can't bring to mind what it is. In his dream Angie had sat directly in front of him. She had leant forward, her forearms on her knees and grabbed hold of his hands. She had held them tightly and stared into his eyes, not saying a word.

"Where to, sir?" Dalton studied Danny, a look of slight bemusement on his face. "Where'd you suggest?" Danny shrugged.

"Well, gee, I don't know. Rodeo Drive? Sunset Strip? If you fancy shopping ... Bijan on Rodeo Drive is the place to go. But you have to make an appointment ..."

"Appointment?"

"Of course."

"No."

"Okay. Er, The Museum of Art? Or we have a great city zoo ..."
And in that instant Danny's dream broke and an image of Jade riding on
the back of a small pony flashed across his mind. She was giggling, her little hands gripping the mane for all she was worth and her blonde hair
cast behind her. Danny reached up to her, but she galloped past him,
turning and looking over her shoulder, a look of worry crossing her face.
Danny stretched out his hand but she was beyond reach. Her mouth
opened wide as if to scream. Then the image was gone.

"What do tourists usually do?"

"Follow the Movie Star Trail, of course!"

"The ...?"

"Movie Star Trail – go and look at the big houses of celebrities,"
Dalton beamed.

"Let's do that, then," Danny said.

The driver turned in his seat and peered at Danny over the top of
his shades.

"Really, sir?"

"Why not?" he said, leaning back into the soft leather cocoon of
his seat.

"You're the boss," Dalton shrugged.

If he was honest, Danny had found the whole party the night
before an unnerving experience. It had been the first time he felt really
out of control has Joss Thwaite. Up until then he had felt that he really
was Joss and Joss was him. But there had been times throughout the
evening that he felt like nothing more than a freak show, brought along
for the amusement of Alex Fry's guests. He resented the way the actor
would pull him by the arm and stand him in front of people.

"Joss here's from England. He's a musician."

The constant questions, however well-meaning, were tiring and
intrusive and he found himself revealing fantastical details that he knew
in the cold light of day he would struggle to remember. As the car cut its
way on to the freeway and dipped back down towards the city, Danny
closed his eyes and tried to piece together the conversations. There had
been Stacey's mother, but he didn't worry too much about her. Like her
daughter, he doubted whether Christie would remember much of the
evening. It had been the men at the party who had been the most inquisitive. The slight arch of a cynical eyebrow, the persistent nagging for
detail, had left him with a cold, exposed feeling. At the driving range a

group of men had circled him. Dean Massey, one of Alex's actor buddies, a tall, plastic-skinned man in his fifties with black boot-polish hair stared at him with a quizzical, unbelieving look. Alex slapped him on the back with a grin,

"Leave the poor guy alone Dean," he said. But Massey just laughed.

"The boy doesn't mind, do ya?" he challenged. Danny hated the way his piercing eyes made him feel so guilty. What films had he worked on? Massey wanted to know. Who was his agent in Hollywood? Which directors had he worked with? Wenders? Burton? Danny had felt naked. He attempted to fend off the questions with self-effacing shrugs, but they only served to fan the flames. They wanted to know about royalties and publishing rights, studio percentages and distribution mechanisms. Danny mumbled his answers, attempting to affect the vagueness of a drunken English eccentric. They didn't appear wholly convinced. He plucked a club from the rail beside him.

"My, a man of many talents is our Mr Thwaite," Dean Massey grinned, replacing the five iron Danny had picked up with a two wood. "Try this buddy, you might have more luck."

The car dipped down into a valley and the coast suddenly appeared again. "Okay," Dalton said over his shoulder. "I'm gonna give you *the* tour."

"*The* tour?" Danny answered half-heartedly.

"Sure, you'll love it. Before this gig I was a private hire guide for tourists wanting to see …" Dalton put-on his show voice, "… the homes of the rich and famous." Dalton peered in his rear-view and Danny, catching his look, smiled back encouragingly.

"Right this is Beverly Hills – ah, even the air smells finer here, know what I mean?"

"If you love it so much – why'd you give it up?"

"What? An' turn down the chance to work for part of the great Fry dynasty? Geez, man, there's nothing like it. It's like I'm a part of history. Hollywood's number one family – and I'm right there, every day." Danny smiled thinly. He didn't really know how to answer that.

"An' I get to meet famous people. Martin Sheen last week. Nice guy." Danny nibbled at the soft pad below his index finger. He suddenly felt an irrational dislike for the man. Why was he so drunk on the fame of other people? What about himself? Wasn't his life worth enjoying for what it was without leaching off the back of others? Danny looked out of the window. On the horizon Danny could just make out where the blues of the ocean and sky were smudged together in a watery line. A tanker hugged the edge as though it might fall off. Danny found himself indulging the driver.

"So, who's the most famous person you've driven around?"

"Driven around, or met?" Dalton challenged. Danny didn't really care.

"Most famous ... hmm?" He enjoyed rolling the thought around in his mind, as though he'd never been asked the question before. "Well, I drove Michael Douglas and his wife to Mr Fry's boat at the marina a month or so ago. But ..." He paused for grand effect. Danny was barely listening. "... I've shaken hands with the great goddess herself, Liz Taylor." He paused for the 'wow'. It wasn't forthcoming. 'Yeah and I've stayed in her favourite hotel suite!' "Okay. Here's Keanu Reeves' pad. And on your right Aaron Spelling's modest abode ..."

And then there had been Stacey's boyfriend. Clearly, for whatever reason, he didn't like Danny. He had caught him looking over at him a couple of times during the evening, his dark eyes boring into him. Danny had shrugged it off and turned his back. He couldn't afford confrontation, especially not with an irrational, hormonal teenager. And then the boy had disappeared for several hours, to follow Stacey around like a lovesick puppy no doubt, until he reappeared just as the party was beginning to disperse. Danny, exhausted by the unrelenting questions and chatter, had sought shelter in the living room. He had poured himself a double bourbon and slumped into one of the deep leather armchairs. He let his head loll back as he studied the small white canvas covered in black and grey etched lines that hung on the far wall. A girl, who had been lying on the settee across the room from him, swung her legs around and sat up straight. "Don't you like it?" she asked, with a smile. Danny looked over at her. She had short spiked white hair and a pierced eyebrow. "Am I supposed to?" he replied.

"Not if you don't want," she giggled.

"It's not really my taste," he said.

And it was at that moment that Taylor had appeared and sat down beside the girl. Even though he hadn't noticed him before, Danny had the uncomfortable feeling Taylor had been in the room for a while, watching them.

"Do you even know what your taste is?" Taylor smirked. The girl, suddenly aware of the prickling tension that spread like a fog through the room, pulled herself to her feet and stumbled towards the door. She blew Danny a kiss. Danny watched her disappear, then turned back to look at the boy.

"Sorry?" he said. Taylor leant back and let his arms spread across the back of the couch.

"We're now approaching Mulholland Drive," Dalton continued. "If you look just ahead of you on this next corner …" he steered the car to the left and let it gently slow. "… you'll probably see people outside a wall on the left. Yep, there they are." Danny craned his neck and saw the driver was pointing at a huddle of tourists all gathered around a gatepost. A couple stood in front of a pair of solid wooden gates while a third person framed them in his view finder.

"12850," Dalton announced. "The man himself." Danny's face remained blank. "Nicholson!" Dalton said with a nod of the head.

"Why are they standing there? Is he going to come out?"

"Nah, of course not. He's probably at one of his other homes anyway." Dalton pulled the car on to the curb and shuffled round in his seat, leaning his elbow against the headrest. "Some camp for days just to get a peep. Occasionally, someone comes out. But it's rare. Most of these houses have a back entrance. These security gates are just for show for the tourists. The bigger the gates the bigger the star. There's, like, a whole gate-envy thing going on out here. " He turned back round and gently eased the car back into gear. "We've got Warren Beatty, Pamela Anderson, all along here…"

"She's not a fool, you know." Taylor said. His streaked hair was lank against his forehead, his eyes wide and round peering directly at Danny through his greasy fringe. Was he on drugs? Danny wondered. Weren't all spoilt little American skater boys? Danny looked towards the window. The glass reflected a surreal collage of inside and out – the two of them sat floating in the middle of Alex Fry's azure pool, palm leaves and wall lights breaking the night sky that hung above their heads.

"I assume we're talking about Stacey, are we?" he replied in a quiet, placating voice.

"Yes, Stacey," answered the teenager irritably. Taylor fidgeted, the baggy denim of his jeans bunched about his crotch. From his belt hung a thick silver chain in a hoop. "She'll work you out in no time. She's not stupid."

"So you said," replied Danny impatiently.

"She doesn't get full access to her money until she's twenty-one, so …" Taylor paused. He knew he was starting to sound petty. That hadn't been the plan. The plan had been to be cool and calculated, to scare the guy, to intimidate him. He didn't appear very intimidated.

Danny shook his head bemused. He leant forward in his chair and rolled the tumbler between his fingers. Outside a splash from the pool and an excited squeal ruffled the otherwise still air.

"Look, sonny," Danny hissed, his voice low and measured, "I've no idea what you are talking about. But don't worry, I've got no intention of stealing your little *girlfriend* away from you." Danny accentuated the word girlfriend and Taylor winced.

"She wouldn't go with you, anyway," Taylor retorted, aware now of how foolish he was beginning to sound. Danny smiled thinly.

"And I've certainly no interest in her money," he scoffed, spreading his arms wide as if to demonstrate how little he needed anybody else's money.

"Whatever," muttered Taylor, his argument floundering. He let his eyes drop to his feet. He started to sulk. Danny laughed.

"Go to bed, boy," he said, placing his glass on the table in front of him and standing up. "Get some sleep and sober up."

Taylor thrust his hands beneath him and started to rock lightly. He lifted his head.

"So who are you? Really?" he said. Danny paused and looked at him. The blood drained from his face and he was aware of a thin rivulet of sweat edging its way down beneath his shoulder blades. The pause was enough to confirm everything Taylor needed to know. He smiled triumphantly.

"Whatever, *Mr Thwaite*," he grinned.

Dalton announced their arrival on Hollywood Boulevard. Danny shuffled in his seat and turned to press his face up against the car window. Well, what could a punk like Taylor do anyway? He was all bravado and acne. The wide, open street was trimmed with tall brown palms and the debris of half-realised roadworks. The buildings either side were set far back from the road and obscured by weathered hardboard signs promising guided tours and cheap fried food. The dollar sign in all its states of printed glory stood proud on every junction and corner; the larger, the more lurid the lettering, the better. Dalton slowed the car to a crawl and let it idle in the slow lane, its low registered hum moaning like a tabletop fridge. Dalton shifted forward in his seat and peered through the windscreen as though mesmerised by the beauty of the scene in front of him. He emitted a low whistle from between his teeth. Danny leant his forehead against the glass. Everywhere grinning families held cameras to their faces. As the car drifted past some tourists turned their lens towards them, assuming the Mercedes' blacked-out windows hid a celebrity.

Danny resisted the temptation to wind down his window and disappoint them. A fat American woman in a pale blue velvet tracksuit jogged beside the car until she ran out of breath. Danny watched her double up, her camera swinging about her neck like a noose.

Taylor had caught Danny off-guard. At the time he had been buoyed up on the bravado of the evening – courted by Stacey's mum and Alex's friends. In the cold light of day the boy's comments made him feel less comfortable. It wouldn't take much for Taylor to plant the seed of doubt in the minds of those about him. And Larry, he was sure, barely tolerated Danny's presence, seeing him as an unnecessary distraction for his client, while the housemaid, Paulita, looked at him as though he'd just stopped off from Mars. A man in an Uncle Sam topper waved at the car with a little flag on a stick. Danny breathed on the glass: a painted cowboy, his lasso around a giant hotdog, slowly misted from view. Maybe it was time for Danny to reconsider his options. He always knew he couldn't live this lie indefinitely. The cold air in the car quickly cleared the window and, like someone switching a light back on, the lurid technicolour of the scene outside reappeared: a bad rendering of Homer Simpson offering a car wash, a blue cat of non-specific gender displaying candy bars. Danny felt an echoing sense of disappointment. This wasn't the glamorous, mystical Hollywood he'd been promised all his life. This was the garden centre Santa's Grotto version of the fantasy in his mind. Dalton eased the car to a halt and Danny opened the door. He blinked his eyes to clear the dust spat up by the coaches that tipped their bewildered contents on to the sidewalk and looked down at his feet. The walkway was studded, to his left and right, with pink granite stars edged with bronze trims. In the centre of each, was a small iconic circle and above that the name of a celebrity. Danny stood on Bette Midler. Then stepped off her. All around him tourists shuffled about as though their ankles were tied together.

"Incredible, isn't it?" marvelled Dalton. "There's Cagney up here, the dirty rat." He laughed at his joke and waddled away, his full pendulous weight now apparent as he stepped from the car. Danny crouched to make out Buster Keaton's name. The lettering was worn and someone had diligently pressed gum into the first three letters of his name rendering them barely legible

An uncharacteristic West Coast breeze had started to build by the time Danny and his driver returned to the actor's home. As the car approached, Danny reflected on the height of Alex Fry's ball-topped pillars and gold painted gates. It reminded him of his mother having the front door painted ruby red when he was a child because the neighbours had just painted theirs burnt orange. Somehow he'd imagined wealth would levitate you beyond such things. Inside the house Paulita directed him to the main living area where he found Fry and Larry bowed in hesitant discussion. Stacey sat curled on a chair in the corner humming a tune to herself and examining the chipped paint on her toenails. The conversation stopped the moment Danny entered the room and he hesitated by the door.

"Oh, sorry, I ...," he muttered. Alex stood up and waved his empty glass.

"No problem, my friend. No problemo." He steadied himself against Larry's leg and stumbled towards the row of decanters on the table by the wall. "You're just in time for a drink. This miserable bastard won't join me."

"Alex, really," Larry began, but a wave of the actor's hand silenced him.

"Mena Suvari's people, apparently," he said spitting the words in derision, "deem me to be an unsuitable prospect." He leant against the cabinet and studied Danny. "What the ... unsuitable prospect?" A dribble of whisky ran down his chin. "What am I, a piece of real estate?"

"Alex, come on." Larry stood up and turned to face him. He towered above the actor but still flinched under his gaze. "You need to get some rest. Let me get Maria to give you a massage. That'll make you feel better. Who's Mena Suvari anyway?"

"Yeah, right. Who is she anyway?" Alex dipped his head and studied his glass. "What do you think Joss? Should a guy be able to choose his own girlfriends? His own life?"

"Guess so. Yes, of course," Danny offered uncertainly.

"Exactly," Alex shouted, clapping his hands then stumbling over to Danny and wrapping his arms about his shoulder. "See Joss, my man, understands," he said, staring accusingly at Larry.

"Get some rest Alex," he said, snapping his case shut and slipping it under his arm. "I'll see you tomorrow. We have scripts to go through."

"If I'd wanted an arranged marriage I'd have moved to India," Alex added with a childish, slightly deranged grin. He laughed at his own joke. Stacey uncurled herself, grunted something Danny didn't catch and wandered out of the French doors to the pool. The actor had already poured Danny a drink and forced it into his hand. Why not? Danny sipped at the burning liquid and watched Stacey unpeel her T-shirt and jump in.

"Glad you're here man," Alex beamed slapping him on the shoulder again. "A voice of reason among the madness." Danny raised his glass in salute. Now was not the time to mention that he was considering leaving.

Bette Midler signed autograph photo / COA, eBay, 2d 09h 57m left, $22.95

5 days before Jocelyn Thwaite's death

Angela would come around to his way of thinking. That was obvious. No mother, presented with the choice, would turn her back on such an opportunity. Anyway, she was probably just playing him along, wasn't she? Isn't that what women did? Jocelyn was quite willing to admit that his knowledge of the 'eccentricities' of the female psyche was limited. But he read the *Telegraph*, caught the end of debates on *Woman's Hour*. He wasn't a complete dinosaur. No, Angela would come round, he just needed to offer her a little 'space'. Certainly, he would admit an element of miscalculation on his part: a degree of unsubtly in his methodology. But that in itself wasn't such a bad thing was it? After all, isn't that what women wanted – the 'grand gesture'? Didn't they yearn for the romantic lead to take control of the situation and wrestle them away from their mundane, inconsequential and dreary lives? Jocelyn scratched irritably at his freshly shaven cheek. He felt the red welt beneath his nails burn. How many of these women living their cold little lives didn't swoon at their Mills & Boons or daydream along to their daily dose of soap opera and wish that someone wealthy – like him – would come along and take them away from their sad little concrete homes? Weren't they all no better than prisoners in their proletarian ghettos: downtrodden by their brutish, drunken, knuckle-grazing husbands? Jocelyn leant forward to peer from his vantage point at the side of the road. He hunched his shoulders amongst the untrimmed privet that gave him his cover. From where he stood, if he bent beyond the telegraph pole that shielded him, he had a clear view of Angela's house opposite. There was a single light still on in the upstairs right hand window. A thin vertical sliver of light, created where the two curtains failed to meet was occasionally broken by the movement of a figure beyond. Presently, the movement stopped and the light dulled to nothing more than the soft translucent glow of a small side light. Jocelyn shuffled his feet and rummaged in his pockets for nothing in particular.

On the other side of the road a group of youths on mountain bikes wheeled past laughing, knocking the wing mirrors of cars and bouncing up and down the kerb. Jocelyn took half a step backwards into the shadows. The youths passed by, either not noticing him or simply not caring. He should have brought Jasper with him as an alibi. And then he thought better of it. This was not the kind of area where one politely walked your dog late at night and nodded pleasantly to your neighbours. Rather this was where you stumbled home drunk past the drug-pedalling thirteen-year-olds on the corner and vomited on your own doorstep after having just frittered away the housekeeping on beer and slot machines. Jocelyn wasn't naïve – he'd seen the *Newsnight* special reports on inner-city deprivation. There was the faint tang of dog crap in the air and he brought his handkerchief to his nose. He half expected to return to his Jag and find it burnt out or, at the very least, bricked up on wheels. So why the hell had Angela turned down the opportunity to escape this? She hadn't even done him the courtesy of an explanation – despite numerous efforts to call her mobile since she had walked out of the house. He had, however, briefly managed to grab Mel's arm as she followed her sister down the driveway. The children were distraught, jumping about their mother's legs pleading for her to reconsider. Mel had been the last one to leave the house. She was still trying to placate the estate agent when Jocelyn reached out to grab her wrist. He pulled at her arm harder than he had meant, spinning her around on her heels. Mel had looked at him in surprise, her eyes wide and questioning. But something in his expression must have softened her because she stopped, pulled the sleeve of her cardigan up and said,

"Look, Angie's very independent, you know ..." No, he didn't know, he wanted to say. "Give her some time, you're rushing her."

"How can I be rushing her?" he said pleadingly. "Get her to think about it." He looked so vulnerable and lost. Mel touched his arm. The muscles beneath his sleeve were tense and rigid. She took a step back.

"Look, I've got to go," she said, "but I'll do my best." Mel sensed that Jocelyn was about to cry. Or shout. Or both. "I've got to go."

The dark brought with it a penetrating chill. Jocelyn pulled his coat about him and turned to make his way back to the car. He had no idea where he would go. Maybe he would pull the car up in a lay-by somewhere and screw himself into a ball in his front seat. It wasn't the kind of thing he had ever imagined himself doing. His fellow college professors would be horrified. Something about that revelation appealed to him. Which was better – somewhere quiet and out of the way, like a country lane, where he might be attacked by a machete-wielding madman, or a well-illuminated suburban street where early morning dog-walkers might peer at him and summon the police? Death or shame? Not an easy choice. The irony, he knew, was that if he wanted to, he could just go home. Elizabeth had never been the kind to create a scene. She wouldn't gloat at the sight of him with his tail between his legs, and she wouldn't make him suffer either. She would just accept. She would place a milky coffee in front of him as he sat at the kitchen table, the Aga warming his back and Jasper's damp muzzle warming his knee. And then she'd leave him to go upstairs, ready herself for bed and settle between the sheets to read four pages of her book. Jocelyn would join her in bed. They wouldn't say a word. He would stare absent-mindedly at the wall opposite and count the rose buds on the wallpaper below the dado rail. Then, she would switch out her sidelight – her gentle breathing slowing and eventually pulling him into sleep.

The sound of a plastic bin wobbling on its rim caught his attention and Jocelyn turned to see the silhouette of a figure feeling his way cautiously along the wall of a neighbouring house. Jocelyn took a step back into the folds of the privet. The occasional sweep of headlights revealed a stooped, youngish man in jeans and filthy denim jacket. He kept pushing the hair back from his eyes. The man stopped when he reached the – Jocelyn stopped short of calling it a gatepost – pile of bricks at the front of Angela's house, turned and looked up at the building. Jocelyn felt his own breath catch in his throat. To his horror, the man stumbled up to the door and lifted his hand to rattle the handle. He reached in his pocket and struggled to find keys that clearly were no longer there. Frustrated, the man slapped the palm of his hand against the surface of the door. Then he peered up towards the window where only moments earlier Jocelyn had seen Angela switch off her light. Paralysed by the realisation that he shouldn't be there, Jocelyn just watched. The man steadied himself against the frame of the door and lowered his head. For a moment, Jocelyn assumed he had given up, but it appeared he was just summoning his breath. He lifted his head and with exaggerated precision pointed his index finger in line with the small plastic bell beside the door. With all the power of his drifting concentration he wobbled forward on the balls of his feet and pressed the button. It had the desired effect and within moments, Angela's bedroom light snapped on. The curtains pulled apart and Jocelyn could just make out the blurred outline of her face appear against the window. Even by the muted silver glow of the cloud-smudged moon, Jocelyn could see the tousled mass of Angela's hair and the outline of her hands pulling her dressing gown tightly around her. He couldn't hear her words, but he could see the shape of her lips mouthing to the figure below. The man stepped back from the door and waved his arms above his head. From his vantage point Jocelyn could make out nothing more than a mix of broken half-sentences. Jocelyn shook his head and smiled to himself.

Only when the dull roar of an approaching car and the familiar soft blue glow of spinning lights filled the street did Jocelyn step away. He placed his mobile phone carefully back into his inside pocket and made his way back to the car. He kept his head down and walked with purpose, aware that it was better not to draw attention to himself. By the time the two disinterested constables had arrived to prise the man's fingers from Angela's front door Jocelyn had long gone, content that he'd done his bit. He was sensitive after all; he understood that some things were private. He smiled again at the memory of the drunken idiot struggling ineffectually between the policemen, his arms flailing wildly and his legs giving way beneath him. And he had heard Angela's shaking voice urging him to leave her alone. Jocelyn flicked the car into drive. She could thank him in the morning.

Angie pulled her curtains together and sat down on the edge of the bed. There were days when she wondered whether her life was her own anymore. Everyone seemed to demand so much from her: her children, her sister, the kids at work, Danny, Jocelyn. She felt as though her sense of identity was slowly being sucked from her. At what point could she put her hand out and stop it all revolving around her? She rubbed her eyes with the ball of her palm and fell back onto the bed. She imagined the duvet was a cloud and that she was drifting away into oblivion. The bedroom door gently eased open, followed by the soft tread of carefully placed feet.

"I thought you were asleep," she said without looking up.

"I heard Danny," said Jordan, climbing onto the bed and lying lengthways across it next to his mother. Angie wrapped her fingers in his hair.

"Sorry," she said.

"'S'not your fault," he answered gently. "He was drunk."

"Yes."

Jordan pushed himself up on to his elbow. He had grown so much just in the last few months. It wouldn't be long before he was a man with his own worries, hopes, friends and family. And then he'd be gone. And so would Jade. And suddenly Angie would no longer need to worry about finding time for herself, she would be swamped by it.

"I miss Danny, too, you know," she said.

"You do?" Jordan sounded surprised.

"Of course I do. Because, you know, you can't switch feelings off just like that."

"Then why …?" Angie knew what her son was about to say. And who was to say he was wrong?

"Come on, it's school tomorrow," she answered simply, ruffling his hair and pulling him towards her. Jordan grinned and wriggled from his mother's grip.

"Yeah, yeah," he groaned.

Danny had looked so vulnerable. She had been shocked at how tired and drawn he appeared. His clothes were a mess and his hair was unkempt, as though he had been sleeping rough. Maybe she should call Steve in the morning and make sure he was okay. That's if the police had let him go. Not that him appearing at her door had merited their intervention. There was no accounting for her neighbours' twisted values. On this estate you could be mugged in broad daylight and no one would come and help, but disturb a night's beauty sleep and all hell broke loose.

Byron 765 wired door chime kit, batteries not included, £16.99

1 week, 6 days after Jocelyn Thwaite's death

The Californian Highway Patrol had found the actor slumped over the steering wheel of his car in a lay-by on San Fernando Boulevard, the engine still running He was so intoxicated that when the state troopers tapped on his window and he opened his door, he fell out of his seat, and lay face down on the road moaning that he could no longer feel his arms and legs. Larry had arrived at the scene within ten minutes of getting a call from the NBC network and groaned at the sight of his client slumped in the back of the patrol car, swearing at the officers.

The night before, Danny had made good his excuses and returned to his room. With Dalton officially excused for the evening, Alex had driven his BMW X5 through the suburbs of Los Angeles and out on to the highway. Larry, keen to unravel the full history of the night before, before the media did, produced a bundle of notes from his inside pocket.

"We can, er, try to keep a lid on this, can't we officer?" he urged, gently pushing the clenched fist of dollars towards the policeman. The trooper peered over his silver shades. There was a gathering crowd. Not only NBC, but also a couple of the smaller independent stations, and a number of local freelance Beverley Hills gossip hacks that the trooper recognised. Add to that a light build-up of general spectators and Trooper Mendes had his audience. In a flash, he could see the future: book deals, Oprah interviews, possibly even that bit part in a movie that he had always kidded his mates he'd one day do.

"Sir, is that a bribe?" he hissed under his breath. Larry looked shocked. How much did this buffoon earn a year that he could afford to turn down his offer?

"Of course not," he said through the corner of his mouth, his eyes darting about him, aware that the longer this particular discourse continued the more likelihood that his career would crumble about his ears. In Hollywood dirt stuck. Ask his mate Bernie Kaufman after the incident with the pre-op transsexual. "It's a gift. A token of my respect for the great work you guys do." Trooper Mendes considered that for a moment and Larry felt the sweat spring out on his forehead.

"Oh, okay, " he replied with a grin. What the hell, he could make both ways if he played his cards right. Take the schmuck's money and clean up with the journos later. Sue me.

Alex, suddenly aware of his surroundings, made to climb out of the car. Larry tried to push him back. It was too late, the actor stumbled barely a foot from the car before Mendes' colleague had slapped a pair of cuffs on him and bundled him back into the car. Larry was almost blinded by the bulbs going off. Shit, he thought – that was the shot they needed. In the mêlée he couldn't help notice Trooper Mendes turn his head towards the cameras and grin. It was a picture that Larry would have to endure over his morning muesli for weeks to come.

Fuelled by a half-bottle of scotch before he set off and spurred on by four bottles of bud at a highway tavern, Alex Fry had then driven along the 210 towards Burbank. He never quite made his intended destination, having taken a corner a little sharply and flattened a water hydrant. After three hours of police ridicule, a $100,000 bail and a number of autographs, the actor was eventually allowed to leave the station. Trooper Mendes swept before the actor, his manager and bodyguard parting the sea of photographers before them. He lingered every now and then to ensure they got his 'good side'. Larry, in the meantime, thrust his hand out to push the huddle of reporters and their foam-bubbled microphones out of the way.

"So where the hell were you driving?" Danny asked. Alex didn't answer and Danny rolled his head to the side to see if the actor had heard him.

"You'll laugh," he said eventually. He sipped tentatively at the glass in his hand.

It was nearly midnight and the two of them had spent the previous hours numbing the horrible sense of reality that threatened to consume them individually. Danny, resolving in his mind that he had little choice but to see his adventure to its conclusion, had spent the day deliberately avoiding Larry, Stacey and her nosey boyfriend. Alex, in the meantime, had slipped deeper and deeper into a dark, all-consuming mood that he refused to be dragged from. A couple of hours by the marina staring at his 200ft yacht was nothing more than a temporary distraction. On return to the house the actor flicked open a fresh bottle of bourbon and gazed out at the pool.

"I was looking for someone," Alex continued, his voice becoming measured and serious. He sat upright and straddled his seat. "A girl, of course." He paused again, pulling the moment out like a thread. "The only girl I think I ever really loved." Danny resisted the temptation to laugh. Was the actor reading from a script? Alex stood up and paced. Outside, the lights beneath the pool's water had dimmed to a pale mustard. The horizon was singed orange by the glow of the city lights below them. Danny wondered if he might quietly get up and retire to bed. "It was just as I was starting to break as an actor. My first film, *Brief Liason* – you know, the original one – had just been released. I was on the crest of a wave. The studio was promising all sorts of deals. They were even talking about Academy Awards. You know, I was on *Jay Leno* one night, *Saturday Night Live* the next. It was so ... so liberating, new and, you know..." Alex was still staring out of the window. But Danny suspected by the tilt of his head and the twist of his hips that he was no longer looking at the view beyond but studying his own reflection. ..."I met Crystal at, er, an exotic bar just beyond Burbank. Is met the right word?" Danny shrugged. "She was a performer there. I didn't pay, you know – honestly – hey, I've never had to pay." Alex spread out his hands on the cold smooth glass and gently lent his forehead against it. He pressed the skin against the solid, unrelenting wall and pushed as hard as he could. He felt the ache below the skin and the chill soak into the bone of his skull. There was a protracted pause in which Danny wondered whether the actor had fallen asleep standing up. The conversation had the slightly disturbing air of a confessional; of someone reaching that point in their life where they feel driven to slap down the red rawness of their heart in front of them and pick over the sinews. Danny had fought hard throughout his life to avoid examining such things. But then maybe it wasn't such a twisted concept. Perhaps if Danny had been more willing to examine his own misgivings and paranoia he would never have slept with that woman. Had he heard right? Had Danny just confessed his own failings? With a shake of his head he scattered the strands of uncomfortable thought from his mind.

"Am I supposed to be able to explain why I fell for her? Does anybody know?" Alex turned around and slid his back down the glass, ending in a pool on the floor. It reminded Danny of a little rubber toy of Jordan's that when thrown against glass slowly tumbled down on its sticky hands and feet. "No, as everyone around me quite rightly pointed out, she wasn't Cameron Diaz, or Nicole Kidman, or Penelope Cruz. Thanks for pointing out the obvious Mom – Jeez!" Who the hell was he talking to now?

"So, what did I do?" Alex lifted his head and stared directly at Danny. Did he want an answer?

"Um …," Danny began.

"Walk out on her, that's what I did. Just dumped her like they told me to. Despite everything my heart told me – I walked away." He stood up and started pacing the room. His shoulders were up, his feet heavy and his eyes hot with resentment and anger. He looked like a trapped animal.

"So," Alex suddenly announced, spinning on his toes and clasping his hands together. There was that maniacal grin again. "I went to find her. Unfortunately, it appears I was a little bit drunk …. "

"But, you know where she is?"

"Where she was. It was six years ago. And, you know …" He seemed to consider his options for a moment. It was obviously the first time he had had an ally to confide in. The temptation was too great. "The Pink Pussycat out near San Fernando."

"Well," smiled Danny, "call Dalton. Let's go there." Suddenly there seemed a reason for the two of them being thrown together – fate *could* exist for a higher purpose. Alex crawled on his hands and knees and picked up his mobile. A strange elation swamped him.

"His wife answered," he giggled. "She didn't seem very happy." The world threatened to spin and Danny felt his way to his feet. His bladder was urgently trying to tell his smudged brain something of great mutual benefit. Minutes later Dalton arrived. His suit was clean and pressed, his freshly polished black hair smoothed down and his shades still perched below a questioning furrow.

"Is it late – or early?" Alex sniggered, levering himself tentatively into the passenger seat of the Mercedes.

"Hey, whatever you guys want it to be," Dalton replied, bemused.

Danny slid back and forth on the leather upholstery in the back of the car and not for the first time that evening pondered what he was doing. Dalton spun the wheel of the car and let its nose bounce out of the driveway.

Dalton dialled the club's address into the sat nav. It was not one of his boss's usual twilight venues – away from the comfort and security that some of the more popular in-town bars would offer. Dalton was a man of the world. He appreciated that movie stars, like everyone else, needed to let their hair down once in a while. But they had their places: clubs with proper security guards with ear-pieces, cocktails with names that you couldn't pronounce and women that in the cold light of day, still looked more attractive than your wife. But discretion, he had learnt long ago was the secret to longevity of service in this town. And he wasn't about to break that code.

The Pink Pussycat, they soon discovered, no longer existed: it had been burnt down by a jealous wife who took her husband's regular visits to 'The Cat' as a personal slight. Having found her husband huddled over a tall black girl called Lia, she stabbed him in the chest with one of his own barbecue skewers, locked herself in the bar's storeroom and poured lighter fluid on the manager's priceless collection of early *Hustlers*. The 1950s wooden building took less than twenty minutes to turn to black smouldering ash, of which only a small percentage was Lucille Bailey and her philandering husband Ron. Alex and Danny studied the grey tenement that now sprouted in its place. Alex groaned – his search over before it had begun.

"You sure this is where it was?" Danny asked. Alex nodded.

"There's a bar across the way," Dalton offered, "I'll go see if any one knows anything."

A piercing sound crackled through the dead, dry dark. It sounded like a gunshot. Danny and Alex hurriedly followed the driver. Inside the bar a round middle-aged woman in a blue, shapeless dress studied them from behind a counter built of pine logs. She watched the unlikely trio: the leader in his dark suit and shades and his two blurry-eyed followers in their expensive slacks and polished shoes. Did she recognise the one on the left? The tables were occupied by lonely, drawn men nursing liquor glasses and lost expressions. The jukebox spun a pre-selected playlist of soulless country rock at half volume, giving the room a distant, hollow echo.

"Jeez, now I want to slit my wrists," Alex breathed from the side of his mouth.

"Two bourbons and a soda, please ma'am," smiled Dalton,

pirouetting his fat arse on one of the stools and flipping his shades up on to his head. The men drank in silence and studied the room. A pool table on the far side of the bar stood untouched, the blue baize splattered with a disturbing dark brown stain. Torn posters on the far wall advertised concerts long since gone. The barmaid sighed. It had been her husband Al's idea to open the bar all night. It was barely worth it. The somnambulists that found themselves lured by the fluorescent tubes in the window were not heavy drinkers: one, maybe two, whiskys every hour. The bar was merely a substitute bed. The man the barmaid thought she recognised turned to study her. She let her hand slip down behind the bar and rest lightly on the butt of the revolver she kept there. Who else's husband would let their wife throw themselves on the mercy of potential murderers and rapists every night while he lay snoring in front of the NFL in the flat upstairs?

"Do you know what happened to the club across the street?" Alex asked. He had small, dark eyes and he looked pale and worried.

"Burnt down, two or three years back," she offered, fingering the gun. Alex nodded, clearly unsatisfied.

"It's a long shot, I know," Danny added, "but we're looking for a girl who used to work there." The woman smiled to herself, 'oh, yeah?'

"Lots of women worked there. Good riddance to the place."

"Her name was Crystal," Danny persevered, ignoring the woman's smirk. "She worked there about six years ago." Danny looked at Alex for confirmation and he nodded. "I don't know her second name ..."

"Peaks," said Alex. Danny stared at him aghast.

"Crystal Peaks?" Danny said. "We're looking for a girl called Crystal Peaks?"

"It was her stage name," Alex added.

"You don't say," Danny groaned. The woman laughed. The other occupants of the bar turned to stare at them. Such amusement was quite unexpected.

"Don't you know her real name?" Danny hissed. Alex shook his head and Danny rolled his eyes. Dalton gulped down the last of his soda and slipped his sunglasses back over his eyes. Pulled out of bed for this? Still, there were worse jobs in this town and the reality was, he'd done most of them. Alex Fry wasn't a bad boss. A bit wired may be, and certainly he drank too much. But if that was a crime then most of the celebrities in town would have been locked up long ago. Dalton held out his arm to Alex's elbow. The actor slid from his seat. The woman behind the bar was still laughing. Her giggles had passed like a childhood cold amongst the men around the bar and they stared at the group amused. At least he'd brought some light into their miserable little lives. He had a palatial, multi-million pound house to go home to. With a pool. And a gym. What did they have?

"Mary," the woman announced. She stopped laughing and laid her palms on the bar. "That's who you're looking for. Mary, Mary Delaney," she said. She leaned forward and Alex could smell her stale breath. "Well, buy another drink first, you ain't gonna get away that easily."

"Las Vegas. God, that's miles, isn't it?"

"Out in the desert. If we keep going we should be there by dawn," said Dalton peering in his rearview mirror. Mary, the bar lady remembered, had been a popular, but desperately naïve girl. She never troubled the management, turned up on time, didn't have sticky fingers and knew how to play the customers. At the end of a shift the girls would often wander into the bar across the road and spill their tales and frustrations onto the bar for her to carefully mop up. The girls fell into two categories: the discarded victims of abusive households, or vacant dreamers lured by the glamour of the city and the silver screen. Mary fell into the first category, kicked out by a mother jealous of her second husband's unhealthy attentions – *It's you or me, love*. When 'The Cat' burnt down, most of the girls found work further out of town. Those that were too old returned home, settled down with abusive husbands and gave birth to daughters that one day would repeat their mother's tormented lifecycle. According to the bar lady, Mary Delaney had hitched up with a piano player who was heading out east and was last heard of working as a hostess at the Booty Bar in Las Vegas.

The car's engine was tuneless and flat. Dalton edged out on to the freeway and let the Mercedes slip into cruise. Danny felt the hum envelop him. One minute he was in the car, the next he was thousands of miles away.

2 hours, 24 minutes before Jocelyn Thwaite's death

Danny hoisted his holdall on to his shoulder and looked down at his hand. The white skin of his knuckles looked dry and worn. A piercing pain behind his eyes forced him to wince.

4 years, 3 months before Jocelyn Thwaite's death

Angie threaded her arm through the loop of his arm. It was a simple gesture but one that never failed to make Danny feel alive. With Angie next to him, he felt in control of the world around him. He could do what ever he wanted. And no one could take that from him. Angie leant into his shoulder and he breathed in the perfume on her hair.

2 weeks after Jocelyn Thwaite's death

The car rocked and jolted Danny momentarily awake. Dalton gripped the wheel and stared into the black that flooded back around them.

2 hours, 23 minutes before Jocelyn Thwaite's death

Danny rubbed his temple. A dog barked several streets away. It was that small gap of time between waking and sleeping, and one by one streetlights snapped off like lids over eyes. Danny stared at the bag in his hand, stared at the dark before him and felt the anger sweep through him. Anger at Angie, anger at Steve and, most of all, anger at himself. He spat on the ground, lifted the bag high above his head and swung it straight through the window behind him. All of a sudden he felt a dull ache seep through his muscles and along his shoulder.

2 weeks after Jocelyn Thwaite's death

Alex rocked Danny by the shoulder. His eyes flicked open, registered the sharp piercing light and closed tight again.

"The Golden Sphinx, our hotel for the night," Alex said, holding the car door open.

They checked in, agreed that their mission was not so urgent that sleep shouldn't get in the way and went in search of their beds. Any memory that Danny had of the approach to his room was unceremoniously swept from him by the deep, all-consuming sleep that pulled him under the moment his head touched the pillow.

At breakfast they ignored the food put in front of them and sipped on mugs of thick black syrupy coffee. The waiter studied them with a disapproving glare. If a celebrity was going to frequent this establishment the very least he should be willing to do was sample the food that he and his staff had spent the early hours preparing just for him. Dalton hovered by the table a slip of paper in hand.

"I've found directions to the Booty Bar," he said, shaking the paper proudly. "Not a very well known hostelry as I've discovered – it's back out on the edge of town on the 215. He paused, unsure how far his opinion might be tolerated. "It has something of an, er, reputation," he added cautiously. Alex was too distracted by his own thoughts to answer. Danny looked quizzical. Dalton took it as a prompt. "It's run by a Mexican family – Cortez. You won't have heard of them but apparently in this city you leave them well alone." Oh, well, he'd said his piece – he was merely the driver. A waitress waved a fresh jug of coffee at them. They shook their heads.

Half an hour later the Mercedes was idling in the parking lot of The Booty Bar. It looked closed. Directly in front of them the main shed-like building cast a hard black shadow over a row of flat roofed chalets to the left – most with their curtains still closed. A plywood cut-out of a gyrating babe in flaking red bikini was stapled to its front. Strings of white bulbs trimming her thighs and breasts hinting at the promise of the light show come dusk. A rusty, emerald green pick-up truck appeared in the rearview mirror, veered to the right and spat chippings in to the air as it juddered to a halt. A broad, dark-skinned man with a shock of black, curly hair, leapt from the truck, shot them a disapproving scowl and vanished into the building.

"Maybe I should go and check out the scene alone," offered Dalton, swivelling in his seat. "I'm perhaps, not quite so, conspicuous."

28" Replica Golden Sphinx, handmade from resin mould, sale price w/FREE shipping, $118.40

4 days before Jocelyn Thwaite's death

The ringing sounds of early morning rattled inside Angie's head. The radio chattered aimlessly beside her, the TV downstairs sang through the floorboards and the clatter from the waking day beyond the curtains pestered her awake. It took her a moment to realise that the phone chiming incessantly amongst it all was her own. She leant over the edge of the bed and dug it from its hiding place amongst the discarded pile of clothes on the floor, then juggled it to her ear and without peeling her sticky eyes apart grumbled a greeting into the handset. Jocelyn smiled to himself. He was no longer in her bad books. She wouldn't have answered otherwise, would she? Ah, see how fickle you girls can be. He sat up straight at his desk and realigned the knot of his tie. When videophones finally became the norm, he for one, would be ready for them.

"Angela. Wanted to catch you before work."

Huh? What time was it? Too early for Angie to remember to arm the answer phone. Damn. She rolled over on to her back keeping her eyes firmly shut. Maybe she was still dreaming.

"Look," he continued, "I need to apologise." There was a pause – Angie let it roll. She wasn't about to make it easy for him. Fill your own gaps – if you want to apologise, apologise. Jocelyn read the silence.

"I rushed you, I know that." Very magnanimous of you, she thought "It was very insensitive of me, I realise that. But …" Ah, here it comes – the but. What was it with guys that there always had to be a but. "But I really thought it's what you wanted. What we wanted …" The silence that crackled defiantly in reply was disarming. Jocelyn shuffled in his chair, the leather welding itself resolutely to his thighs. He had driven straight from Angela's house to London the night before, his mind too alert and excited for sleep. Eventually he had curled up like a cat in the bowl of his office chair and drifted into a stilted, fitful sleep. His arm still ached where his head had rested on it. He rubbed it and looked about. Now that this sad little room was the only haven he had from the world, he felt inexplicably trapped by it. He despised everything about it: the books that lined the walls with their faded jackets and dry, brown pages, the piles of music in their creased cardboard sleeves and most of all he despised everything that the room represented. Old, tired thoughts and irrelevant arrogant dogma. Every inch of it reflected his very being. He felt exhausted – not from a lack of sleep, but from a lack of life.

"I'm lonely, Angela," Jocelyn announced. It was an admission that caught him off guard as much as it did her. It had the desired effect: Angie sighed deeply and opened her eyes. The ceiling needed painting.

"Look Jocelyn, I like you. I do. But, this is too much for me. For the children."

"They loved the house," Jocelyn offered with a whimper, like a small child told he couldn't have another sweet. Angie felt irritable. It wasn't for him to say whether her children liked it or not.

"That's not the point, Jocelyn." She took a breath. It wasn't his fault, he ... "I'm sorry, but I think we ought to stop seeing each other." It was Jocelyn's turn to let the phone cradle in his palm. He stood up and walked over to the window. The stone mullion ledge was cold to the touch. The leaded glass panes were misted with a thin film of early morning damp. Jocelyn stretched out a finger and traced a circle on the glass. He added two dots for eyes and then a single downward curve just below them.

"You know," Angie continued, "we had a great time. And you've been so, so generous." Jocelyn wasn't listening. He was watching one of his students outside running across the grass in the centre of the college quadrangle. She wore a long red evening gown the hem of which she held tightly in the ball of her fist, her shoes swinging between her fingers. She looked briefly over her shoulder as she disappeared into the shadows of the archway below his window, her late-night assignation now the knowledge of at least one more person.

"Do you understand?" Angie added. The finality of the statement drew Jocelyn back into the room.

"Yes. Of course," he said through a creased curve of the lips. "You're probably right. I ..." No, leave it. Now was not the time.

"So, we're okay?" Angie felt the tense ache across the back of her shoulders gently ease. What had she expected from him, shouting and screaming? He wasn't stupid – far from it – he must have known this was coming. But still she couldn't help feel a little surprised that he was taking her suggestion so well. Was a small part of her disappointed? "You know, we can still be friends," she said, instantly reprimanding herself for the triteness of her remark. Downstairs, Jade was squealing at something her brother had done. Angie wanted to put the phone down, pull the duvet up over her head and go back to sleep. "We'll see each other at the nursery," she continued. "You do understand, don't you?" How to end the conversation? "I have to think of the children. They need some stability. They're confused with Danny, and everything ..."

Jocelyn wiped the little scribbled face off the window and turned back to face the room. Was she really going to throw that buffoon into the equation?

"Danny?" He couldn't hide the derision in his tone. But then maybe he didn't want to.

"Well, yes. He was here last night and Jordan got upset," Angie added. Jocelyn felt the irritation rise. Oh, you stupid woman. The cast-iron radiators in the room gurgled awake and Jocelyn ran his fingers up and down the painted metal. There was no helping some people.

"Surely even more reason why you need me with you," he said, the annoyance now naked in his voice. "To protect you and the children."

"Protect us?" Angie shook her head. There he was again: possessing, owning, controlling. "No, Jocelyn. We don't need protecting."

"Well, that's not what it looked like last night," he spat. Angie swung her legs from the bed. Jade was screaming now.

"How I look after my kids and how I deal with Danny is my business and ..." She paused. There was a dull thump starting to tense behind her eyes. "What did you say? Last night?"

"Yes, last night," Jocelyn said indignantly. "Who do you think called the police for you?" The ingratitude baffled him. Who knows what would have happened to her and her precious children if he hadn't been there.

"You," Angie exclaimed, "were here?" Jocelyn shrugged to himself. So?

"Yes. And I could see what a drunken fool this Danny chap obviously is ..." Jocelyn struggled to hold his voice in check. "Angela, look, I'm not trying to control your life. I just want to help you – and your children – to ..." He paused. The line had gone dead.

Without thinking Jocelyn picked up the small bronze statuette he had won for Best Documentary Soundtrack ten years earlier and launched it at the wall opposite. Two small lithographs shattered to the floor.

Victorian cast-iron radiator, painted white, junk shop, £49 (or make me an offer)

114 years before Jocelyn Thwaite's death

A darkness consumed him, like a thick blanket pulled over his head. Satie stumbled drunkenly against his piano and brought his fist down onto the keys. He threw the books and papers in his hand across the room. The unfinished notation for *Danses Gothiques* fluttered feebly to the floor. Suzanne turned her back on him, refusing to look him in the eye.

24 hours before Jocelyn Thwaite's death

Jocelyn spun the lid of his thermos closed and wiped the trickle of dark, luke-warm coffee from its body. He sucked the sour taste from his finger and grimaced. Angela's reaction was irrational and disproportionate. Her ex-boyfriend had a lot to answer for: years of abusive manipulation had left her unable to recognise opportunity when it was thrust in front of her face. Jocelyn watched the driver of the white van he had been following get out and swing open the rear doors. The back was full of identical brown boxes. Nothing about Danny surprised Jocelyn. He was filthy and unkempt. His shoulders were rounded and his head bowed to the floor. He was exactly the kind of person that Jocelyn fondly described as an oik. A word you rarely heard these days but one that Jocelyn had always felt summed up the idle classes rather aptly. It had something of an onomatopoeic roll to it. Danny struggled to balance three boxes at once. The top one slid unceremoniously to the floor and he swore aloud. Oik– perfect.

Jocelyn, he was proud to say, was no snob. But it was obvious to him why the class system had worked so well for hundreds of years. People, he believed, should stick to the role they had been offered in life rather than be encouraged to reach for the non-existent stars. Two hundred years ago the mineworker, the lamplighter and the drayman knew their place – they didn't dream of management and a detached house. These days everyone wandered the streets in a daze of false expectations that very few could ever hope to realise. Because, let's be totally frank about this, only the truly talented ones, like himself, had the ability to grow beyond the mediocrity of the mass. So was it any wonder that women were seduced by the false promises made by men like Angela's ex-boyfriend? Could they not see how ugly and worthless these men were? Jocelyn blamed fantasists like Victor Hugo for fuelling the fallacy that love could be blind: *The Hunchback of Notre Dame, Beauty and the Beast, The Phantom of the Opera* – all wearily improbable nonsense dreamed up by ugly men in the hope of willing beautiful women into their arms. When Angela looked at Danny, what could she possibly see: a wounded mongrel that needed pampering? Well, she needed to understand that bringing strays into her life was not only stupid, but dangerous. And it was Jocelyn's duty to help her. He turned the key in the ignition and pulled the car back into the flow of traffic.

Danny slammed the doors of the van shut and watched the Jag rev its engine. He could imagine himself behind the wheel of a car like that. He wiped his hands across the pockets of his jeans and watched it vanish from view. Inside the van he balanced his clipboard on the centre of the steering wheel and studied the dockets: only four more deliveries left for the day. He would take his time; he had no great urge to get back to Steve's earlier than he needed to. Jenny had made it uncomfortably obvious that he was beginning to out-stay his welcome. His head hurt. He had spent the day trying not to remember the night before. A single large watery droplet landed on the windscreen of the van, followed by a second, and then a third. Danny peered up as the sky above drew like a black curtain overhead. He took a gulp from the tin of Red Bull on the dashboard, opened the glove compartment and pulled out a small pass-port-sized photograph. The couple in the picture laughed at him – their eyes alive and in love, staring defiantly at the lens and challenging the viewer. Danny ran his finger over Angie's glossy lips. God he missed her.

2 weeks after Jocelyn Thwaite's death

"Maybe I should go and check out the scene alone," Dalton had sug-gested. He peered through the car window at the building beyond. Even though he was only the driver, it wouldn't look good if his boss got beaten up on his watch. He wasn't actually convinced that Alex Fry was completely *compos mentis* that morning anyway. Dalton had dragged the curtains from the window and let the desert sun do its worst. The actor had rolled from the bed and stumbled his way to the bathroom sending a small gilt-edged table rocking on its heels. Dalton re-aligned the bowl-based lamp. What was it with movie stars and rich people? Why the urgent need to self-implode? Dalton wiped the lens of his sun-glasses with his greasy index finger and squinted to see beyond the smudge. But for the slightest twist of fate, he could have been sat where Alex Fry was. Like thousands of other feckless, idiotic moths, he had been drawn to the lights of Los Angeles as a youth. And briefly back there it looked like he could make it. Two series of a minor-league cop show on cable and the tantalising promise of a network buyout. But it was not to be. The series was dropped, the 'surfer look' became the flavour of the month with casting agents and he drifted slowly but irrevocably off the radar. Ever since, he had lived in the glow of what might have been and watched others revel in its jaundiced spotlight.

"I'm perhaps, not quite so, conspicuous."

"No. You and Joss stay here," said Alex. It was a statement rather than a suggestion. He threw the car door open and before either Dalton or Danny could protest, he was gone. With no great desire to see whether the inside of the Booty Bar reflected the outside, Danny was content to stay put.

The club was near enough to the highway for its constant rumble to wash over them, but far enough away to present no sense of protection should they suddenly need to flag down help. Danny had a sense of being trapped inside one of Alex's appalling movie scripts: Scene One, cut to a deserted parking lot, two men sat inside a blacked-out Mercedes. Not for the first time since stowing himself away in the hold of someone else's future, Danny Lunt shivered with discomfort. A curtain across one of the chalet windows shifted and fell back into place. A stray mongrel pattered across the concrete, sniffed a dark puddle at the foot of a fire escape and wandered away in disgust. Dalton wrapped his fingers tightly around the leather steering wheel and pulled himself up in his seat. The longer they waited the more he fidgeted, rubbing his arm and scratching his neck. Eventually, sighing deeply, he unfastened the car door and swivelled his legs out. He paused, considering the space that exists between action and inaction. He would give Alex a little more time maybe. Ten minutes passed.

"Shit." Dalton breathed deeply and pushed himself out of his seat. "Wait here," he hissed at Danny. As though dragged by the collar, he stumbled his way across the parking lot to the main entrance. He paused briefly to wrap his fingers around the metal handle. As he did so, the door flew open and Alex Fry spilled out into the sunlight. Blinking, he stared up at Dalton, a smile spreading across his face.

"She's here," he grinned, slapping Dalton on the shoulder. "Thank you *amigo*," he laughed, spinning round to grab the hand of a figure just visible beyond the doorway. "Thank you – we'll be back this evening. What time did you say she'll be here? Nine? Excellent." The Mexican stared at him blankly. He wiped his hand down the side of his crumpled polyester suit, scowled, muttered something in Spanish and slammed the door shut.

The drug of expectation coursed through the actor's veins. Finally he could liberate himself from the stranglehold of the people that buzzed around him like incessant, unforgiving flies. He had spent his life being twisted this way and that, manipulated by these people. As success and money swamped him, he felt the bindweed tighten, not loosen as he always assumed it should. Instead of openly telling him what to do they now simply manipulated him from the safe distance of agents' offices and studio boardrooms. But now, finally, he felt in control of his own destiny. And it felt good. Very good.

Larry and Security Dave powered their combined mass through the corridors of The Golden Sphinx in search of their wayward charge.

Spitting dithering tourists from their path, they fought their way along the main concourse, past the shops, bars, central gambling arena, lounge and towards the exclusive casino rooms at the rear of the hotel. Larry struggled to catch his breath. His eyes bulged in their sockets and the veins that marbled his temple threatened to pop. He was angry at Alex for being so stupid, angry at Security Dave for letting the alcoholic fool give him the slip twice in as many days, angry with Joss for clearly filling his head with wild notions, and angry with himself for not having retired years ago and set up that crab farm off the coast of New Orleans.

Inside the Washington Room – one of a number of rooms that could be privately hired for five thousand dollars a shot with croupiers, unlimited credit and pretzels thrown in –Larry found his client hunched over a craps table eyeing the girl opposite while his English buddy slumped on a couch in the corner, nursing his head and a large tumbler. The croupier, a beautiful long-legged creature in an impossibly self-supporting little black piece of thread, carried on regardless – a removed expression of self-satisfaction toying across her face. Larry took a moment to appreciate the view before grabbing Alex Fry by the arm. Security Dave helped pull Danny to his feet and the wobbling mass of unstable legs stumbled their way back to the actor's hotel suite where Larry forced bowls of strong, black coffee down the actor's neck.

"Christ, man, what'ya trying to do to me?" Larry moaned, crouching down in front of Alex, like an upside-down pyramid. He wobbled and ignored the pain in his tendons. "I've got journalists crawling all over this. They know something's happening –" Alex giggled. "I'm serious Al, this could be bad news. First you crash your car while out of your head ..." Larry took a gulp of air. He could see tiny specks of light begin to spin behind his retinas. "... then you go on some crazy road trip searching for this girl."

"Chill it, Larry, no-one knows."

"You think?" Larry levered himself up with the help of the arm of a chair and rose to his full height. His back ached and his ankles hurt. "Don't be such a dumb ass. Everybody knows. What about the fat-faced barmaid all over every station this morning claiming you forced her to tell her the whereabouts of some stripper?!"

"She's not a stripper. She's an exotic dancer."

"Does she take her clothes off for money?" There was no easy answer to that. "Then she's a stripper." Larry wobbled on his toes. His whole body was screaming to be allowed to close down. It's only a matter of time before you're tracked down here," he said. He looked about. Was he the only one who cared? He ran his hand through his hair.

He was hyperventilating. His therapist had told him to breathe deeply from his diaphragm on stressful occasions. He tried to gulp some air but the air conditioning system in the room had long since sucked out the last remnants of moisture.

"He's not done anything, though," Danny shrugged. Larry shot him a withering look and turned back to his client.

"You're going to have to put a lid on this now, Alex. I mean it. Stop this nonsense." He paused, considering Alex's drained, determined expression. "Look I can get some guys to check out this broad and have her brought to your home. Yeah? Pay her to do a private show?" Larry tried an element of levity. He grinned. Badly. "What you say? All the fun, none of the hassle …"

Alex took a moment to consider his offer. He stood up, wandered about a bit and sat back down again. Danny, Larry and Security Dave all studied him carefully as he did.

"No," he breathed quietly. Larry groaned and slapped his forehead like he was in a cartoon. "Sorry Larry, I need to see her …"

There was a knock at the door. All heads turned. Security Dave, animated by a refreshed sense of purpose, pulled his jacket tight around him, nodded commandingly to the room and peered through the tiny glass knot in the door. The hotel manager's nose loomed large and Dave pulled the door ajar.

"There's a young lady to see Mr Fry," the manager announced, and from behind him a short, thin girl in a sleek red skirt and no-nonsense white blouse appeared. The men in the room, working with their most basic of testosterone-fuelled instincts, watched as she sashayed slowly into the room.

"She, says, she's a, er, friend …" the manager began to say, realising as he did that he might have made a miscalculation. The woman carefully pulled her black and white chequered evening bag from her arm and in a practised move unclipped it and withdrew a microphone. Out of nowhere two men appeared behind her filling the doorway and sending a dark shadow creeping into the room. Security Dave was too distracted to react and the men spilled into the room tangled in a mix of wires and camera lenses.

"Alex Fry, is it true you are having a relationship with a prostitute?" the woman shouted, throwing herself forwards. Dave, unsure who to tackle first, chose the obvious easy option and leapt to wrap his arms about her waist. In the meantime, Larry, with all the stealth of a drugged circus elephant, threw his bulk on top of Alex as though protecting him from a sniper.

"Were you high on crack cocaine when you crashed your car?" the woman continued, as she wriggled wildly beneath Dave's arms. She always knew her daily Ashtanga Yoga would prove useful and she managed to hook her right arm and shoulder below the man's elbow and lever herself out and under him by bending her spine impossibly backwards, leaving Dave waving his hands at empty air. "Do you think this is an example of responsible behaviour for your many young fans?" she continued, thrusting the microphone under Larry's mass in the direction of where she imagined the actor's face to be. "Don't you ..." she began, before Security Dave, suddenly aware he had nothing in his hands, grabbed at her legs. She fell backwards with a squeal and Dave felt his watchstrap tangle with the trim of her skirt. A ripping sound drew a brief halt to the struggle.

"Watch it – I'll sue," she spat, and Dave lightened his grip to manoeuvre himself between her and the actor. He shuffled her towards the door, taking her cameraman and his assistant with her. "Who's your dealer?" she managed to yell through the crack of the closing door. Security Dave leant against the back of the door and Larry peeled himself off Alex, scowling.

"See?" he yelled. "Do you arseing-well see?" Larry could picture his twenty per cent slowly and irrevocably ebbing away before his eyes. Twenty per cent of z-list celebrity slots on cable did not equate to the marina penthouse that bled his income, nor his girlfriend's extravagant taste in shoes that she never wore.

Ray-Ban Model RB3025 sunglasses, peepers.com, list price $99.00, now $95.20

12 hours before Jocelyn Thwaite's death

Stealing Angela's mobile phone had been the easy part: the small children running this way and that, falling over, pinching each other and dropping toys and coats were all the distraction he needed. Jocelyn cradled the small chunk of bright blue metal and plastic in his hand. If he brought it to his nose he could almost taste her familiar, dizzying scent. Of course, it wouldn't be long before Angela missed the phone from her bag. She would probably think that one of the children had found it, moulded it into a slab of Playdoh and flushed it down the loo. Or more likely assume she had misplaced it herself in the rush of early morning pandemonium. He could picture her scooping the surface of the hallway table into her bag without checking what was tumbling in. In would go pens and bills, loose change and, if she was lucky, her mobile phone. Then she would swing her bag thoughtlessly over her shoulder, still unfastened, of course, whilst gathering children around her.

Jocelyn pressed his face against the glass so that it left a near-perfect imprint of his nose and chin. The kitchen was dark and empty. The shrapnel of that morning's breakfast was scattered around the room: dirty bowls by the sink, empty cereal packets on the table, mugs on the sideboard. And Jade had forgotten her coat – her small pink padded jacket draped over the back of her chair where she had left it. There was a spit of rain in the air and she would miss it on the way home. Maybe after he had finished here he should take it to her school. Would Angela thank him for that? It was so hard to fathom what she wanted. Still, it was up to him then to help her – to make the decision easy for her. Jocelyn wobbled the paving slabs under the window with the toe of his shoe. The third one he tried rocked unsteadily and he crouched down, lifted the edge and pulled out the spare backdoor key.

He would be lying if he said it had been easy to stand in front of Angela that morning and pretend that, yes, everything was just fine and dandy. He had greeted her with a civil 'good morning' and she in turn had replied politely. But he recognised the distance in her voice – as though she had already constructed an invisible barrier between them. Still, he noted with satisfaction, she continued to watch him from the corner of her eye as he unpeeled Max from his coat, settled him amongst the Lego and kissed him goodbye. The little boy had peered up at him questioningly, surprised by his father's protracted attention, held out the small sweet he had kept safely in his pocket from the day before and handed it to his Dad. Without looking, he ruffled the boys tussle of blond hair, checked to see if Angela was still watching and left.

The cord for the back-door blind slapped against the glass and Jocelyn steadied it. The house was silent. Like any space used to the bustle of life and movement all around, the kitchen felt lost. It suited his mood perfectly. He ran his hand along the edge of the work surface. Would this melt or burn? And what would it smell like? His fingers toyed with the edge of the toaster and then ran along the trim of the kettle until it reached the top. He pressed the switch and a small red light blinked on. Well, why not? He had all the time in the world. He opened the cupboard doors above his head, found the teabags and sugar and helped himself to a mug from beside the sink. Momentarily he considered whether it had been wise to come without gloves. Had he ever had cause to open these cupboard doors before? Still by the time investigators came to swab the scene, those cheap red plastic handles would probably have melted to tiny blobs of congealed, foul smelling plastic. He sniffed indignantly at the little white bag between his fingers: give him a loose-leaf tea, properly infused, any day. Tea, like so many things, had been reduced to the lowest common denominator. He sat down at the table and sipped the foul brown liquid between pursed lips. Beside the stacked dirty plates was a pile of post. He shuffled the letters into a fan in front of him. In the middle of the supermarket door-drops and free washing liquid samples, was an unopened bill. Slipping his finger under its rim he pulled it open and flicked the page with a twist of the wrist. A sparrow pecked disapprovingly at the window. The bill was printed in large red letters. Really, Angela's ingratitude made no sense. And this evidence just proved him right. He refolded the bill and slipped it into his inside jacket pocket. When the moment was prudent he would use this to prove to her how stupid she was being to not accept his help.

Jocelyn considered himself a sound judge of character. He'd always had an instinct. He could tell instantly which of his students were destined for, if not great things, then at least *some*thing. And which, by contrast, didn't even merit his attention. And he could tell, from just a single night's evidence, what sort of person this Danny fellow was. The fact that Angela couldn't see him for what he was just made the whole business that bit more depressing. Sometimes people couldn't see what was so plainly in front of them. It just needed a friend to point out the facts. It was always hard to accept to begin with, but given time, it could only be for the common good. Angela would see that.

He pressed a button and the tiny blue screen of Angela's mobile sparkled alive. Jocelyn toyed with the small raised buttons before finally scrolling to the text message screen. He had considered what he should write over and over in his mind but had ultimately resolved to keep his message as short as possible. No point in encouraging suspicion due to misplaced abbreviations. Of course, he may well have been worrying unduly – Danny didn't strike him as someone capable of too much linear thinking. Jocelyn considered his message and with a contented sigh pressed the send button. It really was that simple. He lifted the small jerry can that had been by his foot onto the table and loosened the cap. The heady smell of petrol filled the air and he took a moment to enjoy it. The can, he had to say, had been a touch of genius. Borrowed from the lean-to in Angie's back yard the previous evening it even had Danny's childishly painted name down one side. Oh, it really was too much.

Whistling a snippet from the third act of Wagner's *Die Walküre*, Jocelyn placed the cap of the container on the table and proceeded to coat the kitchen, sitting room and hallway carpet with the liquid. He watched mesmerised as it soaked slowly into the settee, leaving barely a mark. Droplets clung to the wallpaper and the screen of the television, tiny rivulets ran down the arm of Jade's coat, dropped off and disappeared into the carpet at his feet. Before long the only evidence of the petrol's existence was the foul stench and a strange mauve otherworldly shimmer in the air, like the heat rays on a dusty Nevada freeway. He frowned at his carelessness, struggling to stop the petrol splashing his own clothes. His lips were dry and his whistle had reverted to a mumbled hum. With the downstairs complete, he headed upstairs. At the top he paused briefly; he had never been this far into the belly of the house before and an irrational sense of resentment passed through him. Angela knew everything about him and yet she had shown him so little of herself. Whilst he had been willing to lay his own wounded soul in front of her, he had always been left with a feeling that she was never being fully honest with him. There were things that, for whatever reason, she couldn't or wouldn't tell him. Had she been scared of Danny perhaps? Was it any wonder that Jocelyn misread what she wanted? If she wasn't going to tell him, then he had had to guess. But that was women for you, wasn't it? Expect you to know the answer without giving you the question. Well, that would change. He stepped on to the small landing. In front of him was a lilac-coloured bathroom. To his right were three white doors. Two of them were plastered with stickers and posters, and the third, which he approached cautiously, was plain white. He ran his fingers lightly over the surface, feeling the rough brush marks and let it swing wide in front of him. Strange that he should linger to consider the morals of entering a woman's bedroom uninvited but think nothing of setting fire to her home. Inside, a large iron-framed bed dominated the room. Against one wall was a tall thin wardrobe, its doors yawning open. The walls were mottled yellow and cream. On the white chipboard dressing table beside the window Jocelyn studied the tiny bottles of perfume and make-up. The air was soaked with a collage of sweet scents. Such feminine things had always been a mystery to him, even Elizabeth's sparse collection. The room was warm, dry heat pumping from a small radiator below the window. Jocelyn felt a sense of peace. He could quite happily lie down on the bed and close his eyes. If he did, would it make everything all right? Would the world stop spinning? Would Elizabeth disappear and Angela fall headlong into his arms? Jocelyn shuffled the bunched curtain edge to one side and peered through the window. This was the spot in which she had stood, watching Danny hammer drunkenly at her door. She deserved better. You heard such far-fetched stories didn't you?

Domineering relationships. Women tethered by invisible strings to bullying husbands. Jocelyn felt his grip tighten on the thin, cheap fabric. Danny clearly looked like the kind who would use fist before thought every time. Angela had never said anything, but then that was consistent with this kind of relationship: twisted loyalty to the last. And now, because of misplaced, warped feelings of guilt she couldn't let anyone else into her life. Even when that person brought her the hope she needed to rebuild it.

Jocelyn took a step towards Angela's bed. He lifted the petrol can and watched with fascination as the liquid slowly soaked into the pattern of the duvet. If Angela didn't realise what kind of fool her ex-boyfriend was, then it was up to Jocelyn to show her. Then, and only then, might she be allowed some release. The fumes stung his eyes and he blinked the tears away. Wagner might have written a short *leitmotif* in honour of the scene: Jocelyn on his tiptoes, his arm raised high above his head describing a trailing pattern of liquid up and down the length of the bed. As he moved his arms he could hear the strains from Act III of *Die Walküre*, 'Magic, Fire, Music'. Wagner would have appreciated the paganism of the scene: the summoning of Loge, igniting the circle of flame to protect Angela, his Brunnhilde. Before he knew it the last drop had fallen from the can. He shrugged. There was more than enough spread about the tiny house to send the place up like a tinderbox. Just to be safe he'd light one match up here and one in the kitchen. Now all he had to do was wait.

It was the first time Angie had contacted him since he had left the house six weeks earlier. At first Danny assumed the message on his mobile was some stupid wind-up from one of his mates. After his late night performance outside her house, Angie was the last person he expected to hear from and, anyhow, it just didn't look like the kind of text that she would send. She always signed off her messages with A xx. But, sure enough, Angie's mobile number appeared on his screen. He slid the last of the boxes along the floor of the van, jumped down from the edge and scooped it into his arms. It could, of course, be Jade or Jordan messing about with their mother's phone. Danny wouldn't put it past them to try some childish attempt at reconciliation. He carried the box across the street, and turning around, pushed his back against the heavy glass door of the large office building. He fidgeted from foot to foot and tapped his fingers on the desk as the grey-haired man behind the reception studied the details on the docket. With agonising slowness he unclipped a pen from his breast pocket and after an impossibly protracted pause scribbled on the paper. Before his pen had barely left the page, Danny had grabbed it and jogged back to the van.

"Don't you dare," he growled at a traffic warden eyeing the van. The next few deliveries would have to be late, but then traffic could always be relied on as an alibi. He jumped the lights at the next junction and took a right. How come Angie wasn't at work? Maybe that was it. Maybe she had lost her job and needed a loan. The thought appealed to him, but it seemed unlikely. Angie, after all, was not the kind who liked to be dependent on anyone. That much he had realised over their years together. And they had been good years hadn't they? Angie had been the only one who had ever really given him the chance to be himself. He had spent so long, before they met, pretending to be someone he wasn't, that he had forgotten how to be Daniel Lunt.

The van eased to a halt outside the house. Danny peered in the rearview mirror and fussed with his hair. He slipped on his denim jacket and drew the collar up. The street seemed unusually still, as though life had taken a temporary break. Inside the house Jocelyn felt his way slowly down the stairs. He could just make out the light sound of fabric starting to crisp and burn, a thin wisp of grey smoke curling from the bedroom door. Timing, as Wagner himself would tell you, is everything. At the bottom of the stairs Jocelyn ducked down to hide his silhouette from the glass panel of the front door and felt a twist of excitement running through his veins. He slipped into the kitchen just as Danny rattled the front-door handle. He had expected to find it locked and yet the door pushed open. Once inside, a familiar smell teased Danny. He called out Angie's name, baffled by the silence. This wasn't the kind of house that ever lay dormant for long. If it wasn't screaming and shouting, voices of giggling children spilling from every room, it was the sound of at least one of the televisions burbling endlessly or Jordan's music thudding inside the wafer-thin walls. He entered the living room, the smell of petrol rushing over him.

"Angie, Ange?" he called again with no reply. And then suddenly he thought his eyes were failing him. He could no longer see the front door clearly. Was he going mad? His mind was several steps behind, the cogs struggling to turn. It wasn't his eyes blurring, but the hallway filling with smoke. Without thinking, he bounded upstairs, taking two steps at a time.

In the kitchen Jocelyn calmly took the box of matches back out of his pocket. He slid the cardboard sleeve aside, took out one small match and studied its strangely pink bobbled end. Ah, the power of one small spark, he thought. He ran the match's head along the box's rough edge and with the *Valkyries* swarming inside his head he dropped the match to the floor. The petrol took instantly, sending thin blue flames leaping about his ankles. He took a step back towards the door, but still he lingered, watching the trail of blue light worm its way over the sideboard and along the floor into the living room. Within moments the curtains were alive with orange, sparks eating at the walls, the distinctive sound of glass splintering under the heat. Above his head Jocelyn could hear the desperate stamping of feet. Of course Jocelyn wished Danny no real harm, but what if he didn't make it out of the house alive, would it matter? Would the world really miss one more leach? Just in case, Jocelyn had called the fire brigade who, if he had timed it right, would be circling the roundabout at the end of the road … just … about … now. Of course he didn't want the man dead, there was no need. Finding out that Danny had set fire to her house would send Angela running into Jocelyn's arms. On the chair Jade's pink coat began to melt and drip like a Dali painting. Jocelyn slipped Angie's phone into the pocket and smiled as the fabric twisted and moulded itself around the little handset, eventually dripping as a puddle of burning plastic on the floor. He closed the back door behind him and turned the key.

Despite the intense heat thrown from the burning duvet and the flames that rose so high that the ceiling had already started to blacken, Danny could see that there was no one in the main bedroom. Downstairs an explosion from the kitchen shook the house and he grabbed at the banister for balance. Sirens filled the street outside. The smoke was growing thicker, the pale blue from the upstairs now met by a darker, heavier smoke curling its way up the stairs. For a moment Danny felt disorientated, his head spinning. And amongst it all a familiar voice was calling. It sounded distant, but desperate. Danny felt the weight of his body as he fell to his knees. And there was the voice again, calling to him, begging him. His head was aching, the smoke groping its way into his mouth, his nose his lungs. He raised a hand, but couldn't see his fingers. And then he recognised the voice. It was Jordan calling to him. Suddenly they were on a beach. Jordan had thrown his Frisbee and it was bouncing on the surface of the water. The boy was jumping up and down, pointing in horror as the waves threatened to drag it away. "Danny, Danny, help," he cried and a big crash of foam hit the shore taking the small red disc even further away from the boy's outstretched hand. And then Danny was touching the boy's fingers. They intertwined and he was pulling the weight of Jordan's body along the hallway carpet, dragging him for all he was worth over the edge of the stairs. A sweep of light like the sun on a foggy morning filled his eyes and he raised a hand to his brow. The last thing he remembered were hands wrapping around his waist and urgent voices all around him as he was pulled out into the day-light, his own hand clasped so tightly to the boy's that his fingers had drained completely of colour.

Die Walküre: The Ride of the Valkyries, Wagner: Overtures and Preludes, iTunes, £0.79

114 years before Jocelyn Thwaite's death

The gendarme stood in the shadow of the simple stone house and looked up at the window above. Satie placed his wrists together and demanded that the gendarme arrest him at once. "I have killed her, sir. My petit biqui." His head was on fire with anger and regret, "I threw her from the window… I am guilty, whether a body lies there or not." The gendarme shook his head and left the poor man sobbing on his haunches below the open window. Petals from a nearby wisteria showered him like the confetti he would never feel.

2 weeks, 1 day after Jocelyn Thwaite's death

There were already trailers and cars spilling their giddy contents of cam-eramen and reporters all over the parking lot of the Booty Bar when Alex and his entourage returned. The journos had done their research: no grubby little stone had gone unturned, no sweaty palm been left ungreased in the twenty-four hours since the woman in the bar opposite the Pink Pussycat had made her initial call to FOX News. Since then she had managed to make herself more money selling her salacious gossip to the vociferous crowd that filled the bar than she had made in the previous five years. Her husband gleefully handed out jugs of beer and rubbed his hands. All the while his wife watched him, preparing to reveal her plans for her newfound wealth. She would, she would announce, never work the night shift, or indeed any shift, again. She was, she would say in a calm and level voice, off to see something of the world: Europe, for example, Vienna and Paris, Monte Carlo and London. He could come if he wished. Or not. She left him to count the dollar bills in the register and crept upstairs to find her old college suitcase. The one she had kept all these years. Just in case.

Alex attempted to side-step a couple of the journalists, realised it was pointless as they filled his footsteps like quicksand, and waded his way straight through the middle of them. Danny, attempting to maintain the pace, found himself tugged and pushed out of the way. Alex pounded on the doors. Two bodyguards appeared, pushing the journalists back and shuffling Alex in through the door. Danny was buffeted backwards by the ravenous pack surrounding him. They vied for space and huddled about him in a circle, prodding at him with their microphones and cameras like a gang of children circling an injured bird.

"Who, are you?" shouted a dismembered voice from somewhere at the back of the crowd. Bags and buckles rattled, flash bulbs strobed. Danny raised a hand to shield his eyes. "Are you a friend of Fry's?" Amongst the shapes and sounds his conscious focussed on the familiar: the short woman in red skirt and white blouse from the hotel earlier in the day. She was thrusting herself up on tiptoe, contorting her body between the jostling elbows. She screamed at Danny as though he was a murderer, her eyes wide and angry. Danny twisted to turn his back on her and bowed his head.

"Who are you?" the pack demanded, picking up the chant and repeating it over and over. Danny pushed himself forward against the tide.

Inside the Booty Bar, the two bodyguards led Alex along the sticky, brown and orange patterned carpet. The walls were black and the air hung with an acrid stench of dry ice, tobacco and stale beer. The corridor wound its way to the left, narrowed briefly, then opened into the cavernous belly of the bar area. At first Danny thought the room was empty, but as his eyes adjusted to the gloom, he became aware of movement by the far wall. Below a large cracked mirror, a couple of heavy-eyed girls watched him, cigarettes dripping from between their fingers. The stage area was illuminated by a puddle of pink light and a curtain of silver tassles hung down at the back of the room. Without the presence of customers and staff stealing attention from the shabby decor, the room was cold and lifeless. Stood by the bar was a thin, stubby Mexican, his elbow thrust up on the lip of the bar. He studied Alex Fry carefully as he approached, choosing not to say a word until he was almost upon him.

"Nice to see you again, Mr Fry," he said, his small hairy hand rising in greeting from the cave of his sleeve. This was the same man that had greeted Alex earlier in the day wearing stained jeans and food-splattered T-shirt – now he proudly plucked at the lapel of his designer suit and smoothed the scuffs from his reptile-skin boots.

"We need to talk business, no señor? I'm Eduardo Cortez. My friends call me Eddie. " He smiled thinly and surveyed the room. Was

156

everybody watching? "You can call me Eduardo." The corners' of his lips lifted ever so slightly. Oh that was clever, he nodded to himself, so very clever. Alex stared at him blankly.

"Where's Crystal. I mean Mary .... Crystal?" Alex asked, unsure whether to arrange himself on one of the stools or remain standing.

"All in good time. Drink?" Cortez didn't wait for an answer. With an effeminate flick of the wrist he gestured to the girl behind the bar. With a practised move she placed two shot glasses in front of them and poured a clear liquid from a thin-spouted bottle. The drink dripped like oil and Alex watched as the Mexican ran the stub of his pink tongue over his lips in anticipation. He purred to himself as he lifted his glass. Alex copied him without taking his eyes off the man. The drink scorched the inside of his mouth and burnt a trail down his throat.

"I think you're looking for Maria," Cortez grinned, savouring the actor's discomfort. "One of my very best dancers, Maria." He swung his little legs around in front of him. "The customers like her. I like her. The gang here like her." He briefly let his eyes wander the room and the audience obediently nodded their muted agreement. This was the big one. The one he had been waiting for all his life. C'mon Eddie, don't blow it now. This boy is big time. "What will I do if you take her away?"

"Do?"

"I've got bills to pay. It's not cheap running a quality establishment like this... And Maria's my star turn." There was a murmur from the far side of the room. Seems not everybody saw it the way the boss did.

"You want money?" Alex said, shocked, and at once reprimanded himself for being so naïve. Of course this ape wasn't going to let Crystal go just like that. "She's not a thing, you know," he felt himself saying, unnecessarily in retrospect. This was hardly the relevant forum for a feminist discussion.

"Don't be so stupid, Mr Big Hollywood Movie Star." Cortez jumped from his seat. He signalled over his shoulder to where a figure was hidden by the shadow of a thick, velvet curtain embroidered with dolphins and sharks playing among writhing, topless mermaids. "Maria." He clicked his fingers and the girl moved uncertainly forward. "Come and sit with your Uncle Ed." The girl was tall, with long, painfully thin legs. A large purple bruise ran the length of her naked right thigh. Her marshmallow pink lipstick collected in the dry cracks on her lips and her vacant, sunken eyes stared back behind a thick veil of clumped mascara and eyeliner. "Now then honey, tell Mr Movie Star who feeds you, who clothes you, who saves you from wasting away that pretty little body on pills and drugs." He held out his hand and wrapped his tiny brown sausage fingers around her wrist. His fingers wound comfortably around the narrow shaft of bone and skin. She smiled aimlessly, her head tilting back to look up at the twinkling lights that dotted the ceiling like tiny stars.

"Why, you do Baby," she said leaning forward and giving him a kiss on the cheek that left the smudged pink residue of her lipstick. Alex stared at Maria in disbelief. Her face was so familiar – yet so unrecognisable. It was like looking into one of those grotesquely distorting fairground mirrors.

"Crystal?" he muttered quietly. Maria wobbled her head backwards and forwards as though finding it hard to disseminate the origin of the voice. A sliver of recognition mingled with confusion and then panic passed across her face. A distant memory briefly threatened to surface. She didn't want it to and her body began to shake.

"What the hell have you done to her?" Alex shouted, instinctively taking a step forward and putting out his arms as though he might pull her close. Maria panicked, squealed and jumped behind Eduardo. He let her hand drop from his grip like a rag doll.

"Don't shout at me. This is my club. These are my girls." Cortez lifted himself lightly on to his toes to demonstrate the fullness of his strictly limited height and placed his hands on his hips. From behind him, Alex felt the shadow of the two bodyguards fall across his shoulder as they took a step forward. "If you want the girl, you are going to have to pay compensation. Lost revenue. Understand?" He waved his arm about him. "Like tonight – it's usually packed in here at this time – who's going to pay for that?" There was a derisory giggle from the other side of the room. Alex shrugged in resignation.

"How much?" he asked.

"$100,000. Cash." Cortez pulled Maria back round in front of him. She whimpered like a scolded dog and grabbed at his arm with her bony fingers. One of her false red nails caught in the threads of his jacket and flew off across the room. She yelped and watched it bounce under a table. Cortez brushed her arm from his sleeve. "And she's all yours." Maria looked up at him, finally beginning to understand something of what was happening in front of her. She slowly slid to her knees, her hands covering her face.

"Hey, Honey, it's okay, Eddie'll see you right." Maria looked unconvinced and reached her hand up towards his leg. He grabbed her arm and twisted it so that she screamed and pulled it away. He slipped his hand inside his jacket pocket and for a moment Alex expected to see the glint of a gun appear. Instead he pulled out a small, clear plastic bag and studied its powdered white contents before letting it fall breathlessly to the floor. Like a starving pack hound Maria grabbed it and clasped it to her breast.

"So, what do you say Mr Fry, have we got a deal?"

Alex looked down at the bundle of bones by his feet and slowly shook his head. Whoever the creature scrambling about in the dirt was, it wasn't Crystal. The actor turned away and, pushing himself between the shoulders of the two bodyguards behind him, stepped towards the doorway.

"It was you who left me," a faint voice whispered. Had he imagined it? No – there it was again. Maria pulled herself unsteadily to her feet. "You left me," she said again, this time louder. There was still something of her in there after all. Alex paused momentarily. Was he being too hasty? Maria stumbled as she leant towards him, her mass of tangled hair falling over her eyes. She scooped it out of the way with a giggle. A small trickle of saliva ran down the side of her cheek. As she drew close Alex could see the blotched marking of her skin beneath the thick make-up. He shivered involuntarily and turned away from her. It had been an almighty mistake to come here. Crystal was as dead as her memory. Without looking behind him he stepped away from her and retraced his way back along to the entranceway. Gratefully he leant the full weight of his body against the handle of the door. From behind him an animal squeal ripped through the air.

The gathering outside had doubled in size in just a few minutes. Unable to fight their way inside the building, the pack turned on the only prey they could find.

"Who are you?" the woman repeated, her voice rising to a screech. Danny raised his hand to push the microphones away from him. The news had travelled like a bushfire through the brittle undergrowth of the media. Along the West Coast they were used to Hollywood stars self-destructing, but rarely was their torment played out as publicly as this. The American audience preferred their news in images they could understand: Hugh Grant with a number around his neck; George Michael slumped at the wheel of his car. These made the portraits of twenty-first-century celebrity and journalists knew their duty – to feed it to the gossip-hungry public. Fists pounded on the club's door, legs kicked, arms nudged and the fervour rippled through the crowd. High above the pink and yellow tinted sky of Las Vegas, the whir of helicopters approaching added an apocalyptic rumble. A couple of cameramen had climbed the front of the building to find a unique vantage point: that one-off shot could be worth millions. There was little doubt that this had the potential to be another O.J. A third and then a fourth helicopter appeared, buzzing like giant wasps readying themselves for the sting. Back at base, editors-in-chief nibbled at thumbnails. The next few minutes could make or break. And then within hours, thanks to YouTube and Google, their footage and logo would ripple across the world, seen by millions desperate to watch the mighty tumble unceremoniously to their knees.

Danny could feel the air move above him. He stooped slightly as Fox News Chopper 7 made to draw off to the east, fooled the competition and doubled back west swooping in less than twenty metres above the Booty Bar's roof. Slowly, but surely, Danny managed to edge his way back towards the car, drawing the crowd around as though towing them on invisible ropes. Those in front of him stumbled backwards. They began to peel off and turned to follow. By the car, Danny could make out Larry's unmistakable bulk hunched by the passenger door. As the barrier of legs and arms in front of him drifted apart, Danny had a clear view: there was a figure inside the car, Dalton presumably, and two others stood behind Alex's manager. Chopper 7 helpfully swept the full glare of its light out in front of Danny, illuminating Larry and, beside him, Stacey and her boyfriend. Danny broke his stride to do a double-take and a couple of reporters tripped over his heels. The sound of camera lenses bouncing on concrete was chewed up and lost to the buzz of the blades eating the air above them. Larry, Stacey and Taylor turned in unison to stare at Danny. The crowd fell expectantly quite.

"Who are you?" squealed that voice again from somewhere at the back. Taylor took a step forward and raised his hand, pointing a stubby finger directly at Danny.

"I'll tell you who he is," he shouted. He stopped just short of the crowd and raised his arms, opening his palms as though beckoning the helicopters above him closer. Their lights washed back and forth as their pilots fought to maintain balance. Cameras focussed, microphone booms appeared in the air above him. And Taylor laughed.

"I'll tell you exactly who he is," he began. "He's an impostor. He's a liar. He's a thief." Stacey grabbed at his arm. But he was enjoying the moment too much to care. He shrugged her away. Danny, caught by the glare, shuddered. He looked to his left and right, but there was no means of escape. "This man is not who he says he is. He's stolen someone else's identity and ..." The sound of a heavy wooden door being thrown wildly against brick, followed by a piercing animal squeal made heads turn. Those that hadn't first registered the noise were quickly drawn by the twisting of the body of the person next to them. Then there was another scream, this time an involuntary shout of shock from one of their own. As one, they pushed back towards the origin of the noise. Taylor yelled after them but it was too late. The doors to the club had been thrown wide and a splash of pink light spilled onto the stone of the parking lot. A familiar black shape filled the doorway. And it was clear something wasn't right. Alex Fry stepped towards them, his movements strangely slow and agonised. His head was dipped forward and his arms hung loosely at his side. His left leg dragged slightly, as though it had forgotten its purpose. You could have been forgiven for assuming he was drunk, but the contorted way his body suddenly folded beneath him told otherwise. Alex Fry collapsed first to his knees and then, after a brief pause when gravity failed to get a full grip of the situation, his upper half toppled forwards. His face lay flat against the dirt and from the back of his head a fine sliver of metal stood up proud, the sweep of Chopper 7's light catching it like a lighthouse beam.

10 grams of cocaine, average street price $700

9 hours before Jocelyn Thwaite's death

Coloured lines, like electrical wires, ran along the length of the sterile, white hospital corridor. Every now and then the lines broke suddenly to veer left or right down further unseen corridors from which dismembered voices could be heard echoing along the walls. Signs hung from the ceiling with arrows pointing this way and that. On the walls, notices warned against using mobile phones, leaving baggage and children unattended, and of visiting out of hours. Angie stood, twisting her head in anguish. People in uniforms flooded towards her, marching with single-minded purpose so that by the time she lifted a hand to call to them, they had already disappeared from view. She had been this way before. She was sure she had. She threw her arms in the air:

"Coleridge Ward," she yelled. "Where's Coleridge Ward." A nurse appeared by her side and steered her by the elbow back the way she had come. She had no idea where she was being lead and all she could hear was the clacking of the nurse's heels and the thump of her own heart echoing inside her chest. An elevator transported them up several floors. The doors jolted open to reveal yet another vast tube of space. Halfway along the wall her ex-boyfriend sat huddled on a chair beside a set of doors. With his body thrust forward and his forearms balanced on his knees, his head hung. Beside him a young constable nursed a small plastic cup. Angie wrenched herself from the nurse's grasp and ran towards him.

"What the hell have you done?" she screamed. Danny lifted his head. The policeman snapped from his daze and jumped to his feet, sending coffee fanning across the floor. He wobbled on his feet and waved his arms, unsure whether he should grab at the irate woman in front of him.

"Now then Miss, I ..." he stammered. Angie ignored him and threw herself at Danny.

"You bastard – you could have killed him!" Danny scrambled to his feet and Angie wrapped her fingers around the collar of his jacket. He wanted to reach out his hands and hold her. The emotion of the last two hours suddenly swamped him and he felt himself falling forwards towards her.

"But I didn't," he said, his head beginning to spin. Suddenly all he could see was smoke flooding his eyes. His arms fell to his side as Angie continued to shake his limp body.

"The police have told me everything." Tears were running down her face. The black around her eyes and the cold hard light of the fluorescent tubes above them made her skin shimmer a ghostly white. Danny wanted her to let go and let him fall to his knees, but she held him upright, urging him to lift his head and look at her. He hadn't the energy to argue. He hadn't the spirit. How could she believe he would do something like that? Did she really think so little of him? Slowly Danny twisted his torso away from her swinging fists. The constable reached out his arms and clasped them about her waist, dragging her away from Danny. The nurse gently took Angie's arm and steered her away.

Danny fell back down into the curve of the plastic chair. He slipped his hands beneath him and rocked back and forth. The lights in the corridor stung his eyes. He felt himself wretch and the dry heaving in his throat made his body convulse. The taste of smoke and petrol returned to his mouth and he gagged. He couldn't remember how many times he had been sick – on the driveway, in the ambulance, in the hospital foyer. Since being pulled from the house, his memory was like a whirling twisted dream: he had felt his body being dragged and pushed, thrust from one place to another.

"Apparently the fire was started deliberately," the young constable with the small, hairless hands had told him, his eyes humourless and accusing. "There is evidence of accelerants being used throughout the property." The inference of guilt hung in the air.

162

"How is he?" Danny asked without lifting his eyes.

"I'm sure he will be fine, sir," the policeman answered. He might well have added; 'No thanks to you'. Danny wanted to hit him. He wanted to grasp the scrawny idiot by the throat and scream at him. Jordan was his son – as good as – and he loved him. The thought that people could think he was capable of hurting him ripped through his very being.

"I need to be sick," he gasped. The constable rolled his eyes and helped him to his feet. He led him along the corridor to the toilets.

"Be quick," the policeman huffed, pushing the door open. Inside, Danny turned on the cold tap and splashed water over his face. He pushed open the cubicle doors, found one with a window and quietly eased it open.

Angie gasped when she saw her son's face. He was so pale she couldn't tell where his skin ended and the bed sheets began. Fresh tears welled behind her eyes and she bit down on her bottom lip to stem them. The nurse placed a hand on her shoulder and Angie struggled with the compulsion to tear it away. Her baby looked so alone and vulnerable, swaddled in the cold blankets of a strange bed. Angie leant over him and cupped his hand.

"It's best to let him sleep," the nurse breathed quietly. How could she possibly be sincere? This wasn't her son with his eyes closed and his arms stretched down by his side like a corpse laid out in a morgue. She had never seen her son sleep like that in his life. He was all twists and turns; even asleep he was awake with life. The nurse offered Angie a glass of water and she took it gratefully, slumping down in the chair drawn up beside the bed. The room was full of wires and tubes and the smell of antiseptic. Angie nodded at the nurse and she stepped away, letting the door click gently behind her. With the nurse gone, Angie let her shoulders drop. All that was left in the room was the buzz of the lights and the hum of the heating. Angie took up Jordan's hand and laid it against her cheek. She breathed in the smell of his soft skin and kissed his fingers. She would never, never let him out of her sight again, she vowed.

Jocelyn switched off the car's radio and shuffled forward in his seat. Now was not the time to be distracted by Dvořák. He narrowed his eyes, squinting to see if they were deceiving him. No. It was definitely Danny – the unkempt hair, the cheap T-shirt and dirty denim jacket and that careless, undisciplined lolloping stride. How on earth had he managed to slip out of the hospital unattended? Jocelyn turned the key in the ignition and let the car idle. The fool looked like he didn't have a clue what he was doing or where he was going. Eventually Danny turned and walked northwards. Jocelyn let the car glide slowly forwards. Every now and then Danny would stop and look behind him, any minute expecting police sirens and screeching tyres. The idiot was playing right into his hands. Only minutes earlier Jocelyn had seen Angela rush into the hospital. Her face had been ashen with worry and he had fought the compulsion to go to her and throw his arms around her. Be patient, he kept telling himself, his chance would come.

Danny pulled his jacket about him and stumbled along the pavement. He had to keep stopping to catch his breath, the taste of smoke still deep in his throat. The moment he had squeezed his frame through the tiny window and dropped to the flat roof below, he had regretted it. The window had swung shut and he stood and stared up at it, feeling suddenly alone. Running away was foolish, he knew, and would only imply guilt. He turned at the next set of crossroads and ducked under the awnings of a row of shops. As he traced his way back to Steve and Jenny's house he was convinced all eyes were staring at him.

He slammed his fist against the plastic doorframe of his friend's house and the frustration swept over him. How little did Angie think of him that she could have him arrested and now believe he would risk the lives of his family? Yes, *his* family – because that's what they were. The last seven years had been the best of his life. Angie and the children had helped him grow and become someone he was proud of. He slapped his hand against the tiny glass panel in the centre of the door. The window shook, considered shattering and sighed back into place with relief. Danny rubbed the palm of his hand, his fingers stung. The house was empty and he kicked the door runner in irritation. Across the street a retired neighbour watched, tenderly wiping the roof of his car with a chamois leather. The sun had begun its final descent for the day. The burning orange reflection bounced off the bonnet and the neighbour had to squint to see. He studied the dishevelled man with undisguised disdain, as he had all the comings and goings at that house over the past few weeks. Further down the road a large, expensive car idled. The neighbour knew all the cars with business in his street and this wasn't one of them. The man across the road kicked the door again and wandered away from the house. His head was bowed and his shoulders hunched up to his ears. The neighbour twisted the damp cloth in his hand into a ball and wrung it until he could no longer feel the tips of his fingers.

Vending machine coffee, plastic cup, 50p

2 weeks, 2 days, 13 hours, 32 minutes after
Jocelyn Thwaite's death

One rule Dalton had learnt long ago was not to linger too long near a dead body. He flicked the Mercedes into drive. The tyres shrieked. A trailing wire caught on the back axel and threw a small portable TV monitor into the air. A station runner took the catch like a wide receiver. Danny gripped the dashboard as Dalton threw the car to the right and then the left. "Get your goddam seatbelt on," Dalton hissed, "we're in for quite a ride."

Dalton had had a simple choice to make: stay where he was, loyal to a dead boss who wasn't about to sign his pay-check any day soon, or accept the wad of dollar bills that the Englishman had waved in front of him. It was true that he didn't exactly trust his passenger, but at times like these self-preservation surfaced like a bubble. In his rearview mirror he saw Larry bounce off the rear wing. "Sorry," he breathed quietly under his breath. Stacey's gawky boyfriend was running after them, his arms waving wildly above his head. A small gaggle of journalists joined in the chase, but soon gave up, their hands on their knees as the car bounced out of the car park. Its nose hit the camber of the freeway before the spin of the rear wheels sent the car rearing up into the air again. An oncoming lorry swerved and shuddered to a halt, a motorcyclist was upended into the scrub that edged the road and a small pick-up shed its load of portable TVs. Taylor followed them onto the main road before admitting defeat and resigning himself to jumping up and down on the spot, pointing. Passersby didn't bat an eye – it was just another normal day in Las Vegas. Through the sunroof Dalton could see the last of the choppers disappear from view. A tiny bit of him was disappointed that the TV crews hadn't followed –he had learnt one or two things from a stunt man friend and was ready to put them into action. As it happened, only one small helicopter briefly considered following, but it quickly gave up and returned to the safety of the pack still hovering over the Hollywood actor's dead body.

It's never easy to know when to stay with something and when to let it go. But at that moment Danny was clearer about what he needed to do than at any other point in his life. There was little doubt that whatever had happened to Alex Fry inside the club meant that Danny would be incriminated by association. It didn't take a genius to work out that his face didn't fit. He may have been the victim of circumstance – wrong time, wrong place – but he couldn't imagine the cops giving that much heed. Then there was the vociferous press who would tear his tissue-thin story to shreds. For all he knew Taylor was in the parking lot right now, selling the rights to his fantastic tale to the highest bidder. The car bounced through the desert, spitting clouds of dust in its wake. At every crossroads and stop sign Danny imagined the sight of black and white Cadillacs swerve on to the road behind, their sirens screaming and lights spinning. As the concrete sprawl of Los Angeles appeared gradually before them, Danny exhaled with relief and peered out of the window. Gone was the city's hypnotic charm. The tall, glass-fronted buildings, the glossy boutiques, the palms, the fountains, now looked ridiculous. He shivered at the ease with which the city had seduced him. But he wasn't alone was he? The parties, the swimming pools, the fast cars and yachts – weren't they what everyone dreamed about? An old woman in bikini and stilettos stood by the kerb waving at the cars. She had long, synthetic hair and red rouge on her dry, wrinkled skin. She still believed. Danny shuddered.

The car screeched to a halt outside the actor's mansion. Dalton frowned as Danny leapt from the car and ran into the building. He closed his eyes. He'd miss this job. But maybe there was a book deal or a film script in it. He'd call his old agent later, see if he couldn't negotiate a better percentage than he had last time. Danny ignored Paulita's questions and bounded up the stairs two at a time. He didn't know how much time he had before Taylor came looking for him, or worse still, the police. He pushed open the door to his room and flung the wardrobe door wide. On to the bed he threw one of the Mulberry leather cases he had bought in London. How long ago had that been? Just two weeks? It felt as though his life had been stretched like an elastic band. Danny was exhausted, but he knew if he collapsed onto the bed he'd never stand up again. He flicked open the case and ran his fingers along the edge of the lining. After a moment's fumbling he found the thin tear in the lining that he had made when he first arrived, felt inside and found what he was looking for. With a thankful slump of the shoulders he sat down on the edge of the bed and fondled the small book in his hand. He opened the first page and studied the familiar blank expression that stared back at him: Daniel James Lunt.

"Welcome back," he breathed quietly to himself. He pushed the passport into his trouser pocket and zipped the case back up.

Adult UK Passport, £72

4 hours before Jocelyn Thwaite's death

Daniel James Lunt sat at the far end of the Ferret wishing he was someone else. Anybody but the sad, lonely failure he had turned out to be; the embodiment of his father's prophetic prediction. He twisted a bottle of Stella backwards and forwards in his fingers, picking the label to shreds with his thumbnail, letting them scatter the table. Merv, the barman, rolled a barrel past his table and shot him a concerned frown. He knew better than to ask. Danny stared at the lights jumping across the front of the fruit machine beside him and considered his ever-dwindling options. A twisted idea teased his thoughts: what if he could just leave all this behind; hitch a lift somewhere, anywhere, even change his name and just vanish? No more hassle, or accusations. He pushed the empty beer bottle away and it gathered with the others at the end of the table like ten pins. Merv arrived at his arm with another.

Outside, in his car, Jocelyn was getting irritated. He had phoned the police over two hours earlier and still there was no sign. What did it take for them to take a crime seriously these days? There was a time when you could rely on the Plod to find your stolen cycle, to give the youth down the road a clip around the ear and to catch people who started fires and absconded from questioning. Angela's ex-boyfriend could have been miles away by now if he had the sense he was born with. It was lucky for the police that they had Jocelyn doing their dirty work. Maybe he should call Angela and let her know he had found Danny? Or perhaps he should wait until the police arrested him and he could go round to her house with the news? She was sure to be delighted. She would invite him in and they would sit together on the settee. Maybe he should take a bottle of wine with him. And then, well, who knows … Still, best not to rush anything; they would have all the time in the world together soon.

Two patrol cars pulled into the Ferret car park. Jocelyn resisted the urge to leap out and lead them right to where Danny sat by the bar. It was better all round if he stayed out of the frame. Let Angela and the police draw their own conclusions. He felt the familiar roll of his stomach reminding him he hadn't touched food all day. Maybe he could take Angela to Paris as a treat? He knew a great place just off the Place de la Concorde that did the most amazing moules frites. Then they could catch a show. Was champagne up the Eiffel Tower a bit naff? Yes, but Angela would appreciate the gesture. Any woman would, wouldn't they? The policemen seemed to take an eternity to peel themselves from their cars, whispering amongst themselves and eventually pushing open the bar doors. By which time, Jocelyn noticed, a shadow had passed through the side door and disappeared behind the back of the building. Damn, he hissed, and turned the key in the ignition once again.

Danny was sweating. Now he really was a man on the run. Of course, it had only been a matter of time before the police came for him, but he had hoped they would find evidence that proved he was innocent first. The sky was black, the moon refusing to appear from behind the clouds and Danny stumbled, twisting his ankle. He cursed out loud. His senses were dull, despite the adrenalin flooding through him. He turned the corner of Steve's road and peered along it, half expecting to see more flashing blue lights barring his way. But instead the road looked as dead as it did at eleven thirty every night. The panel of glass beside the front-door window was ablaze with light and before he could lift his hand to the handle the door swung inwards.

"What the hell have you done?" Steve shouted, grabbing the doorframe and forcing Danny to take an involuntary step backwards. Danny groaned and threw his hands in the air.

"I've not done anything," he said, his voice echoing around them in the still night. Steve shook his head and threw an arm across the door to bar his way, but Danny ducked under it and disappeared inside the house.

"Don't worry, I'm going," Danny grimaced, searching the living room for his things. Jenny appeared beside her boyfriend and clung to his arm. Danny lifted his Puma sports bag onto the settee and began to scoop his clothes into it.

"Look Danny," Steve said, softening his voice slightly, "I know all about it. Angie called me from the hospital. And…"

"And what?" Danny scowled. "That proves that I set fire to the house. Well I didn't, okay, she's wrong." He stopped putting his clothes in the bag and stood upright. He looked into his friend's eyes. There was doubt etched across his face. "Do you think I did it?" He asked. "Do you?" Steve paused.

"Well, didn't you?" Steve said at last. Jenny shuffled uncomfortably beside him. Her hair was wet as though she had just showered. She refused to catch his eye. Fascinating how friendships are made, broken and defined by moments, Danny thought. Steve could have shrugged this nonsense off, used his instinct. Or perhaps he had. Perhaps he really believed Danny capable of such things.

"Oh, what's the point?" he murmured. His legs felt like molten lead and his arms ached. He hoisted the bag onto his shoulder and, without looking at the couple, pushed past them. As he stepped out into the night the cold wrapped around him. A street lamp on the opposite side of the road flickered like a silent movie, illuminating the face of an elderly neighbour watching from his window.

"Sort yourself out, Danny," Steve said from the doorway. Without thinking, Danny lifted his bag off his back and swung it through

168

the air. It caught the frame of the window, sending shards of glass and small pottery figures flying for freedom through the night. Then he turned his back on his friends and walked away. There were better places to be than this. Places where you could be whatever you wanted and nobody knew you.

2 weeks, 2 days, 13 hours, 41 minutes after Jocelyn Thwaite's death

"Señor...?" Danny span round, the blood pumping behind his temples. Paulita stood in the doorway of the bedroom, her hands wound tightly in her white apron. She looked at him nervously.

"There's a man downstairs to see you. He's been waiting for a while," she said, cowering slightly in the shadow of the doorway. Her eyes lingered on the case hanging from his right hand.

"Me? To see me?" Danny was aware that he was acting strangely and Paulita was clearly rattled. She shuffled backwards, looking over her shoulder. Calm. Calm.

"Yes, of course," he said wrestling to compose himself. "I'm coming." He placed the bag carefully on the bed. He didn't need its contents anyway.

At the foot of the stairs a man in a dark green velvet jacket stood with his back to them. Danny gripped the banister and descended slowly.

"Aha, Mr Thwaite," the man beamed, spinning on his toes. "I've found it ... I've found it." It took Danny a moment to recall the face: Marcelo. In his hands he had a small leather folder, which he stared at lovingly, stroking its smooth cover. "See, I said I would," smiled Marcelo, opening the folder and turning it to show Danny the contents.

Danny stared incredulously at the small picture the man was showing him. "*Pommes et Poire*," he announced.

"What?"

"*Pommes et Poire*. Paul Cezanne." Marcelo's exuberance was starting to wain. "The painting. You know, that you asked me to find. I found it." Danny stepped forward and peered at the tiny painting. He had to tilt his head to see beyond the reflection that cut across the gloss of the card. The painting was of a group of apples and pears arranged in a crudely described white dish sat on a ruffled tea towel, that for all the world looked as though it had been sculptured from solid clay. In the background a jug threatened to topple over and in the foreground a further apple appeared to affront gravity and refuse to roll from the table.

"Er," said Danny.

"Private collection in Istanbul. Not yet come up for auction." Marcelo continued. "I can secure it for you for five point five million." Danny resisted the temptation to gulp. He took the folder from Marcelo's hands. His fingers had left a light sheen on the cover.

"Um," he considered again and Marcelo shuffled uncomfortably. He could feel a thin trickle of perspiration travel down the inside of his thigh.

"Too much fruit in it," Danny said, snapping the book shut. Outside a car screeched to a halt and a horn sounded urgently. "Find me something with less fruit," he said, tapping Marcelo on the shoulder and handing him the folder. The next moment the doors flung wide open and a gaggle of bodies fell into the hallway.

27 minutes before Jocelyn Thwaite's death

Haydn used to put unexpected stops in his music to catch out people who were talking during his concerts. That appealed to Jocelyn because people were fundamentally stupid. There had been a moment of undisciplined panic when Jocelyn thought Danny had given him, to use the vernacular, the slip. He was embarrassed that frustration had led him to rev the engine of the Jag at a set of traffic lights, sending a gaggle of squealing girls in short skirts and boob-tubes scuttling. One of them, he was shocked to see, turned on him from the safety of the pavement and raised her middle finger. Girls were allowed to be women far too young these days. He watched them wiggle away and turned the nose of the car back towards the centre of town. Danny couldn't have travelled far on foot. Opposite the newly developed retail park he turned right, sweeping the full length of a wide arc emanating from the Ferret public house. It wasn't long, of course, before he spotted Danny's familiar stooped outline hugging the dark overhang of a row of shops that led towards the main shopping arcade, and the belly of the town. Letting the one-way system guide him, Jocelyn studied Danny from a safe distance. He watched as Danny hesitated by the old Victorian façade of the town's railway station, took a moment to look up and down the street, and disappeared inside. Jocelyn steered his car into a side street opposite. He opened the door, reached across to the passenger seat and grabbed his trench coat. He was about to close the door when his eye fell to the case in the foot well. Leaning back across the seats he gripped the familiar leather handle with its comfortingly worn stitching. Better take it with him. You can never be too careful. He pulled his coat around him and jogged across the main road. A taxi appeared from nowhere and had to brake hard, typres screeching and the driver swearing under his breath. It was late, but Jocelyn felt more awake that he thought possible. His heart was pumping with excitement. This time Danny wouldn't get away from him.

114 years before Jocelyn Thwaite's death

Satie pushed his pince-nez up the bridge of his nose and studied the sheet of music in front of him. 'Work it out yourself,' he wrote as an instruction next to the last line. Let the next person to play this piece understand the pain that existed in every note. Let them suffer, as he did.

2 weeks, 2 days, 13 hours, 46 minutes after Jocelyn Thwaite's death

The oak doors swung violently back on their hinges, bouncing off the plaster pillars either side of the doorway. A flailing triplet of bodies crashed into the hallway. Taylor's arms and legs appeared first followed closely by Stacey. Dalton pulled himself up the steps gasping for breath and attempted to balance his Raybans on the top of his head. Danny twisted his head, looking for potential exit routes, like a hostage-taker under siege. As though anticipating a chase, Taylor outstretched his arm and moved steadily forwards. There was an excited panic about the way he twitched, nervously balancing on the balls of his feet and slowly pointing his finger.

"You, you ..." he stammered excitedly. Danny threw out his arms, his hands upturned, and took a step backwards. "You're not Joss Thwaite!" Taylor squealed, his lank hair falling over his face like a curtain. His pale skin had flushed pink from the neck up and across his cheek like a raspberry birthmark. This was the single most exciting thing that happened to him in his life. Ever. Wait until he told the guys in the band.

"No, I'm not," replied Danny calmly. Taylor's jaw fell open in surprise. He was supposed to deny it. Taylor's cross-examination had been rudely aborted before he had even had a chance to make his opening speech. He struggled in his pocket for the sheets of paper he had printed from the internet. Danny grinned defiantly at the boy.

"No I'm not Joss Thwaite. So?"

"So, so," said Taylor feebly, waving the pieces of paper in his hand, his eyes darting about the room looking for allies. He looked at Dalton. He looked at Paulita. But no one came to his defence. They all stared blankly at him. The silence seemed impenetrable. Stacey smirked and stepped in front of her boyfriend.

"So, who are you, then?" she asked Danny, her voice peppered with intrigue rather than accusation. Taylor stared at her aghast. She didn't still fancy the man, surely? He didn't know what to say – his mind twisting and turning desperately, trying to grasp at the implications of what was happening. Marcelo shuffled uncomfortably and began to edge his way past the stairwell, towards the door. Time to become invisible. Association with a charade like this wouldn't be good for business.

"So did you kill the *real* Joss Thwaite?" Taylor said giddily, fiddling with the chain about his neck, running it this way and that. He leaned in slightly, his eyes wide and expectant. "What did you do with the body?" Stacey shook her head.

"Get out of here Taylor you stupid dumb ass," she hissed, swinging an arm across his chest and pushing him backwards. By the time Taylor could think of a suitable retort Stacey had taken Danny by the arm and led him away from the others.

"I'm not the dumb ass, you're the dumb ass," Taylor shouted, as they disappeared through the doors that led to the pool. "Freakin' girls", he muttered.

Outside, Stacey sat down on the tip of a lounger and held out her hand. Danny took it and sat beside her.

"So, what's your real name?" she asked.

"Danny."

"Danny," she repeated to herself, nodding gently. "Okay. So who's …"

"Look, Stacey," Danny said, cutting through her question. He studied the imaginary fluff on his trousers and wiped it away with his palm. "I didn't mean to hurt anyone – I certainly didn't kill Joss. It all just got a bit out of control. All I wanted to do was get away from life for a while, you know." Stacey watched the dark dot of his pupils intently. "And," he added, "I had nothing to do with what happened to your uncle back there. You must believe me."

"I do," she said simply. And for the first time since he had met her, over two weeks earlier, Danny saw genuine emotion in her face. "I know you didn't." She sighed, a tear escaping from the corner of her eye. "It's us that did that to him – this place." She stared out towards the horizon. The edge of Los Angeles appeared as a silvery blue streak jutting up to the sea. In the sky above the city, tiny darts of silver brought more people hoping for the Midas touch of this promised land. "If only he'd been allowed to fall in love with whoever he wanted ..." She sniffed and pulled her cuff across her nose. "I need to get high," she laughed.

"No you don't," said Danny simply. He reached for her hand again. "No you don't – stop trying to escape from yourself, trying to be someone you're not. You're an amazing, beautiful girl – be *her*." Stacey studied Danny's face: it was different somehow, as though by revealing his true identity, he had physically shifted bodies.

"Isn't that what you just did?" she said. "Pretended to be somebody else? Tried to escape?" He shook his head.

"No, I didn't. I'm still me. Always was. But that's fine now, that's who I want to be. I want to go back home."

Stacey jumped to her feet suddenly "I know!" she squealed excitedly. "Take me with you!" She crouched down in front of Danny and laid her arms on his knees. "Please – I don't care where you're going – take me with you." Danny smiled. Her enthusiasm was infectious.

"No Stacey, I can't," he said peeling her fingers from his leg. "Anyway," he said waving an arm about him, "it's not quite what you're used to." Stacey looked hurt, her face crumpled like a disappointed child's on Christmas morning.

"But I want to," she said.

"Stacey," Danny continued, "you need to make your own life, find your own things and not rely so much on these," he waved his arms, "possessions." Finally Stacey seemed to understand what he was saying. She rolled back on her heels and sat back down on the edge of the lounger. The reflection from the pool rippled a crazy light show at their feet. "I've got my own life to get back to. And," he smiled at her, "my girlfriend."

"Oh," Stacey teased, "your catwalk model fiancé."

"She's not a catwalk model."

"You surprise me."

"And she's not my fiancé."

Stacey thought for a moment, then reached inside her pocket and pulled something out. Taking Danny's hand, she placed it in the centre of his palm and curled his fingers around it.

"Well, you'd better have this then," she smiled and leant over to kiss him on the cheek.

16 minutes before Jocelyn Thwaite's death

Jordan opened his eyes and looked around the hospital room. He stared at his Mum and a tear ran down his cheek.

"I'm so sorry," he whispered.

"Oh, baby boy," she cried, leaning over him and clasping her arm around his shoulders. She felt the weight of his tiny body shake beneath her. He had grown so quickly into a young man that at times she forgot he was still such a little boy. Jordan took a breath and pulled himself out from under her.

"I was bunking off school, Mum," he said, the torment of his confession etched across his face. "I won't do it again, I promise." Angie tried not to laugh.

"I don't care Jordie," she smiled, "You're safe, that's all I care about." He shook his head.

"Is Danny okay?" he asked after a pause. He tried to push himself up on to his shoulders. But his arms felt weak as though they were made of sponge.

"Yes, Danny's okay," Angie replied, more curtly than she had meant, the bitterness seeping from her voice. How could she tell him that Danny, who he trusted so absolutely, who had been the father Jordan had never known, had set fire to their house and nearly killed him?

"Mum ..."

"Shhh, darling. You need to rest now." Angie ran a hand through his fringe. The nurse took a step towards the bed, a small cup in one hand and a tablet clasped in the fingers of her other.

"Mum," Jordan said again, "Your friend Jocelyn was there." Angie stared at him blankly, trying to understand what he was saying. "Just before the fire. I hid in my bedroom. He was in the house."

2006 – 2007 NHS expenditure: £83.8 billion

6 minutes before Jocelyn Thwaite's death

Jocelyn Thwaite was a proud man. An arrogant man. A man who truly believed in the intellectual hierarchy of the human species. It wasn't his fault if everyone else failed to understand it. The smell of stale urine soaked the air around him and he held his hand to his nose. A bundle of rags halfway along the subway that ran between platforms rocked back and forth and Jocelyn turned his face away from it as he scuttled past. Some were weaker than others, wasn't that the whole point of evolution – the strongest survives. A hand crept from under the rags, cupping itself into a bowl. Jocelyn shook his head and headed for the chink of light beyond. The corridor glistened with damp and water dripped from the plastic bowls of light that attempted to illuminate the way. He had lost sight of Danny momentarily after taking a left when right would have been more prudent. But no matter, the man was moving slow and, like a stricken beast was probably searching out somewhere to collapse and lick his wounds. With gratitude, Jocelyn climbed the steps onto the platform. It was empty and a bitter swirl whistled along the tracks and wrapped itself around him. The phone in his pocket began to vibrate and he plucked it out Angela's number filled the screen. He wished she wouldn't call herself Angie. But he could alter that, with time. He pressed the receive button and smiled a sweet and, oh so innocent hello. Don't worry, darling, your saviour is here.

"You bastard, Jocelyn!" Angie screamed. "Don't you ever, ever come near me or my family again," She spat the words out one at a time her hand shaking with anger, the small picture of her children that she kept in her purse crumpled between her fingers. "I hope they bang you up for the rest of your miserable little life."

Click.

59 seconds before Jocelyn Thwaite's death

Jocelyn stared at the screen. Then pressed the red button and slipped it back into his pocket. A small two-carriage train pulled alongside the opposite platform, paused briefly and then slid out of view. A couple of late-night travellers scurried away, heads bowed leaving a single distinctive figure on the other side on the track staring up and down. Jocelyn lifted his case from between his feet and stepped towards the platform edge. Satie's *Gnossiennes* spun inside his head, the notes building and echoing around him, their strangely calming yet foreboding warmth enveloping him completely. For a moment his mother was hugging him again to her chest, wrapping a soft woollen blanket that smelled of cinnamon and candle wax about his shoulders. The illuminated screen hanging above his head warned of the imminent passing of the 1.54 Plymouth to Paddington. It was now 1.58. Was nothing in this world as it should be? He took another step forward. The man opposite was waving frantically. But it was too late. Much too late. Jocelyn took one final step forward, his foot touching nothing but pure air. Satie would have understood. Life had been Jocelyn Thwaite's performance – and he had failed to captivate his audience. Jocelyn gave a slight dip of the head, a nod to an unseen public.

84 years before Jocelyn Thwaite's death

Age had rendered the curtains of the small room useless, sending tiny pinpricks of sunshine bursting in. Erik Satie sat down on the simple wooden-framed bed. The midday sounds of Arcueil rose to meet him. To his left, twelve identical velvet suits hung, their pockets stuffed with unread sheets of music. To his right two old upright pianos balanced on top of one another, their pedals looped with tape and wire. And all about him piles of umbrellas he would never use.

He brought his pen up between his thumb and forefinger.

"Petit Biqui, Suzanne ..." The hearth glowed with its last embers. "All this happened to me because of music. Art has done me more harm than good really." He studied the letter briefly then pinned it to the wall besides the dozens of other letters he had written to Suzanne but had never sent. He gently touched the single lock of her hair pinned beside them. Had he remained a simple cabaret pianist with money to give her, would she have stayed with him? His intestines ached and he pulled his arm across his stomach. He sipped from the bottle on the side and grimaced at the fresh pain the burning liquid brought.

"I am left with nothing," he wrote, "but an icy loneliness that fills the head with emptiness and the heart with sadness."

2 weeks, 3 days after Jocelyn Thwaite's death

The taxi driver slowed and pulled the car to the kerb. Not for the first time he studied his passenger through the rear-view mirror with concern.

"This one?" he asked uncertainly. The man in the back nodded slowly, but made no attempt to open the car door. "That's twelve fifty, mate," the driver said, turning clumsily in his seat. Danny pushed the money through the gap in the grill and opened the door. He stepped out onto the pavement and stared up at the small red-brick house. The front windows were blocked up with chipboard, above which thick black smears of soot rendered the brickwork almost invisible. The paving in front of the house was littered with broken shards of glass, amongst which persistent clinging brown weeds twisted and grew. Next to the fence a yellow metal skip overflowed with distorted strips of twisted black metal and hunks of splintered wood. Broken fragments of barely identifiable furniture matted with the blackened sinews of patterned fabric brought the reality of the fire screaming back into Danny's head. The acrid stench of melted rubber and plastic still filled the air and he shuddered. Danny rubbed at his eyes and stepped towards the side of the house.

2 weeks, 3 days after Jocelyn Thwaite's death

Elizabeth Thwaite placed the china cup and saucer on the tiny round table beside the constable's chair and sat down opposite. She smoothed the woollen fabric of her skirt across her knees and sat upright studying the young man's steely blue eyes.

"I probably shouldn't be bothering you with all this," she said simply. The constable affected a sympathetic expression, nodding encouragingly. He pulled his knees together and sat forward in his chair to mirror the woman's actions as his counselling course had told him to do to 'put her at ease'. He stifled a yawn. "It's been a while now, well, over two and a half weeks. And, you see, I had perhaps expected him to have come back by now, so …"

"You say this isn't the first time your husband has gone away for a few days?" the policeman prompted gently.

"Oh dear, you see, now you make me sound like a silly woman

making a fuss." Elizabeth stood up and the constable swivelled in his seat to follow her movement. By the French doors she stopped and picked at the dead leaves sprouting from the climbing Hibbertia. Its leaves had wilted with the heat of the morning's sun. Really it needed a little more shade. She would put it in the corner of the conservatory. Outside Max was launching small pieces of Lego into the air for Jasper to catch. "And he has sent me a couple of letters. But, I don't know ..." she said vaguely.

"Well, we'll file a report," the constable said, placing the tiny china cup back on its saucer. His finger caught in the tiny looped handle and the cup rattled on its base momentarily threatening to fall to the floor. The long-case clock in the hallway announced the arrival of midday and the policeman pulled himself to his feet. He looked at the entry in his notebook – there had been very little to note – and flipped it shut. "We'll be in touch the moment ..."

"Oh, yes, of course, of course," Elizabeth said, spinning on her toes and waving her hands dismissively as though they were discussing the trifling matter of missing scones at a country fair. "It's probably just me being silly."

"You just wait and see," the constable said, edging towards the door, "he'll wander in through that door come teatime as though nothing's happened." Elizabeth nodded and smiled. She wanted to believe that was so.

"I'm sure you're right," she said.

The young policeman climbed into his car. He placed his pad on the passenger seat and sighed. This job. How come his colleagues always got the juicy cases? He turned the key in the ignition. This was barely worth the time writing it up in the casebook.

2 weeks, 3 days after Jocelyn Thwaite's death

The wooden lattice gate beside the house swung back on itself with a clatter. They didn't notice. They were laughing too hard. Jordan held the stuffed toy high in the air, poor Mr Ted looking down at him with his one remaining good eye with an expression of absolute resignation. His ears had melted into two tight black globules on the side of his head; the fur on his body, once fluffy and golden, was now patchy and black. Both legs and one arm had gone and his other arm was a sorry stump. Angie sat cross-legged on the grass, Jade rolling around giggling in the bow of her legs.

"Has anybody seen my other eye?" Jordan mimicked, wiggling the toy back and forth. A moment later Mr Ted's head left his body and rolled under the dried up mass of a dead bush. Jade convulsed into fits again, tears streaming down her face. Jordan threw himself to his knees in an attempt to retrieve the head. Angie grabbed her son around the waist and pulled him on to the grass, a mass of arms and legs spinning through the air.

"You murderer," she squealed, "You killed Mr Ted."

Danny stood by the side of the house. His mind was numb. He couldn't have pictured a more magical sight. The view from the Dorchester balcony over Hyde Park, the display window of the Prada store on Bond Street, the sight of the Pacific Ocean at night from Beverly Hills, Mulholland Drive, Caesar's Palace, none of them compared to the sight of his family laughing, rolling, playing – just being. He wanted to call out, to shout to them, pull them close and hug them. But he couldn't. Every nerve and muscle refused to click into action. It was all too perfect. Without him.

Angie rocked back on her heels. Something caught her eye and she turned. But the movement had gone and the gate beside the house rattled closed on its hinges.

"Come on guys, let's go," she said, scrambling to her feet and holding out a hand, "we've saved everything we can." Through the thin slats of the gate she saw the shape move again.

"Danny?" Angie said quietly under her breath. She stepped forward. "Danny?" she repeated, louder this time and the children looked up at her. And then she was running, across the lawn, along the side of the house and out into the road. Danny turned and looked at her. His eyes were full. Angie stopped short in front of him. Neither said a word and a hush fell like a fog about them. Jade's squeal cut through the silence; she ran head first towards Danny and wrapped her arms tightly around his waist. He hugged her until his arms arched and he thought he could no longer breathe. Jordan, an unstoppable grin breaking out across his face, stepped forward, leant his forehead against Danny's chest and curled his hands around him. Through a mass of hair, Danny lifted his head to look at Angie. She turned and walked back towards the house. He peeled the children from him and followed. She sat down on the doorstep of her burnt-out home and he knelt beside her.

"Sorry," he said.

Angie lifted her head to look at him. His eyes looked tired, the skin around the sockets dark and creased.

"For everything."

She looked down at the paving by her feet. A smear of red paint ran across the cracks where something had been hurriedly dragged. How close had she come to losing Jordan and Danny forever?

Danny took her hand in his. Slowly he curled her fingers in a ball beneath her palm until only one finger remained, and on to it he slipped a thin circle of silver. Angie looked at her finger. Suddenly it twinkled with the most magnificent light – the sun catching the great stone in the middle of Princess Alexandra's ring and sending its rays cascading about them. She gasped and turned to face Danny. He looked deep into her eyes.

"Marry me," he said.

Angie's body shook. She wanted to hug him. She wanted to cry. She wanted to hit him. And scream. She stood up, the children watching her with wide, expectant eyes. She held her hand up and stared at the ring. It really was the most beautiful thing she had ever seen. She slowly and carefully slipped it over the knuckle of her finger and rolled it around her palm, letting the light paint a rainbow of colours about her. She gazed at it for what to Danny felt like an eternity. And then without warning she raised her hand and threw it across the yard. It bounced off the edge of the yellow skip, rattled amongst the debris and disappeared from sight with one single resonating note. Danny gasped.

"Yes, I'll marry you," she said. Jade squealed and Jordan felt like he was going to cry.

"B... but...?" Danny stammered pointing towards the skip. A magpie perched on an overhanging branch peered enviously in.

"I don't need things. We don't need things," she said. Danny took her hands in his and the children jumped up and down beside them. They turned and walked away from the house.

"Do you know how much that was worth?"

"No."

"A lot."

"Oh."

"Seriously..."

"Right."

"£150,000."

Angie stopped and looked into Danny's eyes. God, she had missed him. Missed that stupid smile, missed that confused frown and missed that arrogant swagger. She shook her head.

"So?" she said.

"So?" he repeated with a shrug. "Yeah, so?"

Love, £0.00